Hacking
His
Code

HACKING HIS CODE

Lark Letter Press
131 Daniel Webster Hwy # 166
Nashua, NH 03060
www.larkandersonbooks.net
mims@mimsthewords.com
Edited by: Natasha Davis

ISBN: 978-1-953191-04-5
eISBN: 978-1-953191-03-8

Any references to historical events, real people, or real places are used fictionally. Names, characters, and places are products of the author's imagination. The following story contains mature content and is intended for mature readers.

BEGUILING A BILLIONAIRE
BOOK 7

Hacking his CODE

LARK ANDERSON

LaRk
LETTER
PrEsS

Also By Lark Anderson

The Beguiling a Billionaire Series

The Billionaire's Board
The Billionaire's Fixer Upper
The Billionaire's Funding
The Bad Girl
The Dis-Graced
The Trainwreck
Hacking His Code

Reckless in Love
eBook Only

Love you…not!!!
Trust you…not!!!
Tempt you…not!!!

Savage in Love

Savage in the Sheets
Savage in the Streets

The Glow Girlz Series

Stacey's Seduction
Tempting Teysa
Desiree's Delight

If you'd like to become an ARC reviewer for Lark, please
email her at: mims@mimsthewords.com.

Arinessa

*B*uzzzz…
Breathe in. Breathe out.
Buzzz…
You can do this.
Buzzzz…
Pick up the phone!!!

"Hello, Ari here!" I chirp into the receiver.

"Arinessa Sylvan, this is Angela calling from—"

"It's okay, I know what you want—that perfect bikini body that will have men drooling and all the women jealous—"

"No!"

"Oh, forgive me. You must be interested in my new goodie box, Makeover Moods—"

"Arinessa, I'm from the university, but I suspect you already know that—"

I inject a sultry inflection into my voice. "What are you wearing, Angela?"

"You have five days—"

"Because for just one-hundred-and-twenty dollars, you could be strutting around campus in some Super Sage leggings as you drink your ImPressed coffee."

"—to come up with your tuition before you are dis-enrolled from the…ehhh…Bachelors of Science in Computers program."

Fuck me…

I gather my courage, knowing it's time to let real-life take center stage, but it's a bitter pill to swallow.

"I know, and I'm trying."

"Against better judgment, you were given an extension—"

"I can't get any more loans! God knows I've tried."

"I supposed that means you'll be disenrolling?"

Panic takes hold as I desperately try to come up with a way to keep myself afloat. I can't stop now, not when I'm so close to achieving my goal. Not when my mother has so little time left.

"I'll do anything—please! Any odd job no one else wants on campus if it will give me a tuition break. I'll tutor. I'm literally the best student this campus has ever had—ask my instructors. I'll scrub the damn toilets—the septic tank if I have to."

"I am aware of your gifts, it's one of the reasons we've been so lenient, but that doesn't mean we can overlook your tuition shortage indefinitely."

"It's ridiculous—especially with how easy the football players have it."

"Football revenue is high—"

"Look, I'm the first person in my family to attend a university—to even enroll in college. I have to finish this, because if I don't…if I don't…"

I don't want to think about my mother, weak in bed, completely oblivious to my plight. I promised I'd get my degree before she passed—her dying wish, but at the time I made that promise, I didn't know how complicated my life was about to get.

Father left shortly after Mother's terminal diagnosis, finding a trailer trash girlfriend with a young son and a drinking problem. What little money Mom took from the divorce went towards her treatment. Of course, she insisted that was silly. Why waste our resources on her when I had tuition to pay? So I lied and told her I had a full-ride scholarship.

Then, things got worse. She couldn't afford the apartment we'd lived in for eighteen years, so I had to find another. I went apartment hunting and moved into a one-bedroom just last week. She's set to move in next month.

She couldn't even afford to die in the place she had called home for more than half her life.

It's so unfair.

Now, I'm drowning in debt with destroyed credit and little hope that I'll ever climb my way out of this monstrous black hole I've dug for myself. But I have to get that degree.

For her.

"I'll call back in a few days," Angela says, irritated. "Take care."

I exhale a ragged breath as I try to formulate a plan. How do I stay in school with no money, terrible credit, and a mountain of debt?

Of course, there are the obvious answers. Stripping would bring in some easy cash, but unfortunately, I came to that conclusion rather late, and there's no way I can manage to bring in over twenty-thousand dollars in five days, even if I stripped from sunrise to sunset.

I've been donating plasma for two years now, but they've recently cut reimbursement rates. I'd consider selling a kidney, but that's illegal. I've even filled out an egg donation form, but so far, there have been no takers. I have no friends to beg for money because my ability to forge lasting friendships has greatly deteriorated under the stress load I've been shouldering.

My gaze travels over to my computer terminal. The one I haven't touched in years.

You promised you'd never do that again.

That's not entirely true, I reason. I promised I'd never hack a government system, but I never said anything about hacking private enterprises.

I know I'm just trying to logic myself into a bad decision—one I could go to jail for.

I exhale slowly, taking a seat at my desk—not my main one, the other one. The one that got me into so much trouble.

I shouldn't have moved it over, but for some reason, I can't part with it. It calls to me every now and then, and the pull has never been this strong.

I boot up the computer, and because it's been six

years since I last hit the power button, it's slow, which only edges me closer to panic.

You're breaking a promise.

I'm doomed to break one promise or another with the hole I've dug for myself, and if I'm careful, no one will ever find out.

I type into the mainframe until I find myself on the dark web.

Hello, old friend.

It doesn't take long to familiarize myself with the screens. The ease at how I slip into my past self causes a caustic feeling of dread to bloom inside me.

Growing up, my family lived paycheck to paycheck, struggling to gain a foothold in the world. I was singled out and tested in grade school, and they determined that I was all kinds of smart. Because of my big brain, I got to go away to camps for free as well as attend expensive schools, all bills paid.

At fourteen, I was slipping in and out of places on the web I shouldn't have been for fun. I didn't know what I was doing was wrong until a teacher clued me in. I smiled, thanked her for the insight, and never crossed that line on school grounds again.

Unfortunately, I didn't learn my lesson. My new hobby was fun, exciting, and WAY too tempting for me to stay away from.

I got better, learning new skills, and I joined chats with people who shared my interest.

That was a mistake.

If I had just gone on having fun, I wouldn't have been caught, but real life took hold, forcing my eyes open.

One of the hackers I was acquainted with worked at a

police department. He was frustrated because the stuff he found on who he called 'the worst of the worst' couldn't lead to an arrest because of how it was acquired. At the time, I was fifteen, but they didn't know that, and they posted things that burned into my brain, alerting me to the seedy underbelly of the world that I had only been vaguely aware of.

There was a network of traffickers that traded drugs…and other commodities. I was angry, at the police, at the world, at everyone.

I thought I was being smart, collecting evidence, bouncing signals, cleaning my trail, and delivering a cache of evidence that was anonymously sent to various agencies.

SPOILER ALERT: I got caught.

A huge investigation was conducted. They talked to my parents, my school, my teachers—everyone. It became a national headline. Since I was a minor, my name was never released, but I got expelled from school all the same, and a juvenile record to boot.

That was six years ago. I'm smarter now, and if I stay away from FBI and CIA hotspots, I could make good money doing low-level hacking. Rich women seeking a better divorce payout would pay well enough, and who knows, maybe I could squeeze a few jobs in over the next two days and make enough to at least get the university off my ass.

I scan forums for hours and set up a few shell accounts. I put together a list of potential clients ranging from an heiress who didn't demand a prenup when she married her boy toy, to a twenty-one-year-old whose eight-five-year-old husband died and is now having to fight his family for her part of the estate.

A message pops onto my screen.

That's weird.

> **Chicken Dinner:** *I need you to retrieve a jpeg file from a server and post it to a Chatter account. If you successfully complete the mission in thirty minutes, twenty-five-thousand dollars will be wired to you. Shall I send over the information?*

I blink, trying to see if I've gone insane, and when I realize my eyes are working, I know it can only mean one thing.

Oh-my-GOD—I've been caught.

My first instinct is to press the power button and be done with hacking altogether, but I'm paralyzed, unable to move, unable to even breathe.

My brain attempts all kinds of logic until it finally reaches some state of reasonability.

I've done nothing wrong…yet.

Chicken Dinner is no police officer, and if the police were to hire me this way, they wouldn't be able to charge me due to entrapment laws. Not only that, but I doubt the FBI spends their time monitoring my computer activity.

> **Chicken Dinner:** *Twenty-seven minutes and counting.*

Shit!

This one hack could solve my big problem. I could complete the mission, get paid, forward the balance of my tuition to my school, and get my degree before my mom passes.

I have to risk it.

Ari: *send the info*

Less than a minute later, a clickable link pops up, and I download a file to my system.

The job is surprisingly easy, or at least it is for me. Some would consider it advanced. Five years ago, I could have done it in fifteen minutes flat. Now, I'm coming in at twenty-eight minutes with zero room for error.

Retrieving the image from the server wasn't too hard, but hacking the Chatter account had me nervous for a minute.

My fingers fly over the keyboard, racing to get a ChitChat up to post in. The picture is surprisingly innocuous: two little girls, one behind a computer, the other dressed as a princess. They look identical.

Enter.

Done.

Twelve seconds to spare.

Chicken Dinner: *Winner, Winner! Now, you wait.*

Wait? My stomach twists in knots, suddenly sure this was a bad idea.

Ideally, I would have demanded half my fee up front, but with the timer going, I thought it best to collect on the backend. And it appears Chicken Dinner might be stalling.

I exhale an angry breath, flex my fingers, and begin typing a scathing message into the text box, telling Mr. Dinner that if he doesn't pay up, he's going to find himself hacked out of a house and home.

As I'm typing, a pounding sounds against my apartment door. Dreadful slamming that shakes the windows.

Oh, no...

After three loud bangs, the door flies open, and men dressed in black come pouring into my living room.

"This is entrapment!" I yell, jumping to my feet.

But it's no use. These aren't your average cops. They're not even FBI, for that matter. I don't think Homeland Security operates like this, but I guess there could be some covert branch.

A man reaches for my arm. "You're coming with me."

"Like hell, I am!" I shout, taking a paperweight from my desk and hurling it at his face, connecting with his chin.

"Mother-fucker!" the man gasps, cradling his jaw.

I fight like a banshee against arms reaching for me, grabbing, pulling, subduing.

It's no use.

Apparently, I really was being watched. They were just waiting for a slip, and now, instead of getting due process, I'm probably going to be thrown into some black hole for posing a national security risk.

Hunter

A gruff voice crackles through the walkie talkie. "Sir, we've subdued the subject."

That's funny.

I press a button to respond. "Subdued? What do you mean by subdued? I asked you to take her in."

"And that's what we're doing."

"You're not using force, are you? I merely said take her to me, not kidnap her."

"Sir, you hired a group of mercenaries and bounty hunters to bring a target to you. This is how we operate."

"Target? She's not a target—"

"We'll be there in twenty," the voice cuts in. "Over."

Shit!

Chapter TWO

Arinessa

Fighting back was useless. I was easily bested.

As soon as they subdued me, a hood was thrown over my head, and shackles secured over my wrists, which were bent awkwardly behind my back. They didn't even bother to read me my rights.

Instead of going down the three flights of stairs to the bottom floor, the burly men drag me up to the rooftop. For a brief moment, I had worried they were going to throw me off the building, but when the maintenance door opened, instead of being murdered, I was loaded onto a helicopter and thrown into a cage.

Thankfully, it was only a short ride to our destination,

and now that the helicopter has landed, I wait for what comes next.

When something terrible happens, waiting is the worst part. I know that sounds insane, but it's the absolute truth.

When I was caught hacking all those years ago, the part that damn near gave me a heart attack was waiting in that interrogation room for someone to show up. It took hours, and I swear, I developed a full-blown ulcer from it.

"Whaddaya suppose he wants with her?" a husky voice says.

"She's cute, but I doubt a man with his deep pockets and pretty boy good looks needs to do this to get laid," a masculine voice says back.

Get laid?

Suddenly, I worry that I'm going to pass out. It hadn't occurred to me that I might be raped.

"He sure went through a lot of trouble to have us pick her up. Wonder why?" the husky voice continues.

The other guy exhales in frustration. "That's not for us to know."

Hinges creak as the cage opens. Hands grab me, removing me aggressively from the cage first, then the helicopter. I'm dragged, my knee scraping on cement.

Maybe I'm being sent to Guantanamo Bay? Or some black ops location that no one knows about? That doesn't make sense, though. With how the men were talking, I doubt it's a government operation.

Which means it's a personal grudge.

Finally, the men stop, and someone shouts, "Seventy-eighth floor," indicating that I'm on an elevator.

The floor lurches. The sound of heavy breathing sets me further on edge.

I can't believe I was so stupid. I'm never going to see my parents again, and they're never going to know what happened to me.

Bile fills my throat, but the last thing I want is to throw up in the hood, so I choke it down.

"Bossman's gonna like this pretty thing." I feel a hand caress my elbow, and I jump away, colliding with one of the other men.

"Leave her alone," a voice growls. "That is not what this team is about."

"Have you seen her pretty thighs, though?"

Oh my God—I'm being sex trafficked! Is this revenge from the men I spied on before?

Terrified, I kick my leg hard into something solid.

"Shit—"

Arms grab me from behind, and I twist my body back and forth, trying to resist.

There is no way I'm going willingly to whatever devious place they have ready for me. I'd rather die.

The elevator dings, and I hear the door slide open. Hands grab my shackled arms. I lurch my head as hard as I can in the opposite direction, kicking a leg up and connecting with a solid mass.

"Dammit!" a man gasps.

"What the hell is going on?" a new voice shouts.

Ten hands are on me at once, twisting, pulling, dragging.

"What is the meaning of this—let her go!"

"Sir, that is ill-advised. As you can see—"

"What I see is you kidnapping a woman!"

"Sir, our orders were—"

"Your orders were to bring her back to me. If you ran into any trouble, you were to assure her that she'd be handsomely rewarded."

"Hmmm….did you mean to say *she* would be handsomely rewarded?"

"Yeah, what did you think I said?"

"I thought you meant that if the target posed a threat, tell the men that *they* would be handsomely rewarded."

"Jesus Christ—get the bag off of her head. Take her shackles off."

Adrenaline courses through my veins, and even though I clearly heard that I'm to be released, I can't bring myself to trust them, and as soon as their hands drop from me, I dart blindly forward.

"She's loose!" a man shouts.

I get five steps before running straight into and barreling over something in my way, sending me crashing downward.

A groan comes from underneath me. That something in my way was a someone.

Footsteps sound. They're on me again, hands grabbing my arms.

"Would you like us to tie up her feet?" a voice says.

"No—let her go!"

"Even after—"

"What you're doing is illegal. Undo the shackles, remove the hood, and leave so I can make this right."

Hands sit me upright. Pressure is relieved from my wrists. The hood slides off, but I can't see because I'm blinded by my hair, which got disheveled during the struggle. I shake my head, pull my hair back, and look down to see a suited man on the floor beneath me.

He's handsome, a businessman judging from his attire. His hair is chocolate brown, tousled from the fall. His eyes are warm honey, and if I'm not mistaken, he's jovial.

I hate him for that.

Hunter

Dark hair tumbles from the hood covering Arinessa's face. Her newly-freed hands frantically smooth the unruly strands, tucking them behind her ear.

"You're going to be alright," I assure her.

"Who the hell are you? And what the fuck am I doing here?" she says frantically, falling back on her butt and shimmying away.

"You can all leave," I say to the mercenaries as I climb to my feet.

A big one named Bruce says, "Are you sure you don't want us to stay? She puts up quite a fight and a pretty boy like yerself—"

"Pretty?" I blink my eyes in disbelief. I work out five times a week and can bench press nearly two-hundred-fifty pounds, but I guess that might be hard to notice under the suit I'm wearing. "Trust me, I can hold my own."

The leader, who goes by Snake, shakes his head, circles a finger in the air, and shouts, "Round it up, boys. Back to the chopper."

After they depart, I approach Arinessa, who is shaking violently from fear. I squat low so I'm not talking down to her, and open my mouth to speak, but before I can utter a word, her leg flies up, connecting with my jaw.

Oof...

Unprepared, I fall backward, bringing a hand up to my face as she angrily charges me, and we fall to the floor.

I raise a hand in surrender. "Please—"

"You filthy pervert," she shouts, pummeling me with her tiny fists. "You can't get laid, so you hire muscled thugs to kidnap—"

I shield my face, allowing a couple punches in for her benefit before grabbing her wrists and setting her straight.

"Oh, I assure you—I can get laid. And even if I couldn't, it's certainly not something I'd look for from you."

She narrows her eyes at me, and I realize how that sounded.

"I mean—"

"Good, because I am never, ever, in a million years— EVER—going to fuck you!"

That's a shame.

Even in times of extreme duress, men never truly get their heads out of the gutter, and I can confirm that my mind has already envisioned three ways of fucking her since she was dragged into the reception area from the elevator.

But this is business.

Arinessa's anger is a mask for her fear, and I realize

just how terrifying this whole experience must be for her. I never intended to scare her or make her feel unsafe. I have to make this right.

I release her arms and look into her big, doe eyes. God, I could get lost in them.

"Arinessa, can we talk?" I give her a reassuring smile. "I'd like to straighten this misunderstanding out."

"Misunderstanding? So I misunderstood my kidnapping?"

"How about instead of using the word kidnap, we go with guide? You misunderstood your guide."

Her jaw gapes at my audacious suggestion, her full lips forming a perfect 'O.'

My cock twitches at the thought of what I'd like to do with that mouth of hers. I know I should shove the thought from my mind, but it would be a fruitless endeavor. It's not just that she's attractive; it's that she's intriguing, spirited, and oh so fucking hot.

To make matters worse, she's wearing a tank top, and her nipples are jutting through the thin fabric. It's impossible not to stare at them, and don't get me started on her shorts. With the way she's squatting, they come up so high that a sliver of her round ass can be seen at certain angles.

Fuck me, I should have told the boys to allow her to get dressed before taking her to me.

"Would you care for a drink?" I offer.

"A drink? I want to go home! If you think you can just kidnap women—"

"It was an accident."

"We'll let the cops decide that."

A chuckle escapes my throat. "Do you really think

they're going to believe you? You'll march out the door, call the authorities, I'll feign ignorance…but…well…I might have to hand over all the evidence I've gathered concerning your recent online activities. With your history, that could land you some serious time."

Her hand flies to her mouth. "How fucking dare you —"

"I want to offer you a job," I cut in.

"—think that you can just—"

"It pays one-million-dollars."

She plops back down on her fabulous rear, looking at me intensely. "I'm listening."

"I need you to help me find someone. I know you can hack, which makes you perfect for the job."

Her eyes flutter open and shut at least a dozen times before she finally says, "Like, what does this person mean to you?"

"That will be disclosed upon your compliance."

"Let me get this straight: you want to hire an out-of-practice hacker and offer them one-million-dollars? Oh, almost forgot—you had them kidnapped from their home —while still in their pajamas!"

My eyes inadvertently rove her lush body. "Not complaining."

Her eyes widen at my out of place comment. "Just who the-who the hell are you?"

"Hunter Davies—"

Her jaw falls open. "Oh my God—you're *the* Hunter Davies!"

"The one and only."

"The one that people aren't even sure what he looks like because he's a reclusive asshole?"

"Yeah, that was my father's doing."

"Your mom was a famous Hollywood actress—a legend! And then she just became a hermit. Was it because of the kidnapping?" she blurts out, then quickly downcasts her eyes. "Sorry, I wasn't thinking."

You mention the name Davies and people think of two things: tech juggernaut Rand Davies marrying Hollywood starlet Ernestine Whitmore and Ernestine Whitmore's missing twin, my Aunt Lucy.

Over twenty years ago, she just up and disappeared, a cyclone of chaos left in her wake in the form of various offshore bank accounts, emails with foreign militia, and connections with various shady organizations.

My mother was heartbroken, forever left to wonder what had become of her. There was no evidence of foul play. Her personal belongings were simply left behind, with nothing pointing to where she would go.

I offer my hand out for Arinessa to take, which she accepts. Her soft skin against mine makes my heart skip a beat, like I'm a damn teenager.

Once she's righted, I say, "It's alright. It happened a long time ago. I can't even say I remember her."

Her mouth twitches to the side as though she's unsure of what to say. If we'd met under different circumstances, I'd be kissing her lips right now.

I give her a moment to adjust her disheveled clothing and hair before continuing. It's entirely possible that Big Foot's hair is more manageable but not nearly as sexy.

"My Aunt Lucy worked for my father. One day, he saw Lucy out with my mother, and it was 'love at first sight,' as he calls it. There was a short courtship during which I was conceived, and they decided to marry.

Things were going great for a couple of years, until my aunt went missing. You should know the rest."

"That all happened before I was born, but still, I know the story. Most everyone does," Arinessa says.

"It was all over the papers. My mother couldn't even grieve properly. After Lucy's disappearance, Father went into 'lockdown' mode. We were never photographed out, and we'd shuffle between homes. He even went so far as to put out fake images of me, so people would debate what I looked like."

"Gosh, that's gotta be rough."

"It is what it is, but it all happened for a reason, and it's why I've summoned you here."

She casts me an impish look, her brow arching dramatically. "Summoned? Is that what we're calling it now?"

There's an addictive quality to the way she addresses me. Most women agree with and nod at everything I say, which is boring, and even exhausting at times. Not Arinessa, though. She has no problem calling me out.

"For lack of a better word."

She fake coughs, uttering the word 'kidnapping' under her breath, and I can't help but smile. She's just so…different.

"Tell me more about your aunt."

"Lucy disappeared when I was three, twenty-four years ago, so I know precious little about her, other than what I've been told."

"Do you think she's still alive?"

"The truth is, I have no idea, but if I can find a way to give my mother closure, I'll take it."

"And of all the professionals in the world, you think I

can find her?" Arinessa spikes a brow and points to her chest.

"I can't think of many better, actually."

"I don't know, maybe someone from Anonymous. Or an actual hacktivist that hasn't been out of practice for six years."

"I would never let a member of Anonymous gain access to any of the Davies' systems. God knows what havoc they'd cause, my family being of the corporate world."

"Good point."

"I know your past, and even though you haven't been hacking recently, you were doing skip tracing with a credit card company last summer, not that I think that will help much."

"Yeah, if you're relying on my skip tracing capabilities to solve a twenty-year cold case, you're sorely out of luck."

I clear my throat, buying myself a moment to carefully phrase what I need to say. "What you did in your past, it spoke to me."

She downcast her eyes. "The hacking? It was amateur."

"Actually, it was quite genius. It wasn't the hacking that got you caught. It was your drive to bring the culprits to justice that did you in."

"Did me in and cost me damn near everything. I wouldn't be in the mountain of debt I'm in now if I had just made better choices."

"Who knows, maybe those choices have a late payoff."

"So, let me see if I have the terms right. You want me

to locate your aunt, who's been missing for twenty-four years, and if I succeed, you'll pay me one-million-dollars."

"That about sums it up."

"And what do I get if I fail?"

"Nothing."

"But—"

"You just admitted to having a mountain of debt. This is your only chance. How else are you going to come up with your tuition, let alone pay your bills?"

"How do you know so much about me?" she asks, her voice tense and full of anger.

"I come from money, and all knowledge can be bought."

She straightens her hair again, a wasted effort with how unruly it's been, but somehow, it only makes her more alluring. Her beauty is organic compared to the plastic princesses I'm used to entertaining. Everything about her feels real, and completely foreign.

There's not even a trace of makeup on her face, and it doesn't seem to bother her. Almost every woman in my orbit dresses in high-end fashion, never a nail unpolished. Arinessa is almost primal looking with her short shorts and her hair fighting its way out of her poorly-done up ponytail, but instead of being put off, I find myself imagining the caress of her thighs around my waist.

"I have school—"

"Hopefully, you'll be done before it begins. We have seven days, and I have the case files collected for you and scanned onto a computer. The hard copies are available as well. I have the numbers for every single person that worked the case."

Her mouth gapes open. "You expect me to find a missing person in a week? Someone who's been gone for twenty-plus years?"

"Yes."

"Do you think I'll succeed?"

I exhale a breath, choosing my words carefully. "For the past twenty-four years, my mother has been a shell of herself. I've heard stories of what she was like before, but I can't remember ever experiencing the carefree look in her eyes I see in any of the movies she's made. Any chance of finding Lucy is worth the effort."

"So you don't think I'll find her then. You expect me to waste a precious week of my life for nothing."

"Oh, I think you'll succeed. We have better technology than we did back then, and if she was kidnapped, whoever did it has probably let their guard down. I'm just careful about giving false hope."

"How did you find me? My name was never released because I was a minor when I committed my crime, and the records were sealed. You said something about money, but who did you pay off?"

"That is a story for another time. Right now, I need to know if you're in. You'll be expected to be on call twenty-four-seven, from start to finish. If you succeed, you go home with one-million-dollars."

"And I get nothing if I fail."

"Not exactly."

She cocks a brow.

"You see, your mother has recently decided to forgo treatment for her condition."

"Wait—what?!?"

"It's good that she did, actually. I have an acquaintance, Cassius Lavinius, who works in pharmaceuticals. I've already given him a call, and he's willing to put your mother on a promising experimental treatment, if you'd like."

Her eyes light in anger. "You want my mother to be some lab rat?"

"The drug has completed its trials, it's just waiting on the powers that be to bless it. So far, it knocks all other available treatment options out of the park. If you agree to call your kidnapping water under the bridge and take my offer, I'll send a text to Cassius right now."

"What kidnapping?" Arinessa says with a smirk.

I send a text to Cassius, a man I barely know, and give him the green light to approach the doctor caring for Arinessa's mother. After I hit send, I return my gaze back to Ari.

"Oh, almost forgot. Mercs gave me this." I hand Arinessa her phone. "I'm sending you something right now."

I pull out my own phone and forward some documents I have ready for her to sign.

Her phone vibrates, and she clicks into the links I sent her.

"You're going to have to sign a non-disclosure agreement. It basically says you can tell no one of your work with me, even the people you encounter here."

"Okay…" she says, her eyes scanning the paragraphs of information.

"And…you're going to have to pretend to be my girlfriend."

Her head snaps up, her eyes round with shock, and if

I'm not mistaken, horror. "What?"

"I can't go telling my mother you're investigating her sister's kidnapping. It will get her hopes up and undo years of progress. Just act like we're dating. That will explain why you're staying with me."

"I don't know if I'm comfortable with that."

"Well, you're going to have to be," I say nonchalantly. "You'll have people coming in to attend to you shortly after you're escorted up to my suite."

"Attend to me?"

"Get you freshened up. Order you a wardrobe. You'll get to keep the clothes, by the way."

"What? Hold on—I didn't—"

"There is no other way. I can't have you meet my parents in that." I gesture to her shorts that are bunched up, exposing a full asscheek. One careless movement from her, and I'll be blessed with a visual I'm pretty sure will have me making her an entirely different kind of proposition.

She curses as she corrects her shorts, and after mulling over the situation a good minute, she says, "Why do I feel as though this is either the best decision I'll ever make, or the worst?"

"So, you're taking the job?"

After signing the eForm, she says, "Count me in."

"Great, we'll go over the details in my office."

As we continue toward my office, her shorts bunch up again, to her utter frustration. She's such a mess, but delightfully so.

Any interest I must show in this woman will not be faked.

THREE

Arinessa

Hunter's office has a modern, contemporary flair, oozing simplistic extravagance. Something you see in both magazines and sci-fi movies.

A wall of windows overlooks the cityscape, creating a breathtaking view. The glass is so clear it looks like you could walk out into the world…and fall to your death.

Hunter gestures for me to take a seat on a sofa, then continues to a cabinet. To my utter horror, I realize I look like a slutty hillbilly. Serves him right for snatching me out of my apartment like he did.

He glances askance at me, holding up a bottle of expensive-looking liquor. "Pick your poison?"

"Do you treat all your guests to kidnapping and poison, or just me?"

He puts down the bottle. "You look like you enjoy a tart red."

"Jokes on you because I can't afford a drinking habit and have no idea what you're talking about."

Hunter chuckles, grinning ear to ear. "Then let me be the benefactor to your slow, downward spiral."

He grabs a glass from a cabinet with one hand and a bottle of wine in the other. The irony that I'm about to drink a glass of wine that may very well cost more than my monthly rent while looking trailer park chic is not lost on me.

But there's no way for me to look less bedraggled. My hair is a crazy mess, my clothes are meant for sleeping, and by the feel of it, my eyes are puffy and red. I'm a hot mess, minus the hot.

Hunter, however, is impeccably dressed in a finely tailored suit that fits like a dream. His hands are large, matching his six-foot-plus frame. I don't think I've ever had a sexual fantasy about a man's hands before, but I just might tonight.

He pours our glasses and whisks one over to me. The deep crimson liquid never seems to unsettle, no matter how grand his movements are.

His cup holds an amber-colored liquid. I can only assume it's some fancy scotch that rich people drink, but it could be tequila for all I know. I've never been a drinker. Not with my workload and barren wallet.

He takes off his blazer, which proves to be distracting. His button-up shirt hugs his muscles in a way that makes me dizzy.

It's not often I'm alone with a man as sexy as Hunter Davies. He doesn't look how you'd expect a tech genius from the Davies family to look. He's every kind of gorgeous whose attractiveness is only enhanced by his arrogance—which he has in spades.

He seats himself in an overstuffed chair, angling it to face me. "Let's begin."

I take a sip of wine, its bitter burn disallowing me from keeping a straight face.

"Jeez. That's one of my smoother blends."

I cough lightly. "I think I've had wine maybe twice before."

His brow furrows. "Ever think about cutting loose and living a little?"

"After getting into trouble, I was terrified of stepping out of line. It's not like my family can afford fancy lawyers like yours can."

"And yet you were still driven to the dark web."

If anyone else had said that, I'd feel embarrassed, ashamed even, but coming from Hunter Davies, who was born with a silver spoon in his mouth, I'm able to meet his gaze with relative ease and say, "Since you'll never have to face any real consequences for your actions, or your upbringing, I don't think you would understand."

"Noted…" He takes a long pull of the amber liquid, then returns his gaze to me. "You must understand that once you begin, it's going to get intense. There's a lot of emotion involved in this. I'm scared of what we might find out."

"If we believe she was kidnapped, who are the suspects?"

"Everyone was looking at my aunt's personal trainer.

She had been working with him for seven months, and they apparently had a fling."

"Casual sex is nothing. What about all the nefarious activities she was rumored to be involved in?"

He exhales morosely, and I almost regret mentioning the big fucking elephant in the cold case.

Almost.

"Although she was undoubtedly involved in some shady dealings, it's not believed to have led to her disappearance. There was just too much confidential information lying around her apartment. It being a random guy that became obsessed with her makes a heck of a lot more sense."

I nod. "The logic checks out."

"Going back to the personal trainer, I actually think we looked into the wrong one. The one they were investigating, Lorenzo Sanchez, had holes in his established timeline that couldn't be filled, and that's the qualifier they've used for the last twenty years to label him a suspect. The trainer she had before Lorenzo, however, left after a messy situation involving money laundering. There was also talk of him hooking up with my aunt, but as you said, casual sex is nothing."

"God, what was it with her and personal trainers?"

"Working out causes all kinds of pheromones."

"I guess. So, what was found on the other trainer?"

"Not much. His name was Clint Easton, and he was in Australia at the time of Lucy's disappearance, removing him as a suspect. The thing is, he could have hired an accomplice."

"Where is he now?"

"About four years ago, he dropped off the radar. No

one's seen or heard from him."

"And you think I can find him?"

"It will be your first assignment, actually." He pulls a slim, black laptop from a messenger bag. "Find Clint Easton."

It takes me a full minute to realize he's serious.

"Where are the files?" I say, looking around. "And I'd like to work alone."

"You'll be given no files for this one, and I'm rather comfortable where I'm seated."

Fuck, it's a test.

With a trembling hand, I accept the laptop, opening it to a secured mainframe.

"Clint Easton, you say?"

"That's his name."

I do a quick search of several databases to find roughly seventy-eight people that share the name.

"Do you know where he was born?"

Hunter leans back in his chair, crossing his arms over his chest.

This is all you. Let's show him what you got.

I take a deep breath and begin gathering information to narrow the search. Based on the fact that he was employed by Lucy twenty-four years ago, I deduce that he must be at least forty-two, living in the United States at the time of his employment with Lucy, eventually moving to Australia.

The search isn't so simple, though, and I find that I cannot find a single Clint Easton that fits those qualifiers.

If you stop now, you'll fail the test. You may not get another shot.

I rack my brain, thinking of what to do next.

Well, if he wants a hacker, hack.

I look up the police department that was on scene for the initial call and find out their records were converted to digital in 2005—a small win.

I go to the department website's login page and prepare for a 'brute force attack' to gain access to the system.

As it turns out, local police departments don't always use strong security measures, and it only takes me twenty minutes to gain access. From there, I have to find the file by way of date since Hunter refuses to provide me with any information.

After locating the file, I scan the documents, taking in every heart-wrenching detail until I find the one that matters most.

"You lied to me. His name wasn't Clint Easton. It was Elton Hartwick."

Hunter smiles. "Don't think of it as lying. Think of it as a lesson well learned."

"A lesson? How is giving me bad information a lesson? I could have been doing something productive."

"Because now you know how easy it is for someone to lie. Don't take any detail of this case as fact. Assume everyone, down to the clerk that entered those documents into the system, is bribable."

I roll my eyes, slamming the laptop shut and casting it aside.

"And now you are officially on the job." He holds up his glass, and I grab mine from the table I set it down on, raising it up before choking down a gulp.

Hunter casts me a wink. "Try sipping."

I now understand the phrase 'panty-dropping smile.'

I've barely had half a cup of wine, but already I feel drunk...on him. He's entirely masculine with a hint of wry mischief. A man that can make a woman laugh is a dangerous thing, they say. One minute you're grabbing your gut chuckling, the next, you're naked and in his bed. Not that I've had such experiences.

The men in my life have always proven to be quite toxic.

"So, when do I get started for real? Do you have me working from a computer lab? I'd like to dig in tonight."

An uneasy look crosses his face. "We start tomorrow. After you leave this room, you'll be escorted to my suite where a team of professionals will attend to you, preparing you for a family dinner."

My brow shoots up. "Ummm...there are all kinds of problems with that. For one: a team of professionals? Like I'm some kind of Neanderthal? And two: a family dinner?"

"Yes. My mother will be thrilled that I'm getting serious with someone. She's been a bit of a recluse, and she'll be happy to have someone to chat with."

"I-I just can't imagine being in the same room as Ernestine Whitmore, let alone talking to her. Like I'll have anything interesting to say."

"You'll do fine." He gives me a reassuring smile. "Oh, and, to make it clear, you will be working out of my suite...and you will be sleeping there as well."

Yes, please!

God—what is wrong with me.

"Your suite? Is that like an apartment?"

"You can think of it as a little studio apartment. It has my bed, a small kitchenette, and an attached bathroom."

I feel a rush of what I can only assume is hormones, every fiber in my body bursting with excitement.

Down, girl!

"You-you can't be serious," I stutter out.

"I can't have you roaming the halls and provoking questions. My mother will just assume we're creating the next line of Davies. She'll approve."

My cheeks flush red as my heart rate quickens at the thought of a carnal week with Hunter, which is most definitely where my mind goes, visualizing him closing the distance between us, his lips grazing mine.

What the fuck is wrong with you?

It's silly because I have so little experience in love. As in, I haven't even kissed a man. Most people would be shocked by that confession, but my teenage years were spent on strict lockdown due to my hacking mishap, and just when I was afforded the tiniest bit of freedom, my mother fell ill.

There was one man in college I was sure would be my first...but he taught me a lesson in trust that forced me to erect a wall, disallowing any man from getting close to me again.

"Is that alright with you?" he asks with a raised brow. "Or would you prefer to dine in what you have on?"

Looking down at my Wish-dot-com outfit, I know that is not an option. "I guess I'll suffer a makeover, although whoever you have has their work cut out for them."

The look he gives me is one I'm unprepared for. It's of disbelief. Like what I'm saying is crazy.

But that's impossible. Hunter Davies is filthy rich with the kind of money that could afford him a bed full of supermodels. And he's attractive—oh my God, he's a level of hot that can only be brought about with superior genetics and hard work in the form of exercising and the strictest of diets.

I look down at my unpolished nails. "Let's get on with it, then."

Hunter's thumbs race over the screen of his phone. "You're going to love the beauty technicians I've assigned to you."

"I can hardly wait."

Chapter FOUR

Arinessa

Hunter's suite is not the black pit I had imagined earlier in the day, with chains fastened to the walls and food lowered down in a bucket.

No, it most certainly is not a torture chamber with its plush furnishings, extravagant decor, and luxurious creature comforts.

The suite is easily one-thousand-square-feet, larger than my entire apartment, every inch of it perfectly designed. The wall-less expanse is segmented into a kitchen, living, dining, and sleeping area, all of them of a similar decor, flowing together seamlessly.

It's meant to feel open and grand with its cavernous ceiling, reaching in some places more than twenty feet high. It certainly creates within me an illusion that I am small.

The bed is one out of fairytales with four tall pillars holding up a decadent canopy of pure white silk. The dressings are equally as stunning, purple and gold threads woven into a masterpiece with decorative pillows complementing the design. My Shabby Chic bedding from Target pales in comparison.

It's then that I remember my mother and take out my phone to give her a call.

After three long rings, she answers.

Arinessa: *Hey, Mom!*

Mom: *Hi, honey. Getting ready to go back to school?*

For the first time in as long as I can remember, my mother sounds excited. The last couple of years, she's pushed me like we were in the middle of the apocalypse. I'm not used to hearing her so cheerful.

Arinessa: *Yeah,*

Mom: *That's fantastic. One more year and you'll finally be finished. I'm so proud.*

Arinessa: *How's your treatment going?*

An audible sigh comes across the receiver, and I wait with bated breath, hoping Hunter made good on his promise.

> **Mom:** *Today, I received a phone call from my doctor. He said that I'm eligible for some kind of new treatment, and I don't know what to do.*

> **Arinessa:** *Mom, don't pass up this opportunity!*

> **Mom:** *I don't know.*

> **Arinessa:** *What did he say about it?*

> **Mom:** *He said it's promising. My best shot, but it's barely out of trial…*

> **Arinessa:** *That's great! Every good treatment goes through a trial.*

> **Mom:** *At this point, I'm not even worried about the side effects.*

> **Arinessa:** *Then what are you worried about?*

> **Mom:** *False hope.*

> **Arinessa:** *Don't give up on your best chance because you're scared of false*

hope.

Mom: *Well, they want me to come in today. In an hour, actually, but I'm supposed to be packing to move.*

Arinessa: *Get your ass off the phone and go see your doctor! We'll move you next week.*

Mom: *I guess maybe I'll see what they have to say.*

Arinessa: *Good. I can't wait to hear the details. I'm not going to be around much next week because I'll be getting the new apartment in order.*

Mom: *Okay, dear. Talk to you later.*

After I hit end, I breathe out a sigh of relief. Whatever doubt I had about Hunter is eroding. I may not take home the big prize, but my mother's health makes this whole ordeal worth it.

My solitude is short-lived, and before I can really process my emotions, the door flies open, and three women enter the room.

One is a bottle blonde with a preference for neon everything. Another has long chestnut hair, donning a more relaxed style. She's wearing jeans and a tee-shirt, but the high-end kind that probably cost more than my entire wardrobe. The third is an Asian woman whose hair is a dark shade of purple. She's wearing shorts with a chain-link belt and a tank top that could have very well come from Target. Her lips are black, her eyes heavily outlined. I guess you'd call the look goth.

All three of them look at me with disdain.

"Who are you?" I ask.

"We deal in glam," Neon says. "We're here to make you look…civilized."

"Oh…I'm Arinessa."

As much as I hate everything about this, the looks on their faces, the implications of their words, I try to reason that maybe this is a good thing. I've never had a makeover, a spa day, or anything more than a haircut from a professional. If you can call Quix Clips professional.

I look down at my body. "New clothes would be nice. All mine are back at my apartment."

"Let's take a look at you," Chestnut says, eyeing me up and down. "Spin for us."

They circle me, each of them inspecting me like I'm some kind of lab specimen.

"She has a dire feel to her," Neon says. "We need to brighten her up."

"I don't know," Chestnut chimes in. "I think we should play up her mystery. Those eyes tell a story.

I snicker because the only story my eyes tell is one of poverty and poor life choices.

"The raw materials we're working with aren't half bad," Purple adds. "Long legs, great bone structure, awesome rack. It's rare that we find such a promising baseline."

"It's like finding a debutant at a trailer park," Neon

japes.

The four of us burst into laughter all at once. Any normal and sane person would be offended, but how can I be mad at something that has me doubled over and grabbing my gut?

"I already like you better than ninety-percent of my clients, and the ten-percent I like more, tip double," Chestnut says.

Purple whips out her phone and begins tapping the screen. "I'm ordering her some capris and casuals."

"No way! Legs like hers deserve to be flaunted," Neon counters. "In lively colors."

"I just want jeans and a tee-shirt." I point to Chestnut. "Like she has, but cheaper."

The three girls laugh in unison.

"I can't remember the last time I looked at a price tag," Chestnut says.

Neon butts her phone in front of Chestnut. "I'm ordering her the Diamond F Jimmy Choo sneakers."

Chestnut rolls her eyes. "God, you're so extra. You know Hunter's going to hate them."

A sick feeling twists in my gut with the mention of Hunter. It hadn't occurred to me until now that they might be well acquainted.

Or rather, how they are acquainted.

It's not like you stand a chance with him, anyway, the logical part of my brain says, but the logical side has thus far been unsuccessful in taming the stark-raving mad side of my brain that is oh so curious as to what Hunter is packing under that suit he had on.

I try to redirect my thoughts, but it's impossible now that images of Hunter have invaded my mind, and I don't much like the feeling of jealousy stirring inside my gut.

As the girls argue over my wardrobe, I go into self-analysis mode, trying to figure out how to fix whatever Hunter broke.

Everything about the man should repulse me. First, he is a man, which makes him untrustworthy by default. And…he was born into wealth and privilege. Let's not forget that he hired thugs to kidnap me. Oh, and he's dangling a carrot just out of my reach—one that I desperately need.

Despite all this, my lady parts have completely forgiven him.

Traitors.

"I'm ordering the formalwear," Chestnut says.

"Oh, no need," I say, cringing at the thought of wearing something too nice. "I'm fine in casual clothes."

Purple snorts. "Silly. This is the Davies family, and they dress to the nines for every occasion. I'm pretty sure Rand Davies dons a three-piece suite just to take a shit."

"That's quite a visual…"

"Your boyfriend really didn't prepare you much, did he?" Neon asks.

Shit-shit-shit! Be cool—casual.

"When we're together, the last thing I want to talk about is work and family," I lie.

"With his body, I don't blame you," Purple says. "Then throw in the fact that he ejaculates cash, and he's a real Prince Charming."

I blink like fifty times, trying to figure out how to respond before finally coming up with, "I had no idea that he had money…but yeah, that body."

"What sound does he make when he comes?" Neon

squeals. "He seems like the silent, stoic type."

I feel my cheeks flush pink. Even Chestnut looks appalled by her audacity.

"He grunts," I blurt out, too stupid to keep my mouth shut.

What the hell is wrong with me?

Three sets of eyes blink back at me.

"I mean, like this," I let out a weird gargling grunt, and when I realize I sound more like a prehistoric dinosaur than a sexy man, I follow up with, "But it's way sexier and very manly."

The three of them break out into laughter, and I join in because fuck, it's as funny as it is stupid.

"You need to get your hormones under control," Chestnut chastises Neon before turning to me. "Oh, by the way, I'm Joey, and this here is Sam," she gestures to Neon, "and Vanessa," she points to Purple. "What's your name again?"

"Arinessa." My name leaves my lips as though I were uttering it to a new college friend. One I never really got to have with how complicated my life has been.

Neon smiles. "Let's head into the washroom so we can get to work."

I follow the trio into Hunter's bathroom, which, aside from being immaculate, has a sitting area and a fireplace.

Neon pulls a chair out from the vanity. "Take a seat. I'm going to draw you a bath, and we're going to get you clean, take care of that unfortunate eyebrow situation you've got going on, fix your hair, and make you good as new."

"Excuse me, but did you just say unfortunate eyebrow situation?"

Neon casts me a firm gaze. "Take a seat."

Hunter

In a lifetime full of disappointments, I hate adding another to my parents' plate, but I see no way of avoiding it.

They've dreamed of the day I'd bring home a lady to introduce them to, ever expectant that I'll eventually settle down and add to the family line. It's especially important to them because they've become so reclusive.

But they aren't the only ones who keep people at arm's length.

Unfortunately, my parents' trust issues, which they inherited from Lucy's betrayal, have rubbed off on me, leaving me with no ability to open up to people, and I don't foresee that changing.

They're going to love Arinessa simply because their criteria at this point are so low. Must not be crazy. Must have a uterus. That's basically it, but I'd be willing to bet they'd overlook crazy for a grandchild.

I used to reason that if I were able to get to know a woman better, the feelings would come, but the lengths I was taught to go through to protect my identity were not conducive to nurturing relationships.

When I travel, I introduce myself as one of my aliases, never using my real name. I have a background I fall back on, happy childhood memories that are not mine.

Because a Davies knows they can never trust.

As a child, my secrecy prevented me from gaining friends, and eventually, when I grew older, lovers. Well, not lovers, I've had plenty of those. Meaningful lovers is what I mean.

As much as I want to blame my parents for being batshit bonkers, I can't. My aunt's disappearance and betrayal forever cast a shadow on our world.

My mother finally came around some and realized I was having trouble forming friendships, but by then, it was too late. The damage was done.

She worried constantly that I'd end up alone in this world and got it into her head that if I settled down, all my problems would be solved. I can't count the number of uncomfortable dinners I've had with the daughters of friends and good acquaintances. None of whom appealed to me.

When they finally got the hint that I wasn't quite ready for matrimony, or even monogamy for that matter, the household went through a staffing change, and I'd wake up to women cleaning my room in their underwear. Because apparently, the most important part of this whole me finding love nightmare is the part where I impregnate a woman with my mother's first grandchild.

And, yes, it was all my mother's doing. It breaks my heart that I'm not at a point where I'm ready to give her a screaming, shitting bundle of joy, but hopefully, one day, I will be.

Don't make a big deal of this. Be direct. Keep his expectations low.

I knock three times on my father's office door.

"Come in," he calls.

I've barely gotten a foot inside when he begins rambling about numbers, digital sales, and returns on investments. I smile, nod, and let him carry on until I find the briefest moment to interrupt.

"Yeah, about that, dad. You see, I was hoping that could wait until next week."

His brow shoots upward. "The Rockford patch will ensure there is no 'back alley' entrance into the mainframe's prototype. What could be more important?"

"It's not work…"

Inhale. Exhale. Break his heart.

"I've met a woman, and I'd like to get to know her a little better. I've invited her to stay in my suite for the week."

Please don't look too happy. Please don't look too happy. Please don't look too happy.

A wide grin spreads across his face. "That's fantastic! Ernestine's going to be delighted! Don't you tell her! Let it be a surprise. I want to see the look on her face."

"It's not a big deal, really. I just need a vacation and don't necessarily want to spend it alone."

"Of course, a vacation! If anyone deserves one, it's you. Take all the time you need."

"We'll mostly stick to my suite."

"Yeah, yeah—that's great. Your mother will be so pleased."

I manage a tight smile, suddenly regretting the whole debacle. Part of me wishes I had just checked Arinessa into a hotel room, but there are risks involved with hacking, and there's no safer place than the Davies Estate, where we work and live out of.

Now, I'm going to be cohabitating in my tight quarters with a woman that not only knows who I am, but is utterly charming.

It's going to be torture.

Father's grinning like an idiot, which only makes me feel worse.

"Ernestine is going to be so pleased," he says.

"I don't want to get her hopes up. There's a good chance mom won't even like her."

"Nonsense," Father says with a glint in his eye. "I knew you'd get that itch eventually. I told Ernestine to be patient, that you needed time."

"Time is so precious," I say morosely.

"Look, I know your mom has been...difficult. You have to believe me when I say she wasn't always like this. It's just—"

"I know, father. It's been hard."

"Please, please—do me the favor of not telling your mother. Not until your little girlfriend enters the room. She's going to be elated."

Dread, sorrow, shame all needle me, and I halfway wonder if I should just marry Arinessa to avoid disappointing my mother. She has a heck of a body, and that brain—there'd be no shortage of insightful conversations.

But that's crazy. There's no way I'm ready to settle down. Not now, and possibly, not ever.

"I'm not gonna keep you. Go on back up to that girl you're seeing. What's her name?"

"Arinessa. Arinessa Sylvan."

"Arinessa Davies—"

"Father—don't you dare."

"What?" He looks innocently at me from behind his desk. "It has a nice ring to it."

I cast him a glare before leaving the office, a sick feeling in my gut.

I pull out my phone and pull up Arinessa's text box.

> **Hunter:** *My father is excited about meeting you.*

> **Arinessa:** *I accidentally blurted out that you grunt when you come!!! Then I tried to replicate it. It was awful. I assured them that it was manly.*

I reread the text three times, making sure I'm not seeing things.

Joey, Sam, and Vanessa must have had a hand in this.

Two can play at that game.

> **Hunter:** *Thanks for telling me. I told my*

father that you liked being choked during sex, and sometimes you masturbate while listening to Micheal Bolton.

Arinessa: *You can't be serious. I'm pretty sure that was a joke, but I need your verbal confirmation, or else I might die!*

Hunter: *I'm not serious, but please shy away from my bedroom habits.*

Arinessa: *They put me on the spot.*

Hunter: *I'll be getting the files ready for the mission while you get ready for dinner.*

Arinessa: *God, this is already going terribly.*

Hunter: *Most women relish a spa day.*

Arinessa: *Does every spa day include getting every hair below your neck ripped out by a small group of sadistic torturers? I don't know if the million dollars is going to cover the therapy I'm going to need after this.*

Fuck, the thought of Arinessa bare and spread out for me on my bed has me painfully hard. This would be so much easier if she were hideous.

Flirting would be a bad idea, and any more

information like that will have me saying things I regret. So I decide to go with honesty.

> **Hunter:** *While we are establishing our professional baseline, I must add that those kinds of details will be ever-distracting to me.*

> **Arinessa:** *Seriously? You probably date supermodels. And you're the one that had them do it!*

> **Hunter:** *I must confess that I did not know how in-depth the spa package would be. And...it doesn't take a supermodel to get the engine going.*

> **Arinessa:** *Noted.*

I pocket my phone, trying to clear my head of the image of Arinessa in my bed, but it's a powerful image that I don't want to abandon.

If I were smart, I'd leave Arinessa to the skillful trio I have tending to her.

But if today proves anything, it's that I'm perfectly capable of making bad decisions.

Arinessa

"**P**hew! The hardest part is done," Neon says with a satisfied grin as I stand naked before the trio of women.

My makeover began three long hours ago. I've been bathed, waxed, polished, tanned, among other rituals that I've heard women do, but had yet to experience myself.

Now, it's time to sift through the racks full of clothing, which sounds awesome, but the women I'm dealing with have a way of making everything feel like boot camp.

Neon grabs an arm full of garments. "This is going to be so much fun!"

Fun, she says. Hmmm…

I honestly think marathons would be less tiring than the rate at which they have me trying on clothes. Within twenty minutes, forty outfits are strewn across the floor, and there's no sign of slowing. It's not until I don an olive green A-line dress that I finally have hope of reprieve.

After zipping me up and backing away for a better view, the girls just kind of stands there, heads cocked to the side.

"I think the V-neck sits well," Purple finally says. "The green doesn't scream for attention, and the way it cascades from the front to the back is going to make for a stunning visual."

Neon shakes her head sadly. "Olive green is so drab."

"You know it's the right choice," Chestnut says. "It shows off her assets without displaying them."

Neon frowns. "I guess the dress accomplishes that."

"Let's get started on her makeup," Purple says. "Maybe we can do something fun."

A loud knock sounds on the bathroom door.

"God, could we have ordered any more clothes?" Chestnut shakes her head, but when she flings open the door, it isn't an attendant with another rack of clothing on the other side.

It's Hunter Davies.

"Hunter!" Chestnut enthuses. "You're going to love what we've done to your girlfriend!"

"May I come in?" he asks, and I pray they tell him no.

"Of course!" the trio calls out in unison.

Fuck!

Hunter

"We haven't done her hair or makeup yet, but we have some great idea," one of the beauticians says, but I couldn't say who. I'm wholly focused on the gorgeous woman in the olive green dress.

"You've done a fabulous job, ladies," I say truthfully. "Arinessa is stunning."

Arinessa's cheeks flush red, but I see the unmistakable hint of a smile playing on her lips.

"I'd like a minute alone with my lady love," I say, and the beauticians quickly leave the room."

Arinessa stands a few feet away, hugging herself and looking like she wants to crawl out of her skin.

Even without her hair and makeup done, she looks stunning. Better than most women fully made up.

"You look ravishing."

My compliment doesn't come across how I'd like it to, though, and instead of her loosening up, she scowls.

"Did I say ravishing?" I smirk. "I meant ravenous. Like you're an apex predator looking for its next meal."

That gets the smile back on her face.

"That dress really does look great on you. What do you think?"

"I can't say. The sadists you hired wouldn't let me look at myself until after hair and makeup."

"Come look, then." I gesture toward the mirror. "I promise I won't tell."

She walks on tipped toes over to the mirror, like she's scared of her reflection.

"What do you think?"

She twirls in a circle, looking at herself from all angles. "The dress is beautiful."

Not half as beautiful as the woman wearing it, I think to myself.

"My parents are going to ask how we met, and I'm going to tell them you applied to a scholarship I assist with."

Arinessa nods. "Please don't tell me we're eating something super fancy for dinner like snails." She scrunches her nose. "I'm totally uncultured."

"You're in luck because my mother doesn't like escargot either. Chances are, we'll be having pasta with some fancy sauce."

She wipes the back of her hand across her forehead. "Phew!"

"The hard copies of the files will be brought up while we're at dinner."

"I can't wait to get started."

As insane as it sounds, the way she goes about her work is incredibly arousing. Watching her on the computer earlier was damn near erotic with the way her eyes were locked on the screen and how she gently nibbled her lower lip.

I'm fairly certain she doesn't have a boyfriend, but I do wonder if she's in some kind of 'friends with benefits' situation. That would be ideal for a woman like her who is most concerned about school and a sick mother.

Seeing as how we'll be working so closely together, I suppose I could dance around the topic. Forging a good working relationship should be of paramount importance, and that requires getting to know each other.

"Am I going to have an angry boyfriend coming at me if he gets wind of our arrangement?" I ask innocuously.

She snorts. "Boyfriend? That would require me tolerating the presence of a man, which I rarely do."

Not the answer I would expect from a college-aged woman.

"If you don't mind me asking, are you gay?"

Her head snaps in my direction. "Huh?"

"It's not a problem if you are. I'm merely curious."

"No, I'm not gay. Unless you count the occasional dream of Gal Gadot as Wonder Woman as being gay."

"Well, that is kind of gay," I reason.

"I promise you, every woman has had that dream at least one."

"As has every man."

Her face brightens as though she's just had a revelation. "I guess deep down, we're all just Gadot-sexual."

It's the equivalent of a 'dad joke,' but it gets me laughing. I can't say I've ever had a conversation like this with a woman before. Plenty have offered up threesomes in order to keep me interested, which is admittedly sexy as hell.

But Ari isn't just sexy. She's also a lot of fun.

"I'll tell you my dreams if you tell me yours," I offer with a waggle of my brow.

"No, thanks. I have enough imagination that I don't need to borrow yours. Gal is probably bored in your dreams, anyway."

"You may have home-field advantage, but I have a desperate desire to please. Don't be surprised if it's my name she screams out."

Ari suddenly looks like a deer caught in headlights, and I wonder if I've gone too far. "Was it something I said? I meant no disrespect."

"No…I just ran out of witty banter."

"Well, next time you meet up with Gadot in your dreams, ask her if I ever run out of anything." I lean down to whisper into her ear. "Spoiler Alert: the answer is no."

Arinessa rolls her eyes then begins sifting through a mountain of shoes.

"It's good that you're single," I say. "Because the last thing I need is some hot-headed boyfriend losing their shit because you dress up for me and not them."

"Ummm, I'm dressing up for your parents."

"Sure." I cast her a wink.

Arinessa slips on a pair of shoes with dangerously high heels and very little surface area at the bottom.

"How on Earth do women even walk in these?" she says, wobbling as she tries to stand upright.

"Careful, Bambi," I warn.

"If twig-thin women can walk around a club in them all night, I can surely walk a couple of feet," she says, carefully toddling forward.

She gets four steps, then turns brazenly like she's walking a runway only to lose her balance, falling against the vanity.

"Fuck!" she shouts as she flounders to stand upright.

When I laugh, she looks over at me with scathing eyes.

"Let me help you." I kneel, offering to take the shoes from her feet.

She complies, and I slip them off.

What I wouldn't give to slip her dress off instead.

"Dammit!" Ari frantically rubs at a makeup smear on her skirt. "It's ruined."

I look over at the racks full of clothing and a pile on the floor. "I wouldn't worry. You have about fifty other dresses to choose from."

"Sorry, I feel like I just wasted your money."

"It's hardly something you should apologize for. I can't remember the last time I laughed so hard."

"It's great that my misfortune is something that brightened your day."

"Let me go get the girls, and they'll help you pick something else out."

"Thanks..."

I exit the bathroom to find the glam trio raiding my fridge.

"While you ladies did a fabulous job of assisting Ari in getting ready, I'm afraid things got a little...out of hand in there, and you're going to have to pick out a new dress."

Their brows shoot up in unison.

"Out of hand?" Sam says.

I give her a wink and let them draw their own conclusion.

"Sure thing, boss," Joey says.

"Oh, and this time try for more of a femme fatale vibe."

Joey's face contorts in confusion. "For...dinner... with your parents?"

"Make it sexy, but not too spicy."

Arinessa

Neon, Purple, and Chestnut come back into the room with sly grins on their faces.

"Sorry about the dress," I say sheepishly.

"I hope it was worth it," Neon says with a wink.

I scrunch my brow in confusion. "Actually, it was pretty terrible. I ruined a nice dress that fit like a dream for—"

"Some hot as fuck sex on the vanity!" Purple pretends to hump Chestnut, who dons a mortified look on her face.

So that's how Hunter spun it.

"Yeah, it was an intense twenty seconds," I reply back, then turn away so they can't catch me smiling.

Purple rummages through the racks, looking for another outfit.

Neon places her chin on Purple's shoulder. "What screams femme fatale!"

Femme fatale? Oh, no—

"Uhhhh, I don't think femme fatale is really appropriate for the occasion."

"It's what Hunter wants," Chestnut says.

That asshole...

"Yeah, but I think I'd rather go with—"

Neon hushes me with a finger to my lips. "We are

getting paid by Hunter. If you have the means to pay us, we'll take your suggestions into consideration, but he specifically requested you wear femme fatale."

When I handed my life over to Hunter for a week, I never expected it would include what I'm supposed to wear, and although I might not love what they're going to pick out for me, it's not worth arguing over.

Besides, if I get a few swanky outfits in addition to my paycheck, who am I to complain?

"Fine."

"Ah-ha!" Purple holds up a black dress. "This one's perfect!"

I'm whisked out of the green dress and into the black one, and while it may be plain in embellishments, it clings to me in such a way that's sure to draw attention no matter the crowd.

"It's kind of crazy that Hunter's wanting to introduce you to the 'rents so soon after meeting you," Neon says.

"Who says it's soon?" I return.

Neon grabs my hand, holding it up so that I'm looking at my newly-polished fingernails. "The state of your nails and eyebrows. When a woman is dealing with a man, their nails and brows are always perfectly manicured."

Wow...I had no idea I was screaming spinsterdom everywhere I went.

Purple pushes me into a chair, and the three begin assaulting me with brushes, creams, and tubes of makeup.

"Can I look in the mirror yet?" I ask.

"Not until the final reveal!" Neon insists.

Chestnut eyes me critically. "We should take off the

red lipstick and replace it with light pink. With the smokey eyes, it's too much."

"You-you gave me smokey eyes?" I stutter out as Purple scrubs my lips.

"Hush!" Neon presses her finger to my lips again.

"Yeah, about this whole 'smokey eye' thing, and those extensions you put on the lashes...I really don't think it's necessary when I'm just attending a dinner—"

"With Hunter Davies' family," Neon interrupts. "We know what we're doing. Trust us."

I look down at my body, suddenly realizing just how much of me is on display. "Does my rack really need to be front and center? Can't we go with one of those sundresses with the flower print?" I gesture to the rack.

Purple dabs a sparkly brush between my cleavage. "Your tits look great. Why not have them on display?"

Oh, great...now I'm glitter tits.

It's become clear that I was raised on a completely different planet than these three. Possibly in another solar system. Each of them has their own signature style of beauty, whether it be outrageous like Neon's or edgy like Purple's. Being around them, I feel like an awkward, lumpy potato.

And trust me when I say it's not because I feel unattractive. I think I look fine. Great even...but in this dress, I exude awkwardness.

I wonder which of the three Hunter would prefer. I always assume men desire supermodels, but what man would complain if they had Neon on their arm? Or...in their bed...

"So, do you know Hunter well?" I ask, trying not to sound jealous.

They glance askance at each other with trepidation. Not a good sign.

"We work with Ernestine frequently. When she tries to shake things up a bit," Neon says nonchalantly. "That's how we got to know Hunter."

"Did you ever think you'd get to work for a living, breathing Hollywood legend?"

"Honestly, I've only ever watched the documentaries," Purple says. "I love the part where they describe Rand and Ernestine's relationship, but what makes it better is knowing that it's real, that in person, they're just as in love as they say in all those shows they've made."

Their relationship unfolded before I was even born, but there are still documentaries being filmed on it today. 'Beauty and the Geek' was branded on every magazine at the time of their coupling, with pictures of them plastered on the cover.

Then disaster struck, and they receded to the shadows. Who could blame them?

"It's ironic that Ernestine requires a glam squad when she doesn't go out much," I respond.

"Are you kidding? She's obsessed with looking perfect for Rand," Chestnut says. "I doubt he's ever seen her with an eyelash out of place."

"And she still attends a lot of functions," Neon cuts in. "She's just very private and purposefully doesn't draw a crowd. Celebrities know how to disappear when they want to."

"I'm changing her hair up a bit to match the style of the dress," Chestnut says. "Large waves will frame her face perfectly."

The three work in unison, seemingly never getting in each other's way, and finally, when they're done with my hair and makeup, Purple sets a pair of shoes down.

"Try these on," she says.

Shit...

The shoes are simple enough, black with three-inch heels, but after what happened earlier, I don't trust myself to walk in them.

"Ummm, can I wear flats?"

"Absolutely, not!" Neon says with bulging eyes.

I try to protest, but Chestnut slips them on my feet, and at this point, I know there's no reasoning with them.

"Walk around a bit," Neon says. "You'll be fine."

Well, here goes nothing...

I walk over to the mirror with relative ease, the heels proving to be structured much better than the previous pair.

"You're gorgeous!" Neon enthuses.

The visual before me leaves me weak-kneed and breathless. My unruly hair has somehow been perfectly tamed, framing my face with large, lush waves of curls. My eyes are indeed smokey, like you see on magazine covers. What I'm most impressed by, however, are my lips, which look far plumper than I know they really are.

What magic is this?

And that's just from the neck up.

The black dress I'm wearing is low cut, yet the cups somehow manage to contain my breasts in such a way that they're both on display, yet fully supported. A quality Forever 21 and Target can't seem to get right. The hem sits a couple inches above my knees, a professional length but far from modest.

I look like I could walk a runway in Milan or head a corporate board. I feel vulnerable and powerful all at once. It's dizzying, terrifying, and if I'm not careful, I think I could get addicted.

Purple appears next to me in the mirror, smiling and bubbly. "Not too bad, if I do say so myself."

Words fail me, not because I'm modest, but because it just doesn't make sense to me. Since when do I have any business looking like *this* on my ramen noodle budget?

"You just went from a low five to a high nine!" Neon enthuses. "We should really put a before and after picture of you on our website."

"Gee, thanks…I guess." Again, I should be offended, but coming from Neon, all I can do is laugh.

Chestnut joins in, saying, "Hunter isn't going to be able to keep his hands off you."

Jokes on her because Hunter's hands will never lay a finger on me. Even if he was interested in me, I want nothing to do with spoiled rich brats that think they can kidnap a woman and then say, "Oops."

Or at least that's what I tell myself.

He does offer a striking visual.

SEVEN

Hunter

T he table is set for five, to include: me, Arinessa, my parents, and Chet, a family friend. Although we're eating in the informal dining room, it will probably feel like a museum exhibit to Ari, who, from what I can tell, has never finely dined.

My father is dressed well, as he always is for family meals. Which is kind of adorable considering the reason.

Before my mother entered the picture, he never left his computer lab and rarely dressed in more than lounging clothes. It was the bane of my grandfather, who struggled to get him to put on a well-fitted suit.

Then he met Ernestine Whitmore, a girl of gold and

glam that brought out a side of him no one knew existed. From that day forward, he dressed in a way he thought would be worthy of a woman like Ernestine.

And even now, after so much time has passed, every time she enters the room, his eyes sparkle.

It may seem with how I've spent my bachelordom that I'd never want that for myself. But the truth is, I want it desperately.

For as far back as I can remember, I've wanted what my father has: to be an utterly devoted husband to a wife who never fails to charm.

But the women I date, if you could even call it that, are less than inspiring. Sure, they're beautiful, many coming from families ripe with old money, but nothing is ever real with them. I'm not even sure they're capable of genuine warmth and love, but they certainly are very good at guessing the number of carats in a diamond.

When the connection isn't there, and the only thing tying you together is money, trust never develops.

It's not that I can put all of the blame on the women for the lack of trust, not when the first thing I tell them is a lie. And by that, I mean my name.

Arinessa is the first woman I've ever introduced myself to as Hunter Davies outside of my family's circle. I'm not entirely sure why I revealed myself, but something about her spoke to me, and my name just popped out before I could give it thought. Perhaps it was because she was wild and helpless just a moment before, or maybe it was because of how guilty I felt over her kidnapping.

Something about Ari has me all kinds of crazy in a way I can't afford to be. Not now, anyway.

"Father," I say curtly.

He nods, trying to keep a smile from creeping onto his lips.

I feel like an asshole, giving him false hope. I tell myself it's necessary, but the truth is, this was all set up on a whim, and I never had a chance to think it through.

Father cocks a brow. "Your lady friend?"

"Arinessa will be down shortly."

"Have you been enjoying your time with her?" he asks, trying to sound innocuous.

"I actually had her treated to a shopping spree and a spa day up in my suite."

"Good man." Father casts me a wink. "That's how you keep a woman."

I chuckle. "Father, with our family name and bank account, it's not going to be too hard for me to keep a woman. It's finding the right one that proves to be a challenge."

Chet walks in, brazen as he ever is. He was my mother's friend from before she'd met my father. They acted in a few films together, and after Lucy disappeared, he proved to be a good man, caring for my mother when others abandoned or exploited her.

"Rand, Hunter, nice to see you both this evening." He sets an intricately wrapped package on the table. "I brought some desserts from Italy that I think you're all going to love."

"I hope you've brought enough for five." Father looks to me with a wide grin. "Hunter here has invited a lady friend to join us."

Chet's brow lifts in surprise. "Well, congratulations are in order. I can't wait to meet the lucky lady."

"Give it a minute, and you'll get your wish," I reply back.

"How is Ernestine today?" he asks, his voice ripe with concern.

Chet, of all people, would know how hard today is for my mother, which is why he came out to see us. Today is the day that everyone is aware of, but no one mentions —my mother's and aunt's birthday. We're forbidden from truly celebrating it because of the emotions it conjures. Still, Chet makes it a point to be here for the hard days.

Growing up, he was something of a fun uncle, but he's come by less and less over the years. He refuses to even entertain the idea of giving up his bachelorhood, though he's no longer the Hollywood heartthrob he once was.

"Chet," my mother says as she walks into the room. "How good it is to see you again. It's been…how many months?"

Chet envelops her in a hug. "Several. Time just slips away from us, I guess."

My mother is dressed in old Hollywood elegance, a silver dress dripping in sparkling embellishments. I can't remember a time I've ever seen her look less than perfect, from her intricately laid golden hair to her impeccable clothing, always tailor fit.

My mother's eyes turn to my father, flooding with love and devotion. I've never seen my mother look at another man the way she looks at my father, which is hilarious because she's beautiful and he's a complete nerd.

Father takes her hand into his, lightly kissing her

knuckles.

"Your son has a surprise for you," he says.

Mother turns to me. "Oh?"

Fuck…why didn't I think this through?

Arinessa being a warm body will be enough to make my mother fall in love with her, as ridiculous as it sounds. She'll see her as her best chance at securing not just a friend, but a grandchild, shower her with kind words and gifts, and then, at week's end, I'll have to tell her that Ari and I just didn't work out. Not enough in common is what I'll say. She'll manage a tight smile. It'll break my heart.

My mother's eyes light up. "Why, hello?"

I look over my shoulder, and my breath leaves my chest.

At first, I don't even recognize her with her hair perfectly set, the messy strands seemingly tamed. Her eyes are what draws my attention next, sultry mystery replacing wide-eyed innocence.

The dress she has on highlights her perfect hourglass figure, her thin waist giving way to the dramatic curve of her hips.

She's not the woman I met just a couple hours earlier. Oh, no. She's somehow captured the ethereal elegance of an angel and the salacious mystery of demoness. The kind you sell your soul to in the blink of an eye so you can grovel at her feet.

I hear my mother utter out some formality, but it's lost on me as I drink in the dramatic curves Arienssa has on display. Shapely legs, round hips, generous breasts—a fucking playground for a man like myself. What I wouldn't give to take her back upstairs, tear that dress off, and bury my cock as deep as it will go—

"Hunter?" my mother's voice finally breaks through my overwhelming fantasy, and I realize that all eyes are on me.

"Do you care to make an introduction?" Mother says pointedly.

"Oh, yes. Of course. Mother, Father, Chet, this is Arinessa Sylvan," I gesture to the brunette beauty that is now standing by my side. "Arinessa, this is my father, Rand; my mother, Ernestine; and my fun uncle Chet."

The hopeful look in my mother's eyes is not lost on me.

"What a pleasure," Mother says. "And why might you be dining with us tonight?"

"Hunter has apparently grown quite close to the lovely lady," Father interjects, wanting to be the one to tell her the good news.

Mother's eyes grow round as her head snaps in his direction. "And you didn't tell me?" A playful hand slaps his arm.

"It's still new," I cut in, "and we're taking some time to get to know each other."

"He's taking a week off from work while she stays here," Father adds.

Mother's hands fly to her mouth. "What fun! We'll do brunch and go shopping. I can't wait to hear all about you: where you're from, what you do, how many children you want."

She just couldn't help herself.

Arinessa's eyes grow round, understandably confused by the forward questions.

"Maybe we should get started on dinner," Chet comes

in with a save. "I'm starving."

And then it strikes me: Chet's here because this is supposed to be one of my mother's bad days, and yet, she's genuinely smiling, ogling my 'girlfriend' in elation.

And fuck—I'm also ogling her in elation. Everyone's looking at Arinessa as though she's some piece of meat, all of us for different reasons.

We take our seats, my mother seating herself next to Arinessa, continuing the conversation without missing a beat, and honestly, I can't be mad at how she's compromising my 'date's' time. She's utterly charming. I knew my mother could work a room, but seeing her so jovial while doing so is like a drug to me.

It's not that my mother was never happy when I was a child, but there was always an edge of sadness to her, and every once in a while, a black hole opened up, and her smiles became rare and strained.

Father loved her and did his best to bring her as much joy as possible, but the pain of losing a twin is great and lasting.

Once the meal is served, we dig in, Arinessa watching each of us before making any moves of her own, too afraid to even lift a fork without confirming its proper use.

If only she knew my mother wouldn't care if she ate cereal with a fork. She's just happy she's here.

My father, well, there's a fucking tear glistening in his eye. He looks over at Mother constantly, practically crying because she's so damn carefree and happy.

I'm literally going to crush them.

Chet quietly eats his meal, a reticent look on his face. It's not like him to be this sullen or without a jape.

Occasionally, his lips form a tight smile before going back to his food.

Maybe he sees through the charade, knowing that it's going to break my mother's heart.

I'm such a shithead.

"Oh, honey, did you hear her say she's majoring in computer science," Mother tells Father.

"Loud and clear."

Chet glances up at Ari, a peculiar look in his eyes.

"Maybe you could give her one of those internships you give out," Mother says. "The paid ones."

Before Father can utter a word, I cut in with, "Best not to mix business with pleasure."

God, I wish I hadn't used the word pleasure.

"Your company is one of the ones I had planned on applying to, but I'd like the same consideration afforded everyone else," Arinessa says, casting me a glare.

"Of course!" Mother places a hand on Ari's. "I'll make sure Rand keeps an eye out for your application."

It's hard not to chuckle at how clueless my mother is regarding some things. I don't even know if she realizes what nepotism is.

Chet sits back, blotting his lips with a napkin. "So, she's a computer science major. How exactly did you two meet?"

My eyes draw to Ari's as hers draw to mine.

"I was looking through scholarship applications for a board I'm on, and while she didn't get the award, her essay was a cut better than the rest, and I asked to meet with her."

"Oh, what was your essay on?" Mother asks.

"The ethical implications of using technology in

criminal profiling," she says without missing a beat, and I suspect it was the subject of a past paper.

"Wow," Mother exclaims, "she's so smart, and Hunter is so smart. Just think of how smart their—"

"You're right, Ernestine," Father cuts in. "They're both brilliant and have their whole lives ahead of them."

Thank God she was cut off before she started rambling about babies.

Arinessa does an amazing job of answering and deflecting questions, every bit as charming as my mother, who's been classically trained.

After finishing off a few of Chet's desserts, we get up to leave, my mother and Ari exchanging hugs.

As they say their goodbyes, Father pulls me aside and whispers into my ear, "I don't know what you have to do to make this work, but I'll leave you the damn company tomorrow if you can make it happen."

I chuckle at his jape before realizing his tone lacks humor.

And suddenly, my life just got infinitely harder.

Chapter
EIGHT

Arinessa

I turn to Hunter as soon as the door closes behind us. "What the hell was that?"

He inhales sharply, raking his long fingers through his shaggy hair. "That was my mother."

"Did she like…up until this moment think that you were gay or something?"

He chuckles. "She's just not used to me bringing women home. You're the first."

"She's kind of awesome, in a weird warm kind of way. I never expected someone like her to be so inviting toward someone like me. I actually felt like she wanted me there."

"Oh, trust me—she did."

The way he looks at me makes my heart skip a beat. Those dark eyes of his have this way of looking not just at you, but into you.

Stop looking at him. You're here to work, nothing more. He's been treating you like a professional, and you need to do the same.

Except, professional doesn't include bragging about our fake sex life.

"Why did you tell the girls that we ruined my dress by…ummm…"

His lips upturn into a smile. "What else would you have me say? That you were learning how to walk in high heels?"

"I wasn't learning! I've just never tried ones so tall."

"What I said was more believable."

He's right, and I need to drop this now. I need to stop looking at him, thinking about him, and even talking to him. This is about work.

There are three large boxes sitting on the table that weren't there before. The cold case files, I assume, and I'm proven right when Hunter begins digging through them.

"Everything we have on the case is either in these boxes or in the computer. You can start whenever you're ready."

"That would be now." I take a seat at the table, lifting the laptop screen and arranging the files next to me.

My heart sinks a little now that I've become acquainted with the Davies family. Before, this was just a cold case I'd watch documentaries on at 2 a.m. Now, the case is real, and I know the people at its center.

I hate that Ernestine suffered the loss of her twin, and I'm more invested in this job as a result.

The computer files are color-coded and in sync with the hard copies, arranged smartly by someone that knew what they were doing. Still, I check each to make sure they align.

I start with recreating the timeline in a way that allows for easier processing, which requires some good old fashion pencil work.

"Do you have a notebook I can write in?" I ask.

Hunter brings me a fancy leather-bound journal.

"Ummm…could it be a cheap Five-Star notebook? I don't want to sound unappreciative, but in order to get 'in the zone,' I can't be writing in that fancy thing."

He shakes his head, chuckling. "I'll have some brought up."

"It's going to take me a while to familiarize myself with the case. It might seem like I'm getting nothing done, but I'm just establishing the known pieces of the puzzle."

Hunter nods. "Understood—oh, and keep the red files separate. Those are documents and items that were illegally obtained, and I want you to look at them last."

"Got it."

With the laptop, I recreate the timeline in corkboard fashion, every document being sorted, placed, and tagged accordingly. It feels like busywork, but I'm learning a lot as I go. Things I never realized about the case."

Hunter plays a supporting role, answering every question, providing me the tools I request, and even going so far as to fetch me water when I'm thirsty. I like that he respects my work and treats me like a professional.

But if I'm being honest, there's a part of me that wishes he saw me differently. The thought of what it would feel like to have his arms wrap around me as he bends to give me a kiss has played on my mind, ever distracting me, and his comment about having 'a desperate desire to please' hasn't helped matters.

The only defense I have against it is getting lost in my work.

"How are you doing?" Hunter says, and I have to shake my head to vanquish him from my thoughts.

"Pretty good. Almost done with the setup."

As much as I don't like bragging, I have to admit, I'm pretty damn good at what I do. At the click of a button, my timeline comes to life, and with another click, I can decide how I want to view the data. It can be by way of written statements, locations, people, or any other variable I've input.

"You're a lot quicker at this than I was," Hunter says, pulling up a chair beside me, "and I wasn't half as good at organizing."

Him sitting so close to me sets me on edge. It's not that he's doing anything salacious; it's that I want him to. His scent doesn't help the matter any, a mixture of wood and sweat that tantalizes my senses.

Get your shit together, Ari.

The slim chance I have at remaining in school relies on me cracking this case, but how am I supposed to do that when I have a thick slice of sexy arrogance seated beside me?

Take a deep breath and show him what you got.

"Once a good base with searchable keywords is set

up, everything becomes infinitely easier." I pull up the file of the garbage man that came by the morning of Lucy's disappearance. "Like this guy, Fred Durmont. When we pull him up, not only does it give us all his personal information, but it provides a timeline put together from the data collected, including his birth date, the year he graduated, and all the things he was doing around the time of the kidnapping. We knew all this before, but now it's digestible and accessible at the click of a button."

Hunter gives a slight nod. "Color me impressed."

"I still have a few more things I need to add, but I'm almost done."

"Don't let me get in your way."

Hours feel like minutes as I compile the cache of data, my fingers flying over the keyboard as I make my way through the files, and after four straight hours of nonstop work, I sit back and admire my accomplishment.

Breathing out a sigh of relief, I say, "I did it. I made a baseline database and corkboard showing all the known data surrounding Lucy's disappearance."

Hunter leans over me, his scent filling my nostrils and sending my mind racing. I had made so much progress in pushing him from my brain, but one single whiff sets me back.

His eyes scan the screen as he clicks through the various files. "You did good, and by that, I mean you're exceptional."

"I input the red files in a way that lets me hide the information with the click of a button. So we can look at them separately."

"Good. Being able to hide it might allow us to better

understand the decisions of the detectives working the case as they didn't have access to some of the information."

For the first time in hours, I look over at Hunter, who is stretching his arms into the air and unleashing a bear-like yawn. Sometime in the middle of my investigating, he changed into sleep pants and a white shirt.

I look down to see that I'm still in formalwear and inadvertently utter, "Oh…" as I realize the ungodly amount of boobage I'm displaying.

Hunter bursts into a fit of laughter. "Good thing you didn't notice them earlier, or else you would have spent the whole investigation distracted by them."

"Seriously, Hunter? You're the one that told those three lunatics to dress me in femme fatale, you asshole. I've been so in the zone that I hadn't even realized I'm still in the slut dress."

He cocks a brow. "Slut dress?"

"I guess our definition may vary. I'm a tech nerd that hides behind computer monitors. I haven't displayed this much skin…ever."

Hunter snorts. "I'm going to have Sam dress you in a real slut dress sometime, so our definitions can align."

I arch a brow. "Sam?"

"Yeah, helped with your makeover. Pixie-like. Perky. Excitable."

"Oh—Neon."

His brow furrows. "Is that what you call her?"

"The trio just barged into the room talking all at once, and instead of remembering their names, I came up with Neon, Chestnut, and Purple."

"Well, Neon certainly suits Sam."

"How well do you know them?" I ask, trying not to sound as jealous as I feel.

"I came to their acquaintance when I walked into my room one day and found all three of them naked and in my bed."

Ouch!

My head snaps in his direction, then I force it back to the screen. Why do I have to be so awkward?

"Oh…um, cool. That must have been nice."

"It was my mother's doing."

"Ummm…wow. Ah, my mother brought me a One Direction poster when I began showing interest in boys, but I guess every parent is different."

"My mother's not well, hasn't been for a long time. She wants grandchildren, so I make it a point not to consort with any of the distractions she sends my way. For all I know, she spikes their food with fertility drugs, and I'll end up with septuplets."

My mouth gapes open. "No…"

"I can hardly hold it against her. She's lonely and refuses to go out much after what happened. I put my foot down, and she's since stopped. She's just so lonely."

"How sad…"

"My father works hard to make her happy, and she often is, but she never feels whole."

"So…did you and the glam squad…" I waggle my brow to get the point across.

He chuckles. "No. They did, however, end up being pretty decent conversationalists, and we chat on occasion. I'm not even Sam and Vanessa's type, but Joey did try to get a little handsy."

"Can't say I blame her," I blurt out without thinking.

A look of surprise washes over his face, and I feel my cheeks flush pink.

"I mean, if you're into, you know, muscular tech heirs."

"Muscular tech heirs?"

My eyes rove his body, an obvious check out. "I mean, yeah."

"Seems like strong qualifiers to me."

I make sure he sees me rolling my eyes before returning my gaze back to my screen.

"Don't think you're off the hook," Hunter says.

"Huh? What hook?"

"You think my mother's going to let you leave without first doing everything she can to entice you into carrying the next Davies heir?"

"That's a hard no," I say too quickly.

His shoulders slump slightly, perhaps from me bruising his ego. "Then you'd be part of the point-zero-zero-one percent of women who aren't looking to get on the Davies' Gravy Train. Fuck, my mother would throw obscene amounts of money at anyone carrying my precious offspring to ensure she'd have access to every part of the child's life. Security. Estates. Luxury everything."

Honestly, I'd be fine just gazing at his body, but I don't want him knowing that.

I bury my nose in a file. "I've always been an outlier," I say nonchalantly, hoping he doesn't notice my voice wavering.

"To be honest, I find that part about you... refreshing."

Don't look too deeply into his words. He's just calling

you a freak in a nice way.

"There is one other thing I need you to look at…" Hunter says hesitantly.

"What?"

"There's a folder. It was created before my aunt went missing, and it hasn't been opened since. It's hidden away, but I found it when looking at old files from before she disappeared. As far as I can tell, no one else knows about it."

"And you haven't opened it?"

"It's encrypted, and I can't gain access."

Hunter takes control of the computer, bringing up a folder titled: Dear Rand.

"What do you think is in it?"

"My aunt was arranging the sale of my father's tech innovations on the black market, so I imagine it's a fuck you letter, maybe telling him why she did what she did. Who knows?"

I bite my lip as I look at its properties, mulling over the intricacies of the folder. An entire program was created from scratch to protect it.

"I'll get to working on this right away, but this isn't something I've seen before."

Hunter goes to the kitchen, opening some cabinets and pulling out some canisters. "I'll throw on a fresh pot of coffee."

Hunter

Staying up until 3 a.m. isn't as easy as it used to be. Waking up afterward is even worse. There are holes in your memory, things seem foggy, your head aches. The whole experience is unpleasant and acts as a wake-up call, slapping you in the face and telling you you're aging.

At least I got sleep, though. Arinessa has been up all night, clicking away at the keyboard, gathering what information she can. I offered her my bed, but she insisted on continuing her work. I was more than happy to stay up, but as time wore on, my mind was finding it difficult to ignore my body's very real reaction to her.

Every part of me wanted every part of her, and I was playing various scenarios in my head of us together. I began looking for excuses to brush my hand against hers, bring my chair just a little closer...it was getting difficult to continue actually working.

I don't even think she's left the chair since she sat down in it, not that I'm complaining. The dress she's wearing does a heck of a job of highlighting her best attributes.

Too bad she's made it abundantly clear that she's not interested in me.

After washing up, I reclaim my seat next to her, but she's so engrossed in the case that she barely notices.

"It's eight in the morning, and you haven't slept," I say, sliding the computer away. "Go get some rest."

She turns to me, tiredness lining her face. "I need coffee, not rest."

"I think you're due for some rest."

"Can't. There's no time."

"What is so pressing that—"

Her eyes grow frantic. "I have one week. One week. If I can just figure this out, not only will I give your family peace, but I can make most of my troubles disappear."

I give a short nod. "I see. What have you found?"

"I couldn't get into the file addressed to your father, so I took a break from it. I did manage to find where Lucy's personal trainer was during his unaccounted for time gap."

My brow shoots upward. "I'm all ears."

"He had a secret email that no one knew about, even the police. It was telling."

"How'd you find that?"

"He emails things to himself under the email catching-you-at-aero-net-dot-com. He's had the email for almost thirty years. Come to find out, he was doing gay porn at the time of your aunt's disappearance."

"Wow…Ari, you've really gone above and beyond."

"When your aunt went missing. He was actually down in Brazil filming, having flown by way of private jet."

"May I have a look?" I nod to the screen.

She pushes the laptop toward me, and I click through the various emails, scanning the dates."

"Oh, shit!" Ari pulls the laptop from me, slamming it shut.

I blink, trying to register what just happened.

"Sorry, but there's something you shouldn't see."

"Ari, what have you been doing on my computer? And how worried should I be?"

"It's nothing?"

"Did that porn lead to other porn? Scared I'll find out your…type?"

"No! It's regarding the case, but it's not something you need to know."

"This is my investigation, so nothing should be off-limits."

"Trust me…you do not want to see what's in those emails…"

"Is it gay pics or something?"

"Let's just leave it at it will in no way change the investigation."

"That's not good enough, Ari."

Her shoulders slump. "Okay, but don't be mad at me.

There are naked pictures of your aunt."

"Jesus…"

"They're just personal pics, and he hasn't distributed them as far as I can tell. From what I gather, he didn't want his gay porn secret getting out, so he never told investigators that he was out of the country during the time gaps."

"Shit…they've been investigating him for years, and it's all been for nothing."

If I'm not mistaken, Arinessa's looking rather cocky with her find. I like a woman who's proud of her work. It's sexy.

"It seems like I'm off to a promising start," Ari says smugly. "Who knows what else we'll find."

Arinessa's intelligence has far exceeded my expectation, and if I'm being honest, I've never been more turned on by a woman.

But she hasn't had any sleep, and the exhaustion is beginning to show on her face.

"Dammit," she mutters under her breath.

"What's up?"

She rubs her eyes, then stretches her arms upward. "I never did change out of the slut dress."

"I'm not complaining," I say, then instantly regret my words when I see her scowl.

"My apologies. I didn't mean to make you feel self-conscious, but you do look lovely. And…well…that dress covers up more than the skimpy tank top and shorts you came in with."

She throws up her hands in frustration. "That's what I sleep in! It's not my fault your hired thugs didn't let me change."

"I am sorry about that. Why don't you go change into something while I check out your progress?"

"I'm going to take you up on that offer."

Arinessa disappears into the bathroom, and I bring the laptop into bed with me. A lure she won't be able to resist.

When she emerges, it takes her a moment to locate me on the bed. Her face registers confusion, then anxiety.

"I hope you don't mind, but I'm not a morning person and was feeling a bit groggy," I say innocuously.

She walks over slowly, an uneasy look on her face. She's wearing a pair of oversized sweats that the girls must have ordered her, every hair on her head is out of place. Even bedraggled, she's stunning.

I sit with my back against the headboard and fluff a pillow beside me. "Climb on in. I promise I won't try anything."

"Your bed is like ten feet high," she says. "There's no way I'll make it up. I'm a computer nerd, not a pole vaulter."

"Well, use the nightstand to climb up."

Grumbling, she hops up on the bed, sitting to the side, far away from me.

"So, you've eliminated personal trainer number two as a suspect. What about personal trainer number one, the one I wanted to look into?"

"Elton Hartwick, as you said, has disappeared. Took a little bit of digging, but I found him."

"How?"

"I looked into what he used to order from Amazon before he disappeared, and I was able to find a bunch of very specific items that renewed automatically. Then I hacked a bunch of shit and found the client lists for those companies, eventually finding someone that had several of the same orders."

"Wow—just wow." My eyes grow round with surprise and admiration. "You really are a genius. I would have never thought of that."

"He is living with a much older woman. I suspect he's after her fortune."

"Anything implicating him in my aunt's disappearance?"

"No. I was able to find forums he frequents along with his daily web traffic, and I haven't seen him looking up your aunt at all, and usually when someone's guilty of kidnapping, they look up the person constantly."

"Agreed."

"That's really all I've found so far."

"You've done great, but I'd like to be able to look at how you constructed the files and the corkboard a little more. You did a much better job of it than myself. Do you care to show me?"

Her eyes go to the pillow beside me. I can tell she's nervous, but she doesn't look suspicious.

"I'm a quick learner. I'm sure it will only take a couple of minutes."

She scoots over until she's next to me, taking her place with the pillow to her back. After clicking through various screens to show me the files, I take the laptop from her, slowly going through them, knowing that if I can keep her on the bed long enough, she'll eventually doze off.

The whole ordeal is painfully boring, but after twelve long minutes of mindless perusing, she's out.

Looking at Arinessa as she sleeps, you'd never realize she's so full of chaos, working odd jobs to get her life in order, caring so attentively for her mother. I admire her greatly, which only enhances how strongly I feel for her.

I let her get deeper into sleep before sliding her down a bit, positioning a pillow under her. She's so exhausted, she doesn't even rouse.

I have to hand it to her, she's doing great work, almost too good. I'd hate for her to inadvertently dig up dirt on my family.

Not that I have much to worry about. I picked Arinessa for a reason, that reason being that she's terrified of landing herself in trouble. No matter what family secrets she manages to dig up, going to the authorities will not be an option for her. That is unless she doesn't mind spending decades in federal prison.

Her hair is back to its unruly mess, scattered across the pillow she's resting on. I pull the blanket up to cover her body and afford her some privacy.

In the short time I've known her, she's proven to be smart, funny, and breathtakingly beautiful. It's easy to find a woman with one of those traits, but all three is like finding a unicorn. I wish we had met under different circumstances, and we could be something other than what we are. I've never 'pined' for a woman before, and I have to say, I rather mislike it. Thinking about someone constantly, the inability to focus, the nervous worry of how they are feeling and if they like you…except I no longer have that worry. She made her thoughts on me perfectly clear.

My phone vibrates, and I check to see a text from

Sabrina, a girl I hook up with every week or so. Lately, I've been so busy with my work, she's been the only thing keeping me sane.

To her, my name is Chase, and I'm a successful real estate investor. She knows we'll never be something serious, but she enjoys it when I take her out for nice meals, and she's always eager to get underneath my clothes.

> **Sabrina:** *I'm flying to Greece tomorrow. Wanna see me off?*

I inhale deeply, reminiscing the soft curves of her body. I could easily rendezvous with her in an hour and get back before Arinessa wakes. Lord knows I need the stress relief.

But for some reason, I don't want to.

> **Hunter:** *Sorry, but I'm otherwise occupied.*

Within thirty seconds, a picture pops into the text box of Sabrina standing on a balcony in only her bikini bottoms.

She's a beautiful woman, and most men would feel lucky to have her on his arm. Any other day, I'd be thrilled to have her in my bed, which is why I can't quite figure out why I'm not pinging my driver to come pick me up.

> **Hunter:** *Definitely call me when you return.*

Sabrina: *Ciao!*

After getting a cup of coffee, I pull out my personal laptop and open up the email that has been haunting me.

The one that could change everything.

For twenty-four years, everyone assumed my aunt was dead. Seventeen years ago, she was legally pronounced dead, based on there being no evidence of life.

Then, just last week, I received an email:

> *Hunter,*
>
> *It's been a while. I'm going to need some things from you, and you're not going to want to tell me no...lest you want unfortunate family secrets coming to light.*
>
> *Tell no one of our communications. You'll be hearing from me again.*
>
> *Sincerely,*
> *Aunt Lucy.*
>
> *P.S. In case you're in doubt, I've attached code from one of the programs I worked on dating back twenty-five years.*

It doesn't take much critical thinking to realize that whoever sent the letter is up to no good. My first instinct was to take it to my father, but he's had to deal with the stress of Aunt Lucy's disappearance for nearly a quarter of a century. It's time I shoulder some of the burden.

It's hard to imagine what she has on my family, but I'd rather not take any chances, which is why I've enlisted Arinessa to investigate.

Initially, I had hoped it was some tech-savvy kid trying to make some easy money by exploiting my family's tragedy. I'd pay him to go away, plain and simple.

But then I looked up the string of code sent with the email, and sure enough, it was from one of my aunt's projects. It might not be Lucy, but it is most certainly someone that knew her or her work well.

Hopefully, this will all get sorted out soon, and catastrophe will be averted. But something tells me it's not going to go as easy as I had hoped.

Chapter TEN

Arinessa

A clean, linen scent is the first thing that draws my attention as I wake, telling me that something isn't right. I douse my apartment in vanilla to cover the smell of cigarettes left behind from a previous tenant, so fresh and clean is a luxury I'm not afforded.

My body tenses into a cloud of softness. The type of exaggerated plushness you see in a Disney movie.

My eyelids flutter open, alert, but the remnants of sleep linger. I'm not scared, though I have no idea where I am.

It takes a moment for my eyes to adjust, and slowly my memory begins placing the chain of events from yesterday together. I was kidnapped, brought to the lavish Davies estate, and given a job by the elusive Hunter Davies himself.

A man who is as handsome as he is arrogant.

And although that's enough crazy for three lifetimes, it doesn't end there.

I was primped and polished to attend his family's dinner, being warmly accepted and even celebrated by his Hollywood royalty mother. Then, I spent all night researching a cold case.

How the hell is any of this even real? I mean, every single thing that's happened to me in the last twenty-four hours is not only unlikely, but downright insane.

I stretch my body, vanquishing the weariness from my muscles. Then, as I turn to my side, I see Hunter seated at the table I once occupied, sifting through files.

My heart races as I try to figure out how to exit the bed quietly as not to draw his attention.

As it turns out, my stealth skills extend only to online perusing, and the moment I hop off the bed, I stumble forward, shouting as I catch myself.

"Did you sleep well?" Hunter asks without turning to face me.

I still don't remember how I got into Hunter's bed, but there's little doubt that I've just had the best sleep of my life. Not that I want him to know that.

"No, barely at all," I lie.

"Nine hours of barely any sleep. That's impressive."

"Nine hours!"

Fuck me—I have only one week to solve a twenty-four-year-old cold case, and I just spent nine straight hours sleeping.

I rush to the bathroom to ready myself for the day. A shower sounds divine, but I feel like I need to assess the situation a bit first.

After freshening up, I tiptoe back into the suite, trying to figure out the best way to get Hunter's attention.

He's wearing plaid pajama pants and a plain white shirt that clings to his muscles. If perfection came in human form, it would take the shape of Hunter Davies.

He has this natural finesse that makes it impossible not to feel clumsy around him; his every movement looks as though it were rehearsed a thousand times before execution.

The only place I have any game is behind a computer screen.

He looks over at me, his honey-rimmed eyes full of amusement. "Hungry?"

"Ummm…yeah."

"We have French pastries, fruit, bagels, all the fixings." He gestures toward the kitchen. "If you'd like anything in particular, I can call it up."

I reach into the fruit bowl at the center of the table. "I guess I'll eat a banana."

"Oh, my mom bought you a ton of stuff."

My hand flies to my chest. "Me?"

"Yeah. A fancy robe, lotions, perfume, chocolates. Literal baskets full of stuff." He points over to a corner of the room, which has various gift baskets piled up.

She really is gunning for that grandkid.

Hunter hikes a brow. "You okay? I swear, I didn't watch you sleep or anything. I'm not a creep."

But I am, I think to myself as my eyes rove his biceps.

"No, it's just that waking up in a new place has me unnerved."

Now ya done it. You managed to make something everyone else has done completely awkward.

"I'm tired. That's all." I take a seat, grabbing a file from the stack.

Thankfully, my answer satisfies him.

"Any idea what you'll be researching today?"

"The best use of my time would be to investigate her ties with foreign entities, but I'm afraid hacking them would trigger some alarms."

"You can hack anything your little heart desires from my family's estate. I have multiple VPNs chained together and signals bouncing all over the world, though I would not say that's a good use of your time."

"Because you're sure it's not them?"

"When my aunt disappeared, she left behind damning evidence that implicated various groups in various crimes, both big and small. The kind of fodder that's great for blackmail."

I nod in agreement. "Your logic checks out. Knowledge is power, and whoever had a hand in your aunt's disappearance didn't care much for it."

Hunter clicks and unclicks his pen as he reads through a file, forcing my attention to him. His hair, though an uncombed mess, looks perfect in its disarray, which is totally unfair considering the amount of time I spend trying to get my hair to denounce its relations to poorly constructed birds' nests.

And his hands...why am I so obsessed with his hands? If anything, they're entirely too large and shouldn't be given critical thought at all.

What the fuck is wrong with me?

Knowing that I'm being borderline creepy, I grab a leather-bound journal and get to work. "I guess I'll look at her day-to-day."

"Good luck with that. My aunt's handwriting was atrocious."

Looking through the files helps me to get a feel for who Lucy was, and none of her attributes strikes me as characteristics of a person involved in corporate espionage. She was smart, obsessed with her work, taciturn by nature, and, if I'm reading between the lines correctly, lonely. There's a familiarity to her I'm not exactly comfortable with. It's like reading a biography of who I'll one day be.

Perhaps the worst part is reading about her unrequited love. She never names him, but there was a guy she worked with that she fancied, and as far as I can tell, she took the secret to her grave, never revealing to him her true feelings.

It's hard to put into words how the passages make me feel, but there's a strong foreboding sensation that seems to overwhelm me. I see my future written in these journals.

And I don't mean to say that I'm undesirable. I'm attractive enough, and if I were to actually put effort into my appearance, I'm positive I could turn a few heads. I'm also smart and reasonably levelheaded. I just have a mountain of debt, poor educational outlooks, and a hatred of men holding me back.

Oh, yeah, in case I didn't make that clear—men are the worst. They simply can't be trusted.

"Any big breakthroughs?"

Hunter's voice cuts through my thoughts, paralyzing me for the briefest of moments.

"N-not really," I stutter out.

Real sly, Ari.

"She did a great job of making herself less than interesting," he says nonchalantly.

"Gee, thanks."

He cocks a brow. "You sound bitter."

"It's just all this is very interesting to me," I say, not wanting to confess how painfully less than interesting my own life is.

"Sometimes I wonder if she wasn't just jealous of my mother and her ability to navigate social situations," Hunter says carelessly.

"Of course, all the computer nerds long to be the prom queen." I roll my eyes to emphasize my distaste for his opinion.

He clears his throat, and a heavy silence falls between us. It's stupid that I got offended because what he said is so blatantly obvious. Lucy was a lonely workaholic that couldn't confess her feelings to the man she loved.

And yet, she banged both her personal trainers and joined at least one sex club.

I force myself to look at Hunter. "It's…fine. I was just being silly."

"And I, rude."

"You know, your aunt was kind of an enigma." I hand the journal to him. "Her love for *him*, whoever *him* was, was so innocent, and yet her exploits with her trainers certainly weren't."

"Yeah, not everything always aligned perfectly with

my aunt. Theories have been tossed around, claiming she may have had some kind of mental illness, a split personality, but I choose to believe that she separated love from lust."

"Separated love from lust?"

"Yeah, the personal trainers and whoever else she laid with never meant anything to her, but *him*, who is some guy from accounting, did."

"You know who he was?"

"He was married with a kid on the way when she disappeared. He was never really a suspect, and he had no clue she had feelings for him."

"How did they figure out it was him?"

"It was one of the few things she confided in my mother."

I scrunch my brow. "You know, she never really mentions Ernestine much in her journals."

"They were from two different worlds, and despite their similar DNA, the only thing that really connected them was my father."

"It's funny how they were so opposite despite being twins."

"Ya know, the biggest difference I've discovered was that one was introverted, the other, extroverted."

"Yeah, one a computer scientist, the other, a Hollywood legend."

"Believe it or not, my mother knew her way around computers, and Lucy was known to act before she decided it wasn't for her."

His hand grazed mine, the sudden contact making me tense and pull away.

Then, I see the picture in his hand.

"Sorry, I was just trying to hand you this."

"Oh." I take it from him, my movements awkward and jerky.

The picture is of Ernestine and Lucy at about ten years old, acting in a play.

"They did theater and computer classes together and were said to be equally good at each."

"Wow, to be born with such gifts, and on top of it all, being drop-dead gorgeous." I snicker. "Some women have all the luck."

"I don't know," Hunter says. "You seem to be quite lucky yourself."

The compliment offends me, though I know it was meant to be nice. I am anything but lucky in this life. In fact, I'm verifiably cursed.

And I don't much like Hunter Davies, of all people, calling *me* lucky.

"Says the man born to inherit a billion-dollar tech corporation," I say, dripping with sarcasm.

His eyes shift guiltily back to the file he had been looking at, and I bring mine to the computer screen.

Fuck, what the hell is wrong with me?

And when did I start asking myself rhetorical questions?

I most certainly know what is wrong with me. It's working so closely with Hunter Davies, a man who possesses a despicable amount of arrogance, a quality I loathe, and yet for whatever reason, I can't seem to vanquish him from my brain.

To make matters worse worse, I have no defense against him and his brand of cockiness. My sharp tongue will never wound him, and all it would take is a simple touch from him and I'd be completely undone.

He's more terrifying than any FBI interrogation room, and even that black hole I was so scared of being thrown down.

As we work, Hunter spends more time looking at me than he does the file in his hands. I pretend not to notice, but it's like working under a spotlight.

"I'm sorry, but is there something wrong?" he finally asks.

Confronted with my awkwardness makes the whole situation worse. I try to bury my nose in a file and ignore the situation entirely, but I feel Hunter's eyes on me.

"Do you think I touched you or something?"

My head snaps in his direction. "No! That never crossed my mind."

"You've been acting weird ever since you got up."

"I'm just working...really hard..."

"I've seen you work really hard, and you're never this tense and angry. And don't think I haven't noticed you bouncing your leg under the table."

It's not that I thought I was hiding my leg bouncing; it's that I didn't even realize I was bouncing my leg. I'm that nervous.

"What the hell is going on with you?"

How could he possibly understand?

"Hunter, just drop it."

"I thought we were getting along quite nicely yesterday, but today you're acting like I kidnapped you or something crazy like that."

It takes me a moment to realize he's joking, making light of my bumbling and trying to get me to smile.

I try to fake a grin, but my lips won't comply with

my brain, and I'm pretty sure I look like Picasso's muse with the face I'm making.

"You look uncomfortable. Do you have gas? Is it your period?"

"No! It's just that," I gesture wildly in the air, "you wouldn't understand."

"Maybe if you clued me in, I would."

My shoulders slump in defeat, and I decide the best course of action is to tell him exactly what my issue is. Or at least that part that doesn't admit that I'm absolutely in lust with him.

"I've never woken up in a stranger's bed before."

"Never had a one-night-stand and stayed the night?"

"Never had any night stand—period. Never even had a boyfriend."

He looks at me in disbelief.

"Are you really surprised? After getting in trouble, I was on lockdown until I moved into my dorm room for college. Then, my mother got sick, my father left, and I had to move back home."

Hunter's mouth hangs ajar. "So, you've never had a boyfriend?"

Of course, he completely ignores the part where I suffered a real hardship, opting instead to focus on my experiences with men...which, at this point, have been almost nonexistent.

"Never," I finally reply, not granting him an explanation.

Hunter says nothing, choosing to look at me thoughtfully, which I appreciate more than any words.

"Your aunt was really good with computers. It's sad that with all the documentaries out there on her, none of them really portray her as the genius that she was."

"She lived and breathed her job. All she wanted to do was sit behind a monitor all day. My mother tried to get her to go out more, but she never wanted to. She was fine in her little apartment, with her computer, and her best friend."

I arc a brow. "Who was her best friend?"

"My father. I know that sounds weird because most people assume it was my mother, but she and Rand got each other."

I go back to the journal I was reading, trying to fully immerse myself in the woman that was Lucy Whitmore.

I swear I can relate to almost everything she says, from her love of coding to her unrequited crush.

And yes, by that I am totally acknowledging that I now have a crush on Hunter Davies. As arrogant and dislikable as he is, there's something about him that makes me feel light, giddy, and sinfully lustful.

And it takes every ounce of my energy to suppress my constant desire to interact with him.

"Your aunt really spoke my language," I say after an extended silence.

"Did she?"

"There's such a strong passion for what she does. She barely talks about your mother or your father. It's all work and a small schoolgirl crush. It'd be easier to read if she wasn't left-handed."

"Left-handed?"

"See how the ink smears? Classic left-handed tell. They smear their ink as they go across the page."

"God, you're smart."

"What's weird is I see no indication in these journals

that Lucy and her physical trainers were lovers, and I can hardly believe she was in a sex club."

"The trainers were pretty upfront about it when questioned, and there's the picture you mentioned in the email. I guess the sex clubs were for pent up energy."

"I just don't get it. She seems so innocent. She has ten years' worth of journaling, and the only person she references romantically is someone she calls, *'him.'* God, I hope I don't turn into her…"

Hunter's hand grazes my wrist, and I look up to see his concerned face. "May I ask you a question?"

"Ummm, sure."

"Why don't you date?"

My eyes grow round, and I grab my arm away, offended he would ask something so personal.

"I'm not trying to judge you," Hunter assures me. "I'm merely trying to figure you out. You have all these reasons that sound valid enough, yet I think there's something more."

"Well, I'm not the mystery here."

"But…you kind of are."

I swallow, trying to figure out what to say, and again, I return to the truth. Or…part of it.

"Remember when I said I hope I don't turn into her?"

"Yeah."

"I already have. Not the sex pot version; the nerdy one. I think a lot about computers, but unlike your aunt, I have a lot of personal struggles as well. My mother getting sick, my father leaving…it's just there's no room in my head for romance. One day, I'll have my own journal, and my own *'him.'* It's actually just easier for me to hate men than face my shortcomings."

"Don't be too hard on yourself."

If only I could tell Hunter that I'd do damn near anything to avoid that fate. That I'd welcome his strong arms lifting me from my seat and throwing me on top of his bed. That as arrogant as he is, I'd welcome anything he'd be willing to do to me.

Wanting someone so desperately is like slow, sweet torture. You don't even know that you're giving away pieces of yourself to be devoured until it's too late.

Calm your fucking hormones, Ari. Lucy's not going to find herself.

As I skim through another journal, a picture falls from the pages. I pick it up to see Lucy and Ernestine standing side by side, one in a wedding dress, the other dressed as a bridesmaid.

"They're beautiful," I finally say, truly in awe of their physical perfection.

"My mother was four months pregnant in that picture."

"You can't tell."

"My father always said he knew she was the one from the moment he first met her; he just had to convince her."

"That's gotta be a powerful feeling. To be so beautiful that the most powerful men in the world bow to your feet."

Hunter gives me a queer expression, cocking a brow and twitching his mouth to the side.

His lips are well-formed with a perfect Cupid's bow. I wonder what they'd feel like pressed against mine. Slow and sensual? Or demanding and greedy?

Stay focused...

"Can I ask you a question?"

He looks over at me, brow raised.

"Do you like forward women?"

He blinks, surprised. "Ummm…while they can be nice, it's not necessarily what I would want all the time. I like a woman that can drive but doesn't mind sitting in the passenger seat on occasion."

"Oh…"

He casts me a grin that I swear is seductive, but my mind can't be trusted at this point.

"Why do you ask?"

"Oh, just because I was trying to figure out your aunt," I lie, burying my nose back in a journal.

I feel his eyes on me, studying me. I'm sure he's not used to spending so much time with a nerd like myself. It can't be that he likes me, can it?

Just the thought of him fantasizing about me sends a strong pulse shooting through my core. Instead of acting on it, though, I focus all my energy on Lucy's writings.

"These journals really don't offer any help," I finally say after spending entirely too long reading about Hack-Cracker and IntroMap. "It reads like a love letter to technology. There's nothing about shady dealings or crazy sex clubs. She doesn't even mention sex, and if I didn't know otherwise, I would assume she was a virgin. All she did was work."

"That's what she was known for."

"And they searched her office?"

"After my mother and father married, Lucy worked out of her apartment more often than not."

"Really? Why?"

Hunter purses his lips, his eyes shifting from me to

no particular point. "I don't know. I guess I never thought to ask that."

"How close was your mom with her sister?"

"Very, when they were little. They were best friends until their interests no longer aligned, at around fifteen. At that time, my mother traveled for acting gigs, and Lucy went to a prestigious school."

"Then she began working for your father."

"Lucy went on to intern at Davies Corporation when she started college. She was just that good. Rand and her really hit it off, becoming fast friends."

"So, your aunt was close with your mother, then became best friends with your father. Interesting. What were the circumstances surrounding your parents' courtship?"

"They met through my aunt, and my father was instantly smitten. Very shortly after they got together, my mother became pregnant."

"Damn, I wish I knew how to crack that file."

"I could probably get my father's best men on the job, but discretion is necessary. I'm not even sure I want my father to know about it. What she said could be very hurtful to him."

Working with Hunter, it's become obvious to me that sometimes people ignore what's right under their noses.

Lucy was not in love with some guy from accounting. Lucy was in love with Rand Davies, and if I'm right, his parents not only knew of her crush, but they did everything they could to deliberately hide the truth, not just from Hunter, but from everyone.

Why they would do that, I cannot say. It could just be embarrassing to them. Or, some fallout may have occurred. Whatever the reason, their secrets aren't safe from me.

ELEVEN

Hunter

S taying a whole week with Arinessa in my apartment is going to be easy. With any other woman, I'd go stir crazy, but something about Ari makes me feel content. I don't get bored, and she's not annoying like the other vapid women I'm used to dealing with.

I know that may sound unfair and even a little misogynistic, but when you choose your lovers based on the number of zeros in their bank account, that's the reputation you're going to get.

Oddly, Arinessa is here for the money, but if she accomplishes what she's set out to do, she'll have earned it. There's no manipulation from her, just data, facts, and an uncanny ability to hack.

Her hair is thrown up in a messy bun, her long fingers tucking loose strands behind her ear every time she turns a page in the file. Every once in a while, she scribbles something in her Five-Star notepad, her nose scrunching as she looks over her writings.

I'm convinced that in a world where women desperately try to copy and one-up each other, Arinessa is different. She's sexy in an understated way and probably the smartest person in every room. That's a line my father has used to describe my mother a thousand times, and it definitely suits Ari. I'd call her humble, but the fact is, in order to be humble, you have to be aware of your charms, and she is completely unaware of her best attributes.

My phone vibrates with a text from my mother, asking to take Arinessa to brunch on Wednesday.

The situation I've put them both in is grossly unfair and wholly selfish. The term 'let sleeping dogs lie' is easier said than done, though, when I have someone emailing me, telling me they're my long lost aunt.

"Ari," I say, hoping my request won't cause her undue stress.

She turns towards me, eyebrows raised. "Yeah?"

"My mother would like to meet you for brunch on Wednesday at a small café less than a block away. Would you be interested in going?"

"With my deadline, I really don't think—"

"You could dig up some information?" I reason.

"You want me to grill your mother on her missing sister? No, thanks."

"You brought up a good point. One that I hadn't

considered. Why did Lucy start working from home after my parents got married?"

She shrugs her shoulders. "I've been thinking about that a lot, actually. I figured that might be when she got into trading secrets."

"Wouldn't she want to stay in office then? To be close to the source?"

"You're the heir to a tech company. You should know when you work on computers, proximity doesn't always matter," Arinessa says, but her voice sounds unconvinced. "Maybe I should do brunch. To clear some things up—but I'll be gentle."

"I think that would be a good idea."

She sighs. "Oh, great. I get to go out in public with Ernestine Whitmore. The legend," she says in a voice dripping with sarcasm.

"First, you look fine. Beautiful even. Second, I'll have the girls come over to get you ready."

Ari's cheeks redden at the compliment. "Seriously? You don't think I can get ready on my own?"

"Don't take that as an insult. My mother has at least two people tend to her each morning."

"Ehhh…"

"Was spa day that bad? Aside from the torturous waxing?"

"It was kind of nice not having to think about what to wear. Though, admittedly, I would have gone with a different dress."

My lips form a smirk, and I reply with, "I'm glad you didn't get your way."

She rolls her eyes, and I decide that I rather dislike her reactions to my attempts at flirting. At first, I thought it was just that she detested me from our initial meeting. But now, I wonder if it has something to do with a self-esteem issue, which would be ridiculous.

"Why did you roll your eyes at me like that?" I finally ask, too annoyed to keep quiet.

She glances nervously at me. "Huh?"

"When I paid you a compliment, you rolled your eyes."

"Yeah, because it's ridiculous."

"Because you don't think that you can look good in a dress?"

"No. I actually think I look really good in a dress, and even just plain, old casual clothes, for that matter."

"Hmmm…that's good, though why the eye roll?"

"Because it came from you, someone who probably dates supermodel-types that spend their days lounging around on beaches. Sure, I look good in a dress, but I'm no catch. I have a mountain of debt and so many obligations that I can barely breathe. I appeal to a different crowd than yours."

"I kinda think you're a catch now."

Arinessa laughs so hard she snorts, causing my lips to twitch into a smile again. Being around her is so easy, and everything about it feels so right.

Too bad she doesn't feel the same way.

Her fingers tap away on the keyboard again, breaking every few minutes to verify something in the records.

"Find anything good?" I ask.

"You have no idea."

"Do tell."

"Oh, it's not to do with your aunt, just technology in general. I've been scanning through facial recognition databases to see if maybe she's been pinged somewhere. It's amazing how much info is out in the world."

"Ahhhh."

"I went through your mother's statements to police, and I have to say, it was pretty heartbreaking."

"Yeah, she was torn up. Her sister went missing, then she finds out she was pilfering company secrets and selling them to rogue intelligence groups."

Ari frowns. "I can only imagine how hard it was to trust, after all that."

"It wasn't just her sister that wronged her. News spread like wildfire, and friends of hers inside and outside the industry were making statements they had no business making, just to get airtime. She cut off nearly everyone after that."

"Your mother is such a lovely woman. I feel bad for the people that made those statements because they're really missing out on someone special."

"Chet stuck around. He's her 'ride or die' as they would call it."

"Has anything ever…never mind."

"Are you asking if they've had romantic relations?"

"Ummm…kind of."

"The answer to that is no. Not that I know of."ther never seemed to worry."

"Chet's statement to the police didn't reveal much. He didn't seem to know Lucy well."

"No one knew Lucy well."

"I guess maybe I'll start looking back at her college years."

"That will have to wait until tomorrow."

"Is there something more pressing you'd like me to

investigate?"

"Nope, it's just that it's going on eleven, and you need sleep."

"We've gone over this. I only have a week—"

"You work for me, and this is nonnegotiable."

"Like hell—"

"I'll cut off the internet to the suite, and if you insist on going over paper files, I'll cut off the lights as well."

Her jaw gapes open in surprise.

"Now, let's get you to bed, shall we?"

"You don't understand...I really need this," she pleads.

"You do realize that if you charm my mother, which you will do by simply having a uterus, she will shower you endlessly with gifts that you can later sell to help keep yourself afloat."

"Is that allowed in the non-disclosure agreement?"

"As long as you don't include my family's name or identifying information." I look over at the pile of gifts my mother had delivered to my suite. "That robe alone probably costs upward two-thousand dollars. Tell her your ovulating, and you could very well find yourself at a high-end car dealership picking out a luxury SUV."

"That poor woman. God, your aunt really did a number on her."

"She did, but I don't think that's what's driving her toward baby fever. I think she's just ready for the joys of grandparenthood."

"I think she'll be great at it."

"The bed is that way." I gesture wildly like I'm assisting a landing plane.

"I'll take the couch."

"Nonsense. You'll take the bed," I insist.

"Your couch is probably way more comfortable than my rock-hard mattress back at my apartment. I'll be fine."

"But I won't be," I say quietly. "Please?"

She gets up, and unlike every other woman that's come before her, hesitantly walks over to my bed, casting an anxious glance over her shoulder at me before climbing onto it, cartoonishly flopping around in exhaustion from the effort.

"I know the bed is a bit dramatic, but so are you."

"Damn, if I were your lover, I'd just go for the couch. I think I pulled my calf scaling your tower of mahogany."

"If you had trouble scaling that tower, my other one would probably throw your back out."

Fuck, I may have just gone too far…

Arinessa blinks at me from the bed. "Seriously?"

"You see, waking up in a stranger's bed isn't the only thing you need to work on. Sharpening those flirting skills would do you good, ya know."

Her brow shoots up in disbelief. "You call that flirting?"

"What would you call it?"

"I don't know—vulgar? It'd be like if I was talking to a man and pushed my boobs together."

"That's advanced level flirting, right there. I wouldn't mind a demonstration."

Arinessa throws her hands in the air dramatically. "It was a joke! But if that's what it takes, I guess I'm doomed to be single forever."

I cross the room, closing the distance between us. When I make it to the bed, she squirms uncomfortably, pulling the comforter over her body.

"Are you really that uncomfortable around men? Or just around me?"

Her shoulders slump, and she looks like she wants to crawl out of her own skin.

"Something happened," she whispers. "You wouldn't understand."

Fire ignites in my veins at the thought of anyone hurting Arinessa, but I force myself to remain calm. I don't want to scare her or make her any more uncomfortable than she already is.

"Care to talk about it?" I say in a tight voice.

"In high school, I was a recluse. Then suddenly, I went to college, and it leveled the playing field a bit. I wanted so badly to be normal and fit in. I ended up meeting a guy, but halfway through the year, my mother got sick, and I had to return home. Teachers let me go remote for some of my classes. Everyone was very accommodating."

"I really hope that this little story doesn't end with me wanting to knock to block off the guy you met."

"He seemed nice enough. He'd bring me schoolwork and listen to my troubles. He kept asking me to go out, but I couldn't. There was too much on my plate. I didn't want to lose what little I had with him, so I grew bold. We started flirting by text, and one thing led to another…" She downcasts her eyes, biting her full lower lip.

"You don't have to tell me if you don't want to."

"No, it's fine. We sexted, which may not seem like much to a guy like you, but it was kind of a big deal for me. It was the only reprieve I had from the hell my life had become. Texts led to pictures, which were thrown into various chats the freshmen boys had showcasing their conquests."

"Jesus Christ—men are such idiots. Scratch that, those idiots aren't men—they're slugs."

"With all the porn out there, I honestly don't care if my pictures are splashed all over the internet. The betrayal is what got to me. I was so depressed when I found out. Humiliated. Ashamed."

"You should be none of those things." I insist, staring intensely into her eyes. "And I promise you, as soon as you're done with college, whatever happened in your life before will be inconsequential. You'll start a job, make friends, and never look back at this time again."

She chuckles dryly. "You just don't get it. I hate men. All of them. I'm destined to be alone."

"Because of one little asshole that showed your picture around?"

"It's not just that though. When my mother got sick, my father got the hell out of there as fast as he could. All I did was blink, and he was gone."

"That's pretty fucking terrible," I say. "And I promise you, not every man is like that."

She rolls her eyes with a sneer.

"You know, we're a lot more alike than you think."

"Yeah, our lives up until now have been so similar," she says sardonically.

"We both don't trust people, and it hinders our ability to form relationships."

She quirks a brow. "You have problems forming relationships?"

"My whole life, I've been taught not to trust people,

thanks to Aunt Lucy. You're the first woman I've ever introduced myself to by my real name that wasn't working for my family or introduced to me by my father."

"Oh…"

"I don't have any real friends."

She looks down guiltily. "Sorry if I seemed insensitive."

"I don't want you to be sorry. I want you to know that there are men out there that you can trust. Men like my father and I, who would never hurt a woman. You can date and live your life just like everyone else out there."

"Except that my major trust issues will never allow me to grow close to a man," she says morosely. "I'm doomed to be a cat-less spinster."

"You know, I can help with that."

"What, are you going to buy me a cat?"

It's hard to bite my tongue, but some things you can't rush. Nothing I say is going to make her suddenly trust men, but maybe by listening to her, she can see that, at the very least, we aren't all assholes.

I hop on the edge of the bed, close enough to listen but far enough away that I'm not invading her space.

"Tell me what's on your mind," I implore. "It can be anything."

She exhales heavily, shaking her head in frustration. "The worst part is feeling so alone. I have online acquaintances, but none of them know me. The real me."

"What about girl friends?"

"I changed schools at fifteen, and it was an awkward time for getting to know people. I was friendly with a couple other women in the dorms, but when I moved out, everything fizzled."

"You know, it's not always going to be like this, don't you? You'll eventually have a career and you'll meet coworkers."

She snickers. "Except that a lot of the jobs I'd be looking at are remote. In my field of study, it's growing more and more common."

"For what it's worth, I think people would be lucky to know you."

"I want to tell you something, but I don't want you to make fun of me."

"I won't."

"I imagine what it must be like to be close to someone. To trust them, but also, to feel them. To lean into them. To feel my skin press against theirs. I'm not just talking about sex, just the intimacy of their flesh. Their warmth. A shared space."

Fuck, I can no longer stay silent.

"I don't think you realize just how similar we are, Ari."

"Oh? Don't tell me you're a virgin. I'm not going to buy that."

"Far from it, but as you said, you're not talking about sex. Every woman in my orbit either doesn't know my real name or knows how many zeros are in my bank account. Nothing about my relations with women is healthy or even intimate."

"Well, I guess we're just two fucked up peas born of pods on opposite sides of the track."

"We could help each other, you know."

"Please don't suggest a hooker."

"Our goals and expectations for each other are clear,

thus, we have no reason to mistrust each other. You say you want a man invading your space, let me be the man."

Her brow furrows like I'm trying to teach her some complex math equation.

"I'm not suggesting sex," I assure her. "Just intimacy. Press your skin against mine. Relax. Share our warmth."

The look of fear in her eyes is unmistakable.

"Either that or I'll pay for your therapy so you can get over whatever PTSD you have."

"No—absolutely not."

"Then you stay as you are and become a self-fulfilling prophecy."

Tears well in her big, doe eyes, and I instantly regret my words. I close the distance between us and take her body into my arms. Initially, she's stiff and resistant, and I almost back away, but then she seems to melt, burying her face into my chest.

"I don't want to be like this. So hateful and full of bitterness."

"Then…let's help each other." I lay down on the bed, stretching my body out, inviting her to curl up against me.

A flicker of eagerness flashes in her eyes. I don't know if it's for me or just the desire to be close to someone, so she can feel her skin pressed against another's.

But then I see the hesitation.

The desire I feel for Ari pales every want I've had for another woman. I love her complexities and crave learning her intricacies. She's better than all those who have come before. But what am I to her?

As desperate as I am to pull her down and cradle her

in my arms, she has to want it, which is why the hesitation in her eyes is torture.

She swallows hard as she looks down at me. "You're going to think I'm weird—no, you already do."

"I think you're interesting, which is very different from weird," I assure her.

"Why?" she asks suspiciously. "I'm not stupid enough to think you're incapable of finding a woman to cuddle with."

"I may have been born into a family of tech juggernauts, but believe it or not, I have other ambitions for my life. I've always fancied myself as one of those cuddlers. You know, the ones they pay to lay there and cuddle you."

"I'm serious. My guess is you have plenty of options for bedmates, so why this?"

The last thing I want is to freak her out and tell her that the more time I spend with her, the less I want to see her go, so I settle for something close to the truth.

"We both have issues, Ari. Not just you. Besides, I hope to restore the reputation of good men everywhere."

She bites her lower lip as she mulls over my words, making her look irresistible, and I begin to wonder if this was a very bad idea. Then she pulls her sweatshirt upward and off her body, so she's sitting in a thin, cotton tank top, which fits her perfectly and leaves very little to the imagination.

Holy Jesus, you just told her she could trust you. Don't fucking ogle her.

"Okay, so…you're now my professional cuddler? Is that how I should introduce you to people?"

Her body slides next to mine, her head connecting

softly with my shoulder. Her light, flowery scent fills my nostrils, and I adjust myself around her.

"See, that wasn't so bad," I say, using my phone to turn off the lights.

Her body is rigid, her hand trembling as it presses against my torso.

"You don't have to be scared of touching me. You're not going to hurt me."

"It's just...very personal," she replies.

"That's the point."

I take her hand and place it against my chest, so she can feel my beating heart.

Big mistake, because my heart is now racing.

For her.

She relaxes, her fingers stretching, gaining more confidence. Her breathing slows, caressing my neck with its warm rush.

I could be content just lying here all night, feeling her cheek against me, breathing her in. It's a feeling unlike any I've had before. A contentness I'm not used to.

"Hunter?" Her voice comes out like a whisper.

"Yeah?"

"Thank you."

TWELVE

Arinessa

I wake with my body pressed against Hunter's, his warm breath gently cascading over my bare shoulder.

My heart should be racing. I should be anxious and trying like hell to find a way to gracefully exit the room —no, the planet.

And yet, I outwardly sigh, extending my arm further over his midsection.

My body fits perfectly alongside his, and despite being solid muscle, his firmness is divine. Snuggled against him, his scent is stronger, more powerful. Intoxicating. It's as calming as any essential oil, the kind of manly musk I've read about in romance novels.

I imagine it's how a boyfriend would smell. One part safe, another part alluring, wholly inviting. What I wouldn't give to roam his body further, exploring his hard muscles with my hand, my leg, my mouth. I hardly think he'd object.

What I wouldn't give for more courage.

Hunter stretches, and I back away, giving him room in case he doesn't feel the same way I do.

"That was a good six hours," he says. "I expect a proper yelp review. A good tip."

His hair is tousled, yet perfect, because he's been given all the gifts in life.

My hair, on the other hand, is in desperate need of a comb and de-tangler.

He hops out of bed with way more grace than I mustered yesterday and proceeds to the bathroom.

To say that last night was significant is an understatement. I feel like another woman, one who wants to live her life, love, and trust again.

Sure, there are a few rotten apples in the barrel, but maybe not all guys are deserving of my contempt.

I must be high on pheromones because this is so not me.

I enter the open door to the bathroom and brush my teeth alongside Hunter, trying not to look too exuberant.

"What do you fancy for breakfast?" he asks.

"You pick. Something carby."

"I have just the thing for you."

Looking in the mirror is slightly mortifying as my hair looks as though it hasn't been properly combed… well, ever.

"I need to take a shower and maybe just shave my

head. What grows back can't be half as bad."

He leans against the counter in the casual way that he does, carefree and without thought. "You've been stressed. Why don't you run yourself a bath?"

A bath sounds absolutely decadent, but I'm on a time crunch. Every minute counts.

You're never going to see a tub like his again, so you might as well take advantage of it. Twenty more minutes washing up won't make much of a difference.

"That sounds nice."

Hunter

After closing the door, I lean with my back against it, imagining Arinessa as she removes her clothes.

Determined to be a gentleman, I've made every effort to avoid making her uncomfortable. I spent an entire sleepless night frozen in place, worried that I was going to pop a boner at the worst possible moment. It was pure hell.

With Arinessa otherwise occupied, now is the perfect time to relieve my pent-up frustration, so I make my way over to the kitchen trash receptacle and slide a hand into my boxers, gripping my hardened flesh.

I brace my other hand on the counter and begin stroking myself as I imagine Arinessa naked in my bath, water lapping at her breasts.

In my mind, she wants me just as badly as I want her,

and her hunger is insatiable. The vision is so powerful, a dozen good pumps do me in, and I spend myself in the can.

Relieved, I call down to the kitchen to have pastries sent up, then I make a pot of coffee, waiting for Arinessa to finally emerge from the washroom.

The wait is excruciating, though I know that when she comes out, I'll see no reprieve. I'll get to spend the day around her, theorizing, strategizing—being right fucking next to her as she studies file after file.

Maybe this just means I need to revisit how I meet women. I think back to the last several conversations I've had with the fairer sex and remember various discussions of purses, Real Housewives, and the best place to buy drugs. All things I have zero interest in.

Arinessa makes me laugh, and watching her brain at work is addictive. Being around her more is going to be torture.

Shortly after breakfast arrives, Arinessa emerges from her bath dressed in comfortable clothes, hair fitted into a towel, phone to her ear.

She's talking with her mother, her face contorting from worry to relief to joy. Seeing her smile makes my heart skip a beat, but I force myself to look away, not wanting to intrude on her private conversation.

Maybe I should convince Ari to wake up here more often.

The thought comes out of nowhere and should scare the ever-living hell out of me. After all, I've only just met her.

And yet, with her, I feel like I'll never get bored. Ari strikes me as the type of woman that would love a good

Escape Room, or even one of those places where you get loaded and recreate works of art to hang on your wall. This isn't just about sex, though my body's reaction to her suggests it's how I'd like to spend a large portion of our time together.

Ari bounds towards me excitedly. "Oh my gosh, my mother said yes to the trial, and they're beginning treatment! They're keeping her in the hospital for the first week to monitor progress."

"That's wonderful," I say, wishing I could take her into my arms but wholly sure that it would be inappropriate.

"They say she could make a complete recovery!"

"I bet she will. You should pick out a gift basket and have it delivered to her. Just send me the one you think she'll like and her room number."

Her brow draws in skeptically. "Really?"

"Really."

She blinks half a dozen times like she's trying to register that she's holding winning lottery numbers. I've never met a woman so easy to please and can't even imagine how she'd act if I actually bought her something of value, like a car.

Her thumbs move over her phone, and a minute later, my own vibrates. She's sent me a link to a treat basket with various chocolate-covered fruit.

"I'll have it delivered this afternoon, but I'm ordering one that's double the size. She's going to go through those rather quickly, I presume."

"Oh-okay!" Arinessa says, her voice ripe with hope.

And just like that, the two-hundred-dollar gift basket I purchased for Arinessa's mother has brought me more joy than anything money has afforded me in…years.

Arinessa pulls the towel from her head, tossing it into the hamper. Damp waves of hair cascade down her back, soon to be a mess of tangles if history is any indication.

Arinessa reclaims her seat from yesterday. "Let's get down to business."

I most definitely agree that we should be getting down to business, though my idea of how we should do that would differ vastly from hers.

Calm yourself. This is a professional acquaintance you're seducing in your head.

She logs into the mainframe, her fingers never slowing. Everything she does is so laser-focused that she doesn't realize how closely I'm watching her, how I'm studying her jaw as it shifts when she's reading, how her brow lifts when she's puzzling together information. I want to remember every part of her.

Without taking her eyes from the screen, she says, "Your aunt was way ahead of her time."

"She had quite a brain on her, or so I've been told."

"This damn folder holds up to every attack I throw at it. She didn't just think about infiltration in her time. She looked to the future and the technology that was probable and protected against it."

"In the tech world, you kind of know what's coming, but even I wouldn't be able to account for the factors my aunt did."

Her fingers fly over the keyboard, typing at least ninety-words-a-minute as she enters data into various screens, trying to find a backdoor into the file my aunt named: Rand.

But my mind is lightyears away from where it's

supposed to be and entirely focused on the problem-ladened beauty before me.

I have to tell her.

"Ari…" I say, my voice trailing off as I try to gather the courage to say words I've never spoken to a woman.

"Yeah," she replies, eyes glued to the screen.

"We are a lot more alike than I could have ever imagined."

She chuckles dryly, casting me a sardonic look.

"Hear me out," I implore. "We are good at what we do, and we have a hard time trusting people."

She crosses her arms over her chest. "Maybe you're good at what you do, but I've yet to have any real wins."

She goes back to the computer screen, and I notice that her hands are shaking ever so slightly.

I can't let this moment get away. Not when I'm just now beginning to accept my feelings and what they mean.

"I don't think you understand the point I'm trying to make."

Arinessa turns back to me, and unruly strands of her hair break free from behind her ear. I long to get close to her, to tuck those strands back into place.

"What are you getting at?"

I swallow hard, trying to come up with the right words that would show her how serious I am without sounding crazy. Simply telling her the truth, that after only forty-eight hours I'm completely smitten by her, would probably scare Ari, especially with her experiences with men.

But I can't let this moment pass because I don't know if I'll ever have the courage to have this conversation again.

"It's just that—"

My phone vibrates, and I lose my train of thought. I look down to see an email that makes my stomach twist with dread—good old Aunt Lucy.

Without thinking, I open the message, frowning when I realize that it contains exactly what I was afraid of: demands.

It takes me a minute to realize Ari is still looking at me expectantly, though I know the moment for heartfelt confessions has passed.

"I'm going to have to tend to some business," I mutter.

"Oh, okay."

"I'm not sure how long this will take me, but there's plenty of food in the fridge, and if there's something you need, you can use the intercom button and someone will assist you."

In ten minutes, I'm dressed. In twenty, I'm out the door, making my way down to my car.

"Where would you like to go," my driver asks.

"The FBI."

THIRTEEN

Arinessa

Finding someone in today's world, with modern technology, shouldn't be that hard. Everyone leaves a mark.

Which is why after three days of searching, I've come to the conclusion that Lucy Whitmore is dead.

Remembering my brunch, I went to sleep at a reasonable hour last night and woke up alone in Hunter's bed, him never returning from yesterday's business.

My body missed Hunter, however illogical that sounds. I tossed and turned all night, craving his scent. Everything about that man screams: WARNING!, but he does something to my soul. He makes it sing.

But now's not the time to dwell on men I'll never have.

Come on, Lucy...

I tap my foot impatiently under the table, eager for any break in the case. I may never be able to recover her from whatever shallow grave she's in, but if I can provide Hunter with new information, maybe there will be some kind of constellation prize in it for me.

A knock sounds on the door, startling me, and I check my phone to see I have two hours until my brunch rendezvous.

I look through the peephole at a rainbow-haired Neon in an audacious orange and green dress.

I open the door and pull her inside the suite. "Thank God you're here!"

Her face contorts into a concerned expression. "So, that hair of yours...it really has a mind of its own, doesn't it?"

"And that mouth of yours really doesn't know when to shut up, amirite?"

"Touché!"

We proceed to the bedroom, and Neon grabs all the toiletries and cosmetics we used the other day, setting them out on the vanity.

She presses the shampoo and conditioner bottles into my hands. "Go shower while I look through the outfits."

My stomach twists with anxiety. Yesterday, a quick Google search told me that the shampoo alone is $240 for only twelve ounces, which is more than the price of every shampoo bottle I've ever owned put together because my poor ass doesn't spend more than two dollars a bottle.

This is nothing to him. Just wash your damn hair and get on with it.

I shed my pajamas and enter the shower for the first time, wishing I were taking another bath. It extends back further than I would have imagined, into a cove lush with foliage.

It's a sight to behold, like I'm entering a jungle. A week ago, I had no idea that showers like this existed.

My own shower fixtures are rusted, with only three tiny streams of water that trickle down. I have no idea how I'm ever going to return back to my slum of an apartment, but it's going to be soon, so it's best I not get too comfortable here.

A panel on the wall contains several buttons and dials, and I figure that must be how to turn it on. I push a button, and a heavy mist fills the air. I push another, and jets come to life. I toggle the temperature dials, getting it to the perfect level of heat before entering the misty stream, stretching my body as every inch of it is doused at once. The smell of the shower plants invigorates me, and I wonder if they were strategically picked out like how some use essential oils.

I exhale out my anxiety, determined not to let life overwhelm me, but I'm about six years too late. I've been struggling to survive for far too long, and for the first time since my juvenile mishap, I realize that I have to let go and work towards actually living instead of bracing for whatever inevitability is coming my way.

I can't continue on the way I was, and from this day forward, I'm going to focus on becoming the best version of myself. Starting with learning how to relax.

It is an indisputable fact that I would have

significantly less stress if I woke up to the Hunter Davies' shower treatment each morning. The only thing I reckon that could make it better is having Hunter in here himself. His body pressed against mine. His hands on my hip. His lips pressed on my neck. Like I've seen in so many movies.

But then I guess that wouldn't exactly take away the stress. It would introduce a completely different form of it.

"Hurry your ass up!" Neon shouts.

My shoulders slump at the thought of leaving the tranquil cove, but the last thing I want is to keep Ernestine Whitmore waiting, so I allow myself one more glorious minute of divine water pressure before exiting the shower with my hair in a towel.

Neon motions for me to take a seat and grabs one of several combs set out on the vanity.

She rips off the towel and sighs, taking a few strands between her fingers to investigate. "Your hair really does a good job of weaponizing moisture."

"A war I've been fighting my entire life. My mother used to hack off my hair when I was little. It was so embarrassing."

Her hands move quickly, pulling and pushing my head as she works her magic. "The sad thing is you have great hair; it just takes a lot of work."

"So, where's the rest of your squad?" I ask.

"We had a bridal party scheduled for today, so Vanessa and Joey are working that. Hunter pays too well to ever deny him."

"What's it like working for Ernestine?"

"She's not at all what you'd expect her to be like.

I've signed an NDA, so I can't really say too much, but she's fun. One of my favorite clients."

"I'm so nervous about having brunch with her."

Neon snickers. "Don't be. I have clients that are outright aggressive, making you feel inferior. Like you're not even worthy of breathing the same air as them. Ernie is not like that."

"Ernie?"

"That's what we call her."

In no time at all, Neon has my hair done perfectly, not a strand out of place.

"Thank God you came. I feel like Ariel from The Little Mermaid with all the crap you guys left behind."

"I'll write up what each product is for, so you can make sense of everything. You have a great base to work with. Your skin is enviable, and your hair, though difficult, is full and capable of many different styles."

I look at my phone, hoping for a text from Hunter, not that he owes me one. I'm just an employee, after all. He probably hooked up with someone and fell asleep at their apartment.

Oh well.

Maybe it would be better to just call this whole thing off. I'm already positive that Lucy is dead, and chances are, I'll never find her. At this point, I'm basically just putting together a psychological profile, which is not my area of expertise, and puzzling together interpersonal relations.

It's just not worth embarrassing myself.

It's not like it's going to matter. You're never going to see her again, unless maybe it's serving her breakfast at some café you end up waiting tables at, and even then, it's not like she'll remember someone like you.

I push all thoughts of Ernestine from my mind and force myself to look at the racks of clothing with Neon.

Everything she pulls out is just too much. The last thing I want to do is draw attention to myself, and the outfits she picks all have either extreme glitter or a color palette as blinding as the sun.

I'm pretty sure I shouldn't wear a gown, but I don't want to look too casual either. I'm half-tempted to send a text to Hunter, but I don't want to bother him with trivial things such as wardrobe choices when he's probably out making big company decisions.

Or fucking some high-classy woman.

Ouch! I wince at the thought of Hunter wooing some proper lady, which is silly because in no universe would I ever stand a chance with a man like him. Someone so handsome that he could turn the heads of an entire room and with enough money to buy a small island to boot. Or…several small islands. Perhaps a large island. Who the fuck knows?

I grab a strapless dress from the rack, examining it closely. It's mauve, which works great with my hair, and I like how it's smocked at the waist.

"This is what I'm wearing."

Neon frown. "It's—"

"I don't care that it's Hunter that pays you. This is what I'm wearing."

"Fine. Let's get you dressed."

FOURTEEN

Hunter

"I've completed all the upgrades to the InKrypto platform. It's locked down tighter than a nun's asshole."

My father's sullen face stares back at me from behind his computer terminal. "That's good to know, and I appreciate the colorful language."

"I hear R&D is ahead of schedule."

"Also good."

"Our Formidable Businessman ranking will probably take a hit this year, especially with Icor and Dallanger teaming up, but we haven't lost any customers. If anything, we've expanded—"

"That's really great. Now, is there anything important you have to tell me, or are you just killing time?"

"Killing time? That sounds—"

"You come in here and tell me a bunch of shit I already know, then carry on with more shit I already know, when you're supposed to be up there with your girlfriend doing...well, I shouldn't have to spell it out."

"Arinessa is fine. She's hanging out up in my suite while I—"

"I know you were working all night."

I downcast my eyes, hating that I've disappointed him.

After seeking out an old acquaintance from the FBI yesterday, I couldn't return to my suite. I couldn't face *her*. So, I hid out in my office and slept slumped over onto my desk. It wasn't comfortable, but I couldn't afford the comfort of my bed...or Arinessa.

"What can I say? I couldn't stay away too long. I'm married to my job."

Father leans back in his chair, massaging the bridge of his nose in frustration. "Yeah, that's the problem."

Guilt needles me, but I met with my father for a reason, and I have to see this through. I need to find out more about his friendship with Aunt Lucy.

"Nothing wrong with a son following in his father's footsteps, and doing a damn good job of it, if I may be so bold."

"If only you'd follow in other ways..."

I deserve everything he's throwing at me. I'm the one who brought us to this point. It's my price to pay.

"Pardon?" I say innocuously.

"You're mother's getting ready for brunch right now,

thinking that girl you got up there is someone special."

"First, her name is Arinessa. Second, she is indeed special."

"If she's so special, why have you been at work all night?"

Be calm. You can do this.

"Father, I need to talk to you about something."

You're such an asshole.

"Which account has you worried?" Father says sarcastically.

I pull out a chair he has reserved for guests and take a seat.

"How did you know mother was the one for you?"

Father blinks back at me, mouth slightly ajar.

You fucker.

"How'd I know your mother was the one?" he repeats back as though in a daze. "I guess it was her looks that caught my attention. Then I found out she was the smartest person in every room."

I chuckle. "Bold statement coming from a man who owns one of the world's largest tech corporations."

"And one-hundred-percent true."

I swallow hard, unsure of how to lead into the question I so desperately need answered. The subject is so difficult to navigate. My mother didn't just lose her sister when Lucy went missing; my father lost a friend, and a big part of my mother.

Bingo!

"I'm sorry for what you've lost."

He looks up uneasily at me. "What do you mean?"

"Oh, just that Mother was young and vibrant, and that was taken from you the moment Aunt Lucy went missing. I often imagine what Ma would have been like had that not happened. The movies she would have made. The adventures we would have had."

Father exhales a long breath. "Don't be sorry for me. If anything, I love her even more now than I did then. When you go through something traumatic with someone, it binds you."

"But you also lost a friend," I reply back. "You and Aunt Lucy were close."

A long moment passes before Father responds with, "Yeah, I lost a friend."

"What was your friendship like? I know how she hurt you and Mom, but I can't help but feel thankful to her for introducing you both."

"Lucy came on as a junior intern at eighteen through a program for people that test high, but I didn't really meet her until she was assigned to my department. She was so fucking smart, and boy did it annoy the others on the team. I wouldn't let them give her hell, though. I simply promoted her above them."

"Funny how Mother looked exactly like Aunt Lucy, but Mother was the one who took your breath away."

Father's brow raises in surprise, as though startled. "Oh, it wasn't her looks as much as it was her vibe. Seeing her onscreen was…breathtaking."

"Watching her in her old films is like watching a different person from Mom," I say. "She was always plucky and full of energy. Now, she's soft-spoken and slow to emote. A completely different woman."

"Ernestine loved acting. I never wanted to take her away from it. She was signed on for two other movies, but when your aunt disappeared…"

"It must have been hard."

He nods stoically.

"It didn't seem like Mother and Aunt Lucy were very close in the end," I say carefully, hoping I don't sound too ambitious, "with Lucy deciding to work from home."

His jaw shifts and I now know something I did not before: my father is hiding something.

It's funny how I never thought to question him on it, not until Ari brought up things that were blatantly obvious. Things you wouldn't think twice about unless you looked from the outside in.

"It was for the best. Ernestine and I were starting our lives together, and we needed to focus on our growing family." Father's brow draws inward. "God, how did we get so sidetracked?"

"I guess I was just curious how you adapted to all the changes that took place in Mother after Lucy disappeared."

Don't say it. Don't you fucking says it.

"Because I guess a small part of me worries that somehow time will change Arinessa, and no matter how strongly I feel for her now, it could all change if—"

"You can't live your life like that, son," Father cuts in. "If you love Ari, you need to tell her. Time slips away. You always think there will be more of it, but every second is so fucking precious, and you don't realize it until it's too late."

The passion storming in my father's eyes disarms me. I'm no longer an investigator. I'm a pupil.

"I barely know her," I say without thinking. "I mean, everything is happening so quickly."

"Hunter, you're twenty-seven-years-old, and Arinessa

is the first woman you've ever brought to meet us. You're not some young, rash kid—you're an adult. There is absolutely something about this woman that makes her special to you."

"She's not rich or from some legacy line. She's not even middle class."

"Luckily, with our coffers, we don't have to worry about that."

"That doesn't bother you at all?"

"Maybe it would have ten years ago, but the only thing I really care about right now is that you and Ernestine are happy. I love you both with every ounce of my nerd soul."

Despite how unsure I am about everything, I manage a chuckle. I really am lucky to have been born to such loving parents.

"Anything else?" he asks.

There is so much more I want to ask, but the last thing I want to do is turn into a babbling mess.

It's funny how I came to my father's office with every intention of plying information from him, and instead, I'm discussing Arinessa, a woman I met seventy-two hours ago when I sent hired muscle to kidnap her.

"To be honest, I don't think Ari feels for me the way I feel for her."

"Well, I can't imagine she'd be up there right now if she didn't like you."

"It was supposed to be about a job," I say honestly. "I was considering hiring her for a position. She's quite talented, and you know how competitive it can be to land someone with her skill set. Then, I don't know…she kind of overwhelmed me in a way I didn't expect."

"Sounds like what your mother did to me."

"But I don't think Ari will ever really go for me. Not seriously."

"Why not? You got my good looks," he says jokingly. We both know full well I got my looks from my mother.

Thankfully.

"She doesn't trust men. And...I don't think she was prepared for dating a Davies. She didn't fully realize who I was until I brought her here. It's a lot for her to take in."

"Most women would climb on the backs of friends and enemies alike to get in the vicinity of a Davies."

"Not Arinessa."

"Hopefully, your mother will make her feel welcome. I have a feeling they'll speak the same language."

I burst into laughter. "I don't know about that. Arinessa is an introverted computer wiz, and Ma is, or was, a Hollywood socialite. If you ask me, she'd be a lot more comfortable with Aunt Lucy."

Father sighs, his shoulders slumping. It's obvious he hasn't gotten over the loss of his friend after all these years, or maybe he just hasn't gotten over the betrayal.

And once again, I wonder what he's hiding.

"Thanks, Dad," I say as I get up from my seat.

"Don't mention it."

His phone vibrates, and he picks it up, grinning. "Your mother is excited to take Arinessa out to brunch. She's on her way now."

"Arinessa is scared out of her mind."

"She shouldn't be. Ernestine is relieved you picked someone smart, with a good head on her shoulders. She reminds your mother a lot of your Aunt Lucy, ya know. Intelligent, computer-oriented, reticent."

"She got all of that out of one dinner?" I ask with a cocked brow.

"Your mother could. She and Lucy were twins, as close as you could ever be to another person—"

"Until Lucy moved out."

Father glowers, and I know I've struck a chord. "Enough about your aunt."

"Thanks for the talk," I say in earnest. "You really helped straighten some things out for me."

Father's face softens a tad. "Sometimes, you just gotta take that leap."

FIFTEEN

Arinessa

After Neon reluctantly helped me into my dress, she tied a dark grey sash around my waist to highlight the hourglass figure I never realized I had, and now I'm being escorted to a small café down the street by a guy that's a part of the Davies' security team.

He tried to get me into a limo, but after being cooped up in the Davies estate for days, I decided I needed to walk a bit.

Heads snap in my direction, craning to get a look at me. At first, I assume they're staring at my security detail, but when I look back over my shoulder, I see that he's keeping a careful distance, scanning the clusters of people as they approach and pass.

Which means they're looking at me.

Why, oh, why didn't I accept the ride?

Keep your head up. Don't make this awkward. Fuck—it's already awkward.

After getting my ass handed to me as a teenager by the FBI, CIA, and all the hard-ass initials, I've avoided drawing attention to myself. People hear the word hacker, and they assume I've stolen someone's identity and went to town with their credit cards, when really the extent of my illegal activities was hunting human traffickers.

I quicken my pace, relieved when I finally arrive at The Cultured Crêpe. Ernestine, who is seated at a table on the sidewalk, rises to embrace me.

She's a woman that could make overalls look elegant, though today she's chosen a cream-colored pantsuit that fits loosely yet somehow manages to show off her exquisite figure. Everything she does looks graceful and effortless, from the way she slides out of her chair to how she tucks a stray curl behind her ear. Even in the fancy dress Hunter bought me, I look like a pauper next to her.

"You look absolutely gorgeous," she enthuses, her light, floral scent wafting to my nose.

I hug her stiffly, trying my best to return the warmth but failing entirely.

"I hope you don't mind that I grabbed a table outside. The weather is beautiful today."

I force a smile. "Not at all."

My security detail joins hers at a neighboring table, and we seat ourselves across from one another. People passing give us casual glances, but no one seems to recognize Ernestine.

"I've gone ahead and ordered you a morning mimosa." She gestures to two cocktails on the table. "Tell me, how has your stay with Hunter been?"

"Wonderful," I reply back. "Everything is so beautiful."

"It felt so sterile when I first arrived. I spruced up the living quarters, but the work areas are still so bleak."

"Techies don't much care about the finer aesthetics. Case in point: my apartment is decorated with old pizza boxes and Mountain Dew bottles," I say without thinking.

Dammit—now she's gonna think you're a hillbilly.

Instead of making me feel awkward, Ernestine chuckles. "I remember those days."

I cock a brow. "You remember coding all hours of the night for class?"

She rolls her eyes, bobbling her head. "No, I mean Lucy. It got to a point where my parents wouldn't even force her to come down for evening meal."

So, I guess working Lucy into the conversation isn't going to be as hard as I had expected it to be.

"It was probably smart that they gave up. The effort it would have taken each meal would have been an inefficient use of their time."

"Hunter wasn't nearly as bad as she. He's definitely gifted, like his father, but the drive just isn't there."

"I have a feeling he enjoys coming down to eat. He speaks highly of you and Rand."

"He's always been a momma's boy." She frowns, looking down at the menu. "Which is partially my fault.

After Lucy went missing, I smothered him."

The waiter approaches the table, and I let Ernestine order for me, trusting her judgment.

"No one can blame you for being protective. Especially when a very real danger existed."

"Unfortunately, it wasn't just to protect him. I was selfish. With everything that happened with Lucy, not just her disappearance, but her betrayal…I just kept him close. I was so scared of losing another person."

"Well, it seems like everything turned out alright."

She looks up at me with a deadpan gaze. "I'm not so sure of that, and it's one of the reasons I decided to ask you out to brunch."

"Oh?"

"You're the first woman Hunter's ever developed feelings for, but unfortunately, that's not even the worst part of it. He's never even had a strong friendship. It's not that people don't like him, it's just that he never lets them in. He knows all the big names, and they do lunch and rub elbows, but there's no true kinship."

My heart aches for her.

"Trying to fix my mistakes only made it worse. I figured if he found himself a partner, he'd always have someone, like I have Rand. When he wasn't finding them on his own, I tried to help matters."

"I can understand why you did that."

"It was dumb, I fully admit it. He thinks I'm obsessed with him becoming a father so I could have a grandchild, but the truth is very different. When Rand and I are gone, I want him to have an anchor in this world. Someone he can love more than anyone. Someone he can trust. I want it so badly for him."

Ernestine grows reticent, but I'm unsure how to fill the heavy void that lies between us.

Luckily, the crêpes arrive, and we dig into our food.

"This is delicious," I finally say, then fork a savory bite of roasted bell pepper and caramelized onion into my mouth.

"Wait until the dessert crêpe comes. Strawberries and a chocolate hazelnut spread topped with powdered sugar. It's to die for."

"I always figured women like you never ate things like that, which means your figure is entirely genetic and completely unfair."

Ernestine laughs so hard a piece of mushroom flies from her mouth. Her cheeks turn a deep shade of crimson. "Gosh, I hope nobody else saw that."

"Your secret's safe with me." I wink.

Ernestine's face grows serious. "About what I said earlier…I just meant that if Hunter seems distant, it's not you. I've made mistakes, and now it seems he has to pay for them."

"I think you're being a little too hard on yourself. You were protecting your son. Who knows why Lucy went missing. It could have been that someone was targeting you, and they very well may have gone after Hunter next if you hadn't taken such good care of him."

She exhales slowly, her lips pursing in a way that unsettles me. "I appreciate you saying that."

"I didn't mean to imply that it was your fault your sister was taken!"

"That's not how I took your words, though, over the years, that has haunted me."

There are so many things I want to ask, but every

question I have could lead to unfortunate consequences, such as hurting Ernestine or even making her mad. I loathe gossip and would hate to appear nosy, but there are some risks worth taking in life, and digging a little just might be the thing that breaks the case.

"It must have been hard having a best friend to tell all your secrets to one day, only to have them disappear with no explanation."

The look she gives me is not one that I expect. It's serious, not at all sad.

"I'm going to be honest with you, though heaven knows I should lie," she says, sipping her mimosa. "It's good that she's gone."

The truth doesn't surprise me, considering what Lucy was up to. Still, I raise my eyebrows in feign shock.

"And…you're not a good actress."

"Pardon?"

"I was so hopeful that Hunter had found someone that would bring him joy. I guess that may never happen."

I feel myself go numb, unable to even speak.

"Enough of the games, Arinessa. I've known a good number of actors in my day, all better than you. You had me fooled for a bit, but I can see through you now."

"I-I don't know what you're talking about," I sputter out.

"You want to know about Lucy. So many do, and I don't blame you. The thing is, though…it's not just your curiosity. Hunter recruited you, didn't he?"

I feel dizzy, like I'm going to faint. Ernestine is looking at me with narrowed eyes and a tight jaw.

"Just tell me what it is he wants."

"He wants you to be happy," I reply without thinking.

"By digging up old ghosts?"

"He thinks that by finding out what happened to your sister, that you'll heal in some way."

"The thing is, I've already healed."

"Really? I mean, you left your career behind, something you loved."

She looks away, refusing to meet my gaze. "Maybe I did love it once. I don't love it now. I don't miss my sister. I didn't even know her. Not since long before she disappeared."

"Is that why she stopped going to work? Because you didn't get along?"

She sneers, shaking her head in disgust. "Let's just say our relationship was beyond repair at that point."

"That's not what you told the cops."

"But it's what I'm telling you. Back then, we didn't want questions. I did feel guilt, but I didn't miss her. And whatever liability I once felt is long gone."

"Oh…"

"What did my son promise you?"

"If I solved the cold case, one million dollars."

Ernestine laughs. "And if you don't?"

"Nothing."

"Then I'm afraid you're about to go home empty-handed because I'm positive he made you sign an NDA, which would exclude you from profiting in any way."

"Actually, I'm not so sure of that."

Her brow lifts in surprise. "You found something?"

"No. I'm pretty sure the case will stay cold, but I'm not going home empty-handed."

"Are you threatening blackmail?"

"No, not at all. If anything, I owe your son a great debt."

"How so?"

"For one, he got my mother into treatment that she wouldn't have received otherwise."

Her eyes grow round with surprise. "That's good. I'm glad."

"But also, I have a lot of demons of my own when it comes to personal relationships. Hunter is…helping with that."

"My sister was an introvert, so I understand."

"Oh, it's not just that. Sure, I'm an introvert, but that never really affected my relations with people. Recently, however, well, let's just say I was hurt by someone."

"I know betrayal."

"Hunter is the only man I've trusted since, though admittedly, I barely know him."

"I'm going to go out on a limb and say your trust is not misplaced."

"What little good it does me now. I imagine he'll send me home after he finds out you know why I'm at the estate."

"Then let's not tell him."

I quirk a brow. "Seriously?"

"He needs to think he's done everything in his power to solve my sister's cold case, so when you come up empty-handed, maybe he can finally let it rest."

"Like you said, I'm not a great actress."

"Then, don't act. Do everything you can to solve the case, but don't let him know I'm aware of what you're doing."

"You make that sound so easy."

"Just focus on the work. I promise you, though—you're not going to find anything. Rand owns one of the biggest tech corporations in the entire world. Whatever computer skills you have aren't going to best the teams of people he's had scouring for any tidbit of information over the past twenty-plus years...legally or otherwise."

"I figured." I sigh heavily, my shoulders slumping. "So, is there anything you can tell me? Any clue that hasn't made it into a file?"

"My sister is probably dead. If I had to guess, she was taken from some running trail by a pervert, and her body was never recovered. It's horrible and grotesque, but the closest thing to the truth we'll ever know."

There's no hint of skepticism in her voice. It's clear that she's come to that conclusion long ago.

"There's something I want to tell you," I say shyly. "If we're keeping secrets, mind keeping another?"

"What is it?"

"Hunter is...so amazing. Everything about him. I know you probably think I'm saying this because he's a rich Davies, but that's not it."

"You don't strike me as the gold digger type, and trust me, I know how to spot them."

"It would be easy if this were just about money," I chuckle dryly. "This...hurts."

Her face grows serious, and her hand reaches across the table, grabbing mine.

"Arinessa, you listen to me. I made the mistake once of not telling someone I loved how I felt about them, and it led to chaos you can't even imagine. Before you leave, you better tell my son how you feel, regardless of the consequences. I promise you, you'll regret holding it in."

"Oh, my heavens—is that Ernestine Whitmore!" a voice cries out.

We look over to see an older woman, her hand covering her mouth. A little boy tugs at her arm.

"Grandma, I want donuts! Not some fancy pancake. Do-nuts!" the boy pleads.

Ernestine flashes a toothy grin. "Why, hello. It's not too often I get recognized."

"Who could miss you!" the woman says in disbelief. "You're like royalty. Could you sign something for me?"

"Absolutely."

"Grandma—I'm hungry!" the boy whines.

"Just-just give me a moment, dear. Imagine how you would act if Spiderman were here."

She digs in her purse, pulling out what looks like a little notepad she uses for her grocery list, turns to a fresh page, then hands it to Ernestine. "Could you make it out to Elenor?"

Ernestine smiles, taking a pen from her clutch, and positions the notepad to begin signing. By now, the child is in a fury that his grandma stopped on the way to breakfast, and smacks his hands down angrily on the table.

My mimosa tips over, drenching me with the orange delight. Ernestine, however, managed to catch her own glass with her right hand, never taking a break from signing with her left.

To be honest, it was a more impressive feat than any of the acting I've seen her do in the movies.

"Hughie! Look what you did!"

The child glares up at his grandma, pleased with himself.

The woman's face contorts in horror. "I am so sorry —"

"It's fine," Ernestine assures her.

"Her outfit—"

"Is replaceable," Ernestine cuts in. "And look on the bright side, now you have quite a story to tell your friends."

I already liked Ernestine, but now, I adore her. She's down to earth, completely unlike what I would expect a woman with her accomplishments to be like.

She hands the small notepad back to Elenor. "Here ya go."

After they leave, Ernestine turns to me. "Why don't we head back to the tower. You can get cleaned up and continue on your mission, and I'll act charmed by you."

"Okay…I do want you to know that I'm sorry for any deception."

"Oh, no reason to be. I don't blame you for taking the job, and I sincerely hope you get something out of it."

Chapter SIXTEEN

Arinessa

After a confusing brunch, I enter Hunter's suite to him pacing the floor, an anxious expression on his face.

Sonnets could be written about his flawless features, though I would not be the one to write them as I suck at rhyming and balancing syllables. Every inch of him is exquisitely chiseled, from the shape of his brow, to his strong jawline, to his muscular chest my hand was against the other night. He is perfection, in an absolute science kind of way.

The way he looks at me lets me know that I'm not the only one with something on their mind, though I doubt he carries the burden I do.

Nothing feels good about lying to him. Not after our most recent interactions. It's not like I'm going to stop my work. I'm going to do everything I can to help him solve the case. I just can't let him know that Ernestine is aware of why I'm here.

His eyes rove my body, an appreciative look on his face. "You look...splendid."

Happiness bloomed inside me. The dress is gorgeous and fits me like a dream. I'm glad he's noticed.

"Thanks. Some kid knocked the table and my drink spilt on me, but you can barely tell now that it's dry."

"Other than that, how was brunch?" he asks.

"It was nice. Your mother is a lovely woman."

"Did she try to convince you to carry the next Davies heir?"

My gut twists. Every part of me loathes this conversation.

Still, I smile. "I could tell it was at the forefront of her mind, though she managed to control herself."

He casts me an ambiguous smile that doesn't seem at all joyful.

Oh, God—he knows!

"How are you?" I ask.

"While I was away, I did some reconnaissance."

"Oh?"

"I asked my father some questions, trying not to let it seem too much like an interrogator."

"How did that go?"

"I learned a lot, though nothing about the case," he says. "All in all, it was a good chat."

I decide not to question him further, though I have no

idea what the hell that meant. Instead, I take my place behind the laptop, entering into the mainframe.

Why are you still here? Ernestine all but confirmed you'll come up with nothing, and you don't get paid for nothing.

But I knew what I was getting into long before my talk with Ernestine. The reason I'm still here is the same reason I was still here yesterday: Hunter.

Some insane part of me craves him. He's become like a teenage crush, that one that you have when you first realize that boys turn into men and they're so much more than the spit wads they threw in grade school.

I never got to act on any teenage crush, and when I finally had my first experience bordering on romance, it ended in disaster.

And while I'd love to be able to confess my feelings as Ernestine suggested, she has no idea what it's like to suffer rejection, which is the inevitable outcome to any confession I make to Hunter.

Staying is torture.

I have to leave.

"Hunter, I'm wasting my time here."

I look away, because I'm too much of a coward to face him, but I hear him stop and pivot in my direction. I can't recall a time I've ever felt this naked when fully clothed.

"Giving up so soon?"

"You know as well as I do that your father owns a tech company. He employs some of the best technical minds on the planet, and I'm sure he's done everything he can to find your aunt. What I'm doing is—"

"Insightful. To be honest, you got me thinking about

things in a way I haven't before."

"But that doesn't solve the case, and that doesn't pay my tuition."

"Your tuition was paid the day you were taken to my family's estate."

My head snaps in his direction. "Huh?"

"The check's dated to be cashed the day before you go back to class."

"But…why?"

"I'm not a complete asshole, but I wanted to keep you hungry. Wanting it."

"Well…thanks."

"Will you get back to work now?"

"I don't think so."

"Why?"

"There's this saying: know when you've been beat. There's no way we're ever going to find out what happened to your aunt. The best of the best have already been on the case. There's nothing I can find that they wouldn't have already."

"I don't trust them, though."

"You don't trust your father?"

His mouth opens slightly, like he wants to tell me something, but no words come out.

"It's okay to want answers, but sometimes you have to realize that you just need to move on. Sometimes there are no answers."

"I received an email," he says quickly, like the words burn his throat.

"An email?"

"The person who sent it says they are my aunt."

"Your Aunt Lucy? Why didn't you tell me?"

"She, or whoever is claiming to be her, is making demands." He runs his fingers through his tousled hair. "I really need you, Ari."

"Why didn't you go to your parents with this?"

"She demanded discretion. Said that if I told anyone, she'd release information that would be damning to my family."

"Oh…"

"My parents aren't monsters, I can tell you that much, but every family has their secrets."

"How do you know it's a serious threat and not some fifteen-year-old kid, like I was?"

"They sent a string of code that Lucy wrote over two decades ago. If it's not her, it's someone that knew her."

"What does she want now?"

"Some old program called ScrptX. I found remnants of it, but it's inaccessible and I wouldn't give it to them anyway. When I left yesterday, it was to meet up with a friend at the FBI. That didn't pan out how I had hoped, though."

I think back to my brunch with Ernestine and the surprising turn of our conversation. She wasn't a sister mourning her twin. Nor was she riddled with guilt. She was positive that I would find no answers to her sister's disappearance, and now I can't help but wonder if there's a reason for that. Perhaps Lucy is still alive.

But I can't ignore the darker logic in Ernestine's confidence, which provokes the question: what if Ernestine or Rand had a hand in Lucy's disappearance?

It's hard to believe a woman like Ernestine could be capable of something so dark, but if she and her family were threatened, it's hard to say how she would react.

But the logic doesn't check out. If they were somehow involved, they would have done a better job of cleaning up after themselves. The information found in Lucy's apartment forever cast a shadow on the Davies' empire as it's never good having your technology sold to the highest bidder and even enemies of your nation.

"How did you find me?" I demand, deciding it's finally time I knew.

"You know how my parents have had 'round the clock security on me since my aunt disappeared?"

"Yeah."

"About three years ago, an FBI guy started working for us part-time. We did some traveling together, chit chatted, and he told me about the cases he'd investigated. He was assigned to your case, and I swear, when he talked about you, he was filled with such admiration. He couldn't believe that some girl attending private school on a hardship scholarship spent her free time hunting the world's worst predators instead of finding ways to pad your family's income. He's a man that's seen the worst in society, and he said that you restored his faith in humanity."

My jaw drops in shock. "No…"

"I actually went to see him yesterday, but I guess he received an injury a year ago and has been medically retired."

The FBI was the absolute worst, treating me like I was a hardened criminal. I'd been yelled at, lectured, and told that I had ruined their case. Never praised.

"Wait-wait-wait—all that time, they admired me?"

"Uh-huh," Hunter says, nodding his head.

"But they yelled at me…"

"Have you ever heard of the term 'scared straight'?"

Tears well in my eyes as heat floods my cheeks. "Oh my God...all this time I thought I was despised—loathed."

Hunter hands me a napkin to dab my tears with. "Not even close. They wanted to approach you with a job right out of high school, but it's standard to wait until someone has completed college. I wouldn't have contacted you at all, except some huge twist of fate had you wandering around the dark web, and I had an alarm set to trigger if you made such ventures. You see, Davies could use smart minds like yours, and I was going to make a competing offer when the time was right."

"You're serious? I'll really be offered a job with the FBI?"

"If the plan hasn't changed, yes."

All I can do is stare back at him, slack-jawed and confused. For so long, I felt I was adrift on a raft, waiting for someone to save me, but I was never alone. People I didn't even know of were silently cheering me on.

Hunter takes a step towards me, his eyes locked on mine. "I hope this means you will stay on and continue to help me dig."

As intriguing as the whole situation is, I can't bring myself to work under such torture, and by torture, I mean so close to a man that has completely and utterly broken through all my defenses.

"I can't."

He snickers, turning away. "I should have known. Women are all the same. They can't be trusted."

"Excuse me?"

"You found out your tuition was paid, and now

you're hightailing it out of here."

I wince at his words. "That's not it at all."

"Oh, really?" he says, his voice thick with sarcasm.

"It's just that…getting close to you has…complicated things."

He looks over to me, eyes narrowed. "How so?"

"I don't know if it's a good idea that we talk about this. You wouldn't understand."

"Why wouldn't I?"

My hands fly dramatically into the air. "For so many reasons. I'm supposed to hate men. Despise every fiber of their being."

"I think we've established that you don't hate me."

"Exactly, and that's terrifying."

"It makes me happy."

"Would you like me to share a secret with you?"

"What? That living with no attachments makes life significantly less complicated?" I roll my eyes to emphasize my distaste.

"No, it's that I have developed an attachment as of late. One I'm not quite sure what to do with."

My heart sinks, but I shouldn't be surprised. It explains where he was last night.

"And who would that be with?"

"You."

I blink, stunned, and not at all sure that I heard or interpreted him correctly.

"You're smart, funny, insanely attractive, though I doubt you'll believe that. You also don't trust people; I don't either. It's one of the reasons I have a hard time forming attachments. For some reason, though, I trust you."

"I'm sure you encounter women with those attributes all the damn time. You know, ones with better pedigrees that aren't poor."

"I have gobs of money and need none from you. Sure, I encounter beautiful women. Frequently. With my line of work, I encounter smart ones too. But I've never encountered the whole package before. That is, until I met you."

"Hunter, I don't think you understand. You hold my heart in the palm of your hands."

He takes a step forward, his hand wrapping around my own. "As you hold mine."

Nothing he's saying makes sense.

"I'll transfer the full million to your account this very minute if you just agree to stay. All I want is your aroundness. Nothing more. Just…to help me make sense of what it is I'm feeling."

This is it. This is your time. Your opportunity to have a slice of what everyone else is talking about. Don't fuck it up.

"I don't want your money," I say boldly. "But I do want something from you."

"Anything."

"I trust you. And…I trust you with me…"

He looks at me, a hopeful look on his face. "Oh-kay…but what does that mean, exactly?"

"Don't make me say it…"

Hunter takes a deep breath, his chest rising dramatically. I couldn't have made my point any more clear, which means he has reservations.

After the longest, most uncomfortable silence in the history of mankind, Hunter finally says, "This is all very new to me."

I roll my eyes. "I'm not stupid enough to believe you're a virgin."

"Not the sex," he says, taking a step forward and cupping my cheek in his hand, "the feelings."

God, is spontaneous heart explosion a thing? Because if it is, someone get me to a doctor.

His honey eyes look deeply into mine. "I can't promise you anything. I can't say whether or not I'll be interested in you tomorrow. This is all very new to me."

"I know," I say breathlessly.

Hunter tips my chin up, forcing me to look him in the eyes. "Do you really want this? No matter where it leads?"

"I do," I reply back, knowing I'm ready for at least the physical aspect of our encounter.

The sex will be easy to handle. I've been waiting years to see what all the fuss was about, but how strongly I feel for Hunter scares me. We're like kindred souls, both wary of outsiders, yet somehow finding each other.

His mouth ticks upwards into a grin. "Then let's take this to the bed."

Chapter
SEVENTEEN

Hunter

Seeing Arinessa climb into my bed, not only willing, but eager, has me euphoric, and I haven't even touched her yet.

I pull my white undershirt off, flexing to display the thick chords of muscles running down the length of my arms. I go to the gym five times a week, and it shows.

Her eyes drink me in, so innocent, so full of desire.

And then it strikes me. She's a virgin. And what I'm doing is morally wrong. I'm taking something from her and giving her nothing in return. No promise of a future, or even of tomorrow.

I pull out my phone, tapping a few buttons.

"Are you really going to do business shit while I'm on your bed waiting for you?" Arinessa chastises.

"All I'm doing is leveling the playing field," I say without looking up at her.

"Huh?" she whispers.

"You've done more than enough to earn your reward, Ari. I just transferred the million into your account. You're free to go…or…you could stay."

She looks at me apprehensively without saying a word.

"Go check. It will be in the transfer stage, but my banks are lightning-fast with their transactions."

"I don't want to check." Her eyes fixate on me with an intensity I feel in my core. "I want you."

I take the few remaining steps to my bed and hop on, advancing toward Arinessa like a predator stalking its prey.

Her chest rises and falls in anticipation. She looks deliciously eager and a little afraid. The good kind of fear. The kind you get from riding a rollercoaster.

I continue towards her until I'm deep inside her space, forcing her body back against the bed.

My mouth crashes down onto hers, my tongue sliding between her lips. She accepts me greedily, moaning with every twist of my tongue.

"You smell like oranges," I rasp against her.

"That's the mimosa."

My hand snakes to her back, locating the tiny zipper that's keeping me from fully viewing her. I tug it down gently. If it were another woman, I might have torn the dress off, but I decide to use more caution with Ari.

But Ari has other plans. Her inexperienced hands

frantically tug at the waistband of my pants, trying to undo the buckle of my belt.

I grab her wrists, bringing them above her head, nuzzling her neck.

"Patience," I whisper into her ear, pinning her wrists with one hand.

"You have no idea how long I've been waiting for this moment," she replies back.

I peel away the dress from her breasts, marveling at their softness. They're lush in size and shape, topped with two perfect rose-pink nipples I'm aching to taste.

Unable to resist, I knead a breast with my free hand, taking the nipple into my mouth and sucking gently. My other hand continues to anchor her wrists to the bed. The ragged breath she releases lets me know I'm having just the effect I want.

I give her other breast the same treatment, moving slowly, drawing out her anticipation.

"Please." Her voice quivers when she speaks.

I move my free hand down to the sash at her waist, untying it so I can reveal the rest of her gorgeous body. She lifts her hips, allowing me to slide the garment off, leaving her in a pair of skimpy lace panties.

The scent of her sex has my cock throbbing, but there's no way I'm going to unleash it. Not yet. It would have me racing to the finish line, and this isn't a sprint. Her knees are glued together so tightly it would take a crowbar to pry them apart. Or perhaps a few gentle words.

"You look beautiful," I say, but it feels like a lie because the word doesn't do her justice. "Will you allow me to see more of you?"

All hesitation leaves her eyes, and her legs gently part the tiniest bit. I trail my hand over her stomach, between her legs, and her knees fall open. She wants to share herself with me, and that's sexy as hell.

"I'm going to release your wrists, but you're going to do as I say, alright?"

She nods, her lower lip firmly between her teeth.

Usually, I love letting a woman explore my body, but that will have to come later lest I spend myself in her hand. Something about Arinessa is turning me into a teenage boy with no finesse, and the last thing I want is for the encounter to be over before it really begins.

I insert a knee between Ari's legs, then the other as I release her wrists and bring my mouth to hers. Her fingers toy with my hair, trembling as she digs through the strands. As much as I love kissing her, by now, I'm eager for more. I want to be able to make a map of her body, her scent, her taste. I want to know every part of her, inside and out.

I kiss my way from her mouth down to her breasts, taking a short detour to suck on her perfect nipples. Her every squeal delights me, letting me know she's enjoying herself.

I continue down until my mouth meets the scrap of lace covering her mons. It hardly meets the definition of underwear, already soaked through. I pull them off, casting them aside so I can fully appreciate the slick folds of her sex.

Sure enough, she's completely bare, leaving nothing to hinder my view. Her smell is intoxicating, and all I can think about is how badly I want to consume her.

"Hunter?" she says with a shaky voice.

"Yeah?"

"You don't have to—"

"Shhh," I silence her.

I delve my tongue deep into her pussy, licking upward towards her clit. The guttural moan she emits makes my cock throb with urgent want.

Arinessa deserves a skillful lover, someone who knows what they're doing, and I'm determined to be that man. I don't rush to the nuclear button. Instead, I lick close enough to keep her escalating, allowing her orgasm to simmer just beneath the surface.

"Do you like that?" I ask as I swipe my tongue against her opening, relishing the juices that flood my mouth.

She moans her response, her hands grasping desperately at my hair, my shoulders, anywhere she can grip.

Unable to hold back any longer, I bring my tongue up in a long lick, formally introducing it to the rise of her clit. She gasps with pleasure, bucking her hips gently upward, begging for more.

After a flurry of skillful maneuvers, I give a gentle suck, increasing the pressure steadily until she's writhing beneath me. Her body twists violently, and I have to pin her hips down with my hands in order to maintain contact.

"Oh God, yes," she pants out, and I can tell she's close.

I increase my tempo, her moans turning to incoherent babbles. Her body shudders as she cries out in ecstasy, arching her back upward as she comes.

My tongue continues its steady rhythm as she rides

the high of her orgasm, flexing, and moaning and cursing my name.

Her body finally relaxes, twitching with sensitivity, so I pull away, kissing her inner thigh.

"That was amazing," she mutters, still drunk from her come. "You're amazing."

I chuckle to myself, not wanting to embarrass her. It's easy to do a good job when you have a sublime partner to work with, who is an absolute delight.

And she's so fucking sensitive.

Her hand massages my shoulder. "I want you. Badly."

I almost come from her words alone. Damn near everything she does puts me into the 'holy fuck I'm about to prematurely ejaculate' range.

I sit up and pull off my belt so I can take down my pants and boxers. Her eyes grow round as my member pops free.

"Wow…"

I arc a brow. "Having second thoughts?"

"Is everyone…built like you?"

"I've been told I'm blessed."

"I hope I'm able to walk tomorrow."

"Your job can be done from the bed," I tease.

She slaps me playfully, and I cover her mouth with mine, giving her a long kiss.

"This might be uncomfortable—"

"I want it." Her voice is as full of want and need as my cock is.

I bring myself to her core, staring into her eyes the entire time. Her warmth makes my head throb with urgency. I wish I could remain a gentleman with Ari, but

I can no longer cage the beast within me.

I plunge into her, harder than I had planned. Her body tenses around mine, and I feel her fear escalating.

Shit—

I freeze in place. I can't even breathe; I'm so anxious. I never intended to hurt her.

"Please, more…" she finally moans.

Inwardly, I give a big sigh of relief, thankful she's okay.

She bucks upward, impatient, and I slowly guide myself out and back in.

"Jesus, you're so fucking tight it's damn near painful," I say with a shuddering breath.

I begin to pump into her quicker, firmer, more forceful. She wraps her legs around me in response, urging me in as deep as I can go.

It's a miracle I haven't come by now. My body so desperately wants to, but I'm able to do enough mental gymnastics to stave it off.

And then it hits me.

I was so caught up in the moment, so caught up in *her*, that I forgot about protection. I've never fucked a woman bareback before, and the realization that Ari is my first sends a surge of lust coursing through me.

I grunt, releasing into her as she cries out in pleasure.

Fuck, I've been missing out.

Spent, I fall against Ari, exhausted and satisfied in a way I've never been before.

"Ari," I whisper, my hand roving her body. I can't get enough of her.

"That was…crazy," she says in a voice barely above a whisper.

I decide not to dwell on the lack of protection. I don't want to ruin the moment, and she was fully aware of what we were doing.

I kiss her forehead, relishing the scent of her sex still lingering in the air. "What can I say? I'm crazy about you."

She rolls into me, and I circle my arms around her protectively.

For the first time in my life, I feel content.

EIGHTEEN

Arinessa

Waking up after my sexual debut has me buzzing with energy. Now that I know the sinful delights of Hunter's flesh, I want nothing more than to explore his body and all the pleasures it has to offer.

But that's not technically why I'm here. Hunter has a problem. One that only I know about, and I'm determined to do everything I can to help him.

After ordering up breakfast, we make our way over to the table after a morning of cuddling. His scent lingers on my flesh, mixing with the smell of our sex in the air. It's the ultimate aphrodisiac, and I'm hoping to reward my good work with a lunchtime interlude.

Unfortunately, I soon realize that the work I'm doing is not good. It's one thing to try to solve a cold case, but this isn't that. Threats have been made.

"We have to tell your father."

"That's what I've been trying to avoid, remember?"

"Whatever it is she wants can't be good, and your family has to be prepared for the fallout coming their way."

His face hardens, his eyes growing dark. "No. We're not asking them for help."

"But why?"

He answers with silence.

Nothing I say is going to convince him to rope his father in, so I decide to drop it and look at the folder titled: Rand.

I reread its properties for the thousandth time, trying to figure out an attack that could possibly circumvent the security measures. "What if this is just some practical joke she planted, knowing that no one would ever be able to open it?"

"Doubtful. I have a feeling that if we crack this folder, we crack the case."

"Yeah, but the password is twenty-eight characters and cycles through to a different preset code with each attempt at it."

"It was a method she pioneered," Hunter says. "It follows some puzzle-pattern that she set it to."

He flips through a file, though it's easy to see he's not actually reading it.

"Does Davies Corporation have ways around it?"

Hunter's mouth twitches to the side. "There are a few home-brewed methods for hacking, but if we use them on a file inside the Davies' system, it will trigger an alarm, alerting my father to our trespass."

"What if we hack into the system from the outside?"

"Pardon?"

"We stay at a hotel, rerouting the signal through multiple VPNs, and actually hack Davies Corporation from the outside and employ the home-brewed systems that way."

Hunter shakes his head aggressively. "It would send my father into a frenzy."

"But he wouldn't know it was you."

"I'm not sure if I'm prepared for the consequences of covertly hacking my father's corporation."

"Then maybe you can enlist Icor or Dallanger. They're both tech giants, and I'm sure they'll afford you discretion."

For a moment, it looks like he's considering the proposition, then he shakes his head.

"I can't. If something incriminating were to be found, lord knows how they'd wield it."

"You're right, but the problem is, someone is contacting you under your aunt's name and making demands. Eventually, whatever she has is going to see the light of day."

He looks morosely at the stack of paperwork on the table. I wish more than anything that I could take his worries away, if only for a moment, and I have a good idea how: down on my knees, taking his impressive member into my mouth.

Though suggesting that while I'm trying to help him crack his aunt's cold case is grossly inappropriate.

Still, a girl can dream, and the thought of tasting him

has me ever distracted.

I set my hand on his lap. "Don't worry, I'm gonna keep looking. This week, next week, and the week after that if I have to."

His expression changes, softening a bit. He exhales a long breath, then throws the file he was looking at on the table. "Fuck it."

"Pardon?"

"I just don't care anymore."

My brow shoots upward. "What do you mean?"

"This stops now."

"Huh? Aren't you worried about what they have on your family?"

"Even if I could give them what they want, they could still release what they have. Telling my parents will only drive them crazy, making all our lives unlivable. I'm not playing this game anymore. If they want the program so badly, they can go to my father."

"Are you sure?"

"No. But right now, more than anything, I want to throw you back onto that bed and have my way with you every way you'll let me."

I arc a brow. "Why does it have to be on the bed?"

"Are you really that put off by how high it is? You're really gunning for a small staircase like they have for dogs, aren't you?"

"No. It's just that for the last thirty minutes, all I've been thinking about is this." I slide from my chair to my knees, placing my hands on Hunter's thighs.

His brow lifts. "I suppose the chair will do."

He relaxing his legs to allow me greater access to his body. I lean forward, pulling at the elastic of his pants until I can pull out his already erect member.

I'm surprised by how soft and silky the skin is and how easily my hand glides over the shaft. It's not at all like I had imagined it, and seeing it so close has my curiosity piqued.

Hunter emits a throaty groan, his hand gently cradling my cheek.

Then, the fear sets in when I realize I'm probably going to give him the worst blowjob of his life.

"I've never done this before," I blurt out.

"I know," he says gently.

"I'm sorry for—"

"You'll do fine."

His head glistens with precum, which I lap with my tongue slowly, savoring my first taste of him. He sucks in a breath, and I get a rush from knowing that I'm in control.

I inhale deeply, hoping I can take enough of his thick cock into my mouth to give him some amount of pleasure.

Stop being so dramatic. He's a man that is about to have his dick sucked. He has no reason to complain.

Still, I want to make this as memorable as I can for him.

I stretch my tongue out, licking the tip before sliding the head past my lips. He gives a husky groan, and I feel his hips flexing with anticipation.

I take him in another inch, then another, making my way down his shaft and using my hand where I cannot reach.

"Look at me," Hunter demands, and I force my eyes upwards to his.

The intensity of his gaze emboldens me, making me want to perform for him. I work faster, taking him as far back into my throat as I can manage and doing a damn good job of it if Hunter's reaction is any indication.

He taps my shoulder. "Ari."

I settle into a faster pace, my mouth and hand working in rhythm.

"Ari," he says urgently.

His body begins to quiver, his legs shaking.

"Ari, I'm going to come." He gently presses against my shoulder, but my desire to taste him is so great that I ignore his warnings.

Three pumps later, he explodes inside me, a hot gush of fluid rushing down my throat.

I don't relent until he pulls me off, though his member is still hard. He tips my chin up, a look of reverence in his eyes.

"Remove your pants and panties and sit your ass on the chair," he commands.

I obey, and as I seat myself, Hunter is already on his knees, lacing his arms around my legs, forcing me open for him.

He stares with lust-filled eyes for almost a minute before he finally brings his mouth to my core. Gone are the careful, well-planned licks from last night, exchanged for a tornado-style assault that brings me to the brink of orgasm almost immediately, and when he slides a finger into my aching cunt, a euphoric burst of pleasure blooms within me, and I'm sent spiraling out of control.

Hunter Davies is pure magic, able to do things to me I didn't think possible.

After my body calms, he lays his head down on my

thighs like they are pillows.

I run my fingers through his hair, cherishing what time I have with him. It's not that I think he's going to send me on my way, but I'm not naive enough to believe this will last. We are from two different worlds. Heck, he may as well have come from Mars. We're so different.

"Arinessa," Hunter whispers from my lap.

"Yeah."

Before he can say another word, my phone rings. Annoyed, I pick it up to see that it's the hospital calling.

"I have to take this."

I hit answer and hold the phone up to my ear.

Arinessa: *Hello?*

Doctor: *Is this Arinessa Sylvan?*

Arinessa: *Yeah.*

Doctor: *I'm Doctor Ryan. I'm going to have to ask you to come down to the hospital. There's been a development regarding your mother.*

NINETEEN

Hunter

We take the company helicopter across the city to where Arinessa's mother is being treated. The entire ride, she refuses to meet my gaze.

There are risks going into any treatment, and Arinessa's mother would have been told these when she signed the consent form with LaviTech Labs, but that doesn't mean Ari will understand, and judging by her interactions with me, or lack thereof, she's already assigned blame.

"I'm going to do everything in my power to see to her health," I assure her, but all she does is blink at me in return.

Once the helicopter lands, we hop off and make our way to the ICU.

Cassius is standing outside of Ari's mother's room, looking in at the team seeing to her.

"What-what's going on?" Arinessa manages to stutter out.

Cassius turns to Arinessa, a friendly expression on his face. "Ah, you must be Arinessa Sylvan," he says with a wide, toothy grin. "My name is Cassius Lavinius—"

"I know who you are. Everyone does. How is my mother?"

Cassius spares me a glance before looking back to Ari. Formal introductions will have to come later.

"Sometime in the middle of the night, your mother's vitals became worrisome."

"Why didn't someone call me?"

"She requested you not be notified."

"Huh?"

"She didn't want to worry you."

Tears spill down Ari's cheeks. "Why is she so stubborn!"

"This morning, we put her in a medically induced coma because of the pain—"

Arinessa's hands fly to her mouth. "Oh my God—she's in pain."

"She was, but she's not right now," Cassius assures her. "We're doing everything we can for her, and once we get a proper diagnosis, we'll know how to best go forward."

Ari looks hopelessly through the window at her mother lying in the hospital bed. I want nothing more than to hold her, but I have to respect her.

"In a moment, I'll have one of my team members take you in," Cassius offers.

"I should have been here…"

Cassius places a hand on her shoulder. "Trust me, this was by her design."

Arinessa starts sobbing, and I feel helpless just watching her.

Cassius pushes a button, and a woman in a white lab coat steps from the room.

"This is Mrs. Sylvan's daughter, Arinessa."

"Hello, Arinessa, I'm Nurse Agnes."

Ari nods, sniffling.

Cassius looks back into the room. "I'd like you to escort Arinessa in to see her mother."

"Yes, Mr. Lavinius," Nurse Agnes says, giving Arinessa a mask.

Arinessa dons the mask and follows the nurse into the ICU room.

Cassius turns to me, a curious look on his face. "I don't believe we've been formally introduced."

"I'm Hunter Davies," I say dryly.

"I know."

"That's all you need to know."

"You're a bit…testy."

"You may have just killed my friend's mother. Forgive me if I lack warmth."

"Yeah, putting her into this treatment was a mistake, but when the world's most reclusive billionaire asks you for a favor, you say yes."

Fire pumps in my veins. "So you knew she wasn't a candidate? You just put her on it to curry some favor, and now it's going to kill her?"

"No-no-no, that's not what I meant. The drug is fine, one of the most promising drugs we've ever produced, but Ari's mother wasn't a good candidate because it looks like she may have had comorbidities we were not aware of."

"Explain."

"There is something else going on with her that hasn't yet been diagnosed, and now, we're looking at a delay in getting the pill to market if we can't get her properly diagnosed."

"Oh, shit."

"Shit, indeed," Cassius chastises. "A lot of people are depending on this pill."

"I'm sorry."

Cassius sucks in a breath. "It's not your fault."

"So, what's going to happen to her?"

"She doesn't stand a chance unless we properly diagnose her and see to the secondary condition. Believe it or not, the pill actually made significant progress in eliminating her primary condition, which may have been keeping the comorbidity in check."

"Fuck, this is all confusing."

"All you need to know is that we're working tirelessly to get her fixed so we can get the pill to market."

"How long will she be under?"

"At least a few days, but it could be weeks. If we could just get her out of hostile waters, she could live for years."

"Do whatever the fuck you have to to make that happen. Forward all bills to me, keep me in the loop on everything."

"Trust me, it's within everyone's best interest that Ari's mother remain alive. We have a good idea of what's wrong, we just need to run some diagnostics to confirm."

The blood rushing through my veins is giving me a headache. I close my eyes and massage my temple. "Fuck! I'm such an idiot."

"This isn't your fault," Cassius assures me. "You couldn't have predicted this."

"Not that it will matter to Arinessa."

Cassius cocks a brow. "Is she your girlfriend?"

"She's an employee," I reply, figuring my personal life is none of his business.

Cassius snickers. "I'm sure you've read how that turned out for me."

"The pleasure pill stunt?"

"Oh, that was no stunt. Come to think of it, we ended up in the exact same situation you did."

"How so?"

"Sadie's mother was having chest pains and saw a bottle of the O Go pills sitting on a counter and thought they were heart pills."

My jaw drops in disbelief. "It was your girlfriend's mother that took the female orgasm pills?"

"Yeah. It was a terrible ordeal, but now that it's behind us, I can finally say that it's fucking hilarious."

"Can I ask you a favor?"

"Another one? The first favor you asked of me put my clinical trial in danger."

"I need you to put me in touch with Gabriel Icor."

Cassius's eyebrows draw inward. "Icor? Why do you care to talk to him?"

"I have my reasons."

Arinessa

Seeing my mother asleep in her hospital bed really puts what's about to happen into perspective.

She's going to die, and I'm never going to get to say goodbye. Not really.

I should have been with her the last few days. The moment I found out that she had stopped treatment, I should have gone to her, demanding she get back on, no matter the cost.

"This is because of me," I whisper.

Nurse Agnes puts a hand on my shoulder and says, "I've been treating your mother the last few days. She talked about you all the time."

"I told her to get on that stupid treatment."

"If she hadn't gone on at all, she wasn't long for this world. I know that must be horrible to hear, but your mother knew it to be true, and she had made peace with it."

"I can't believe I wasn't here with her. That I was…"

Off having sex with Hunter Davies.

"Sweetheart, she would never blame you, so don't blame yourself. I talked to her a lot the last few days. She was so proud of you, so excited to see you achieve what she could only dream of. She would not want you beating yourself up because you didn't have a crystal ball. None of us do, or else we'd all be filthy rich."

Hot tears run down my cheeks. I know if there were

any way to fix this, Hunter would without question. He'd do anything for me, reasonable or not.

But sometimes all the money in the world can't buy what you need the most.

"You can hold her hand if you'd like," a doctor says.

I rush to my mother's side, placing my hand on hers. "What's the plan?"

The doctor jots down some numbers from the machines my mother is hooked up to, then turns to me. "First, we need to figure out what's wrong. It's still unclear, and I have a feeling that it has nothing to do with the new treatment."

I narrow my eyes at the doctor. "Are you just saying that because you're worried about your precious trial?"

"No, Ma'am." A man in a business suit steps forward from the recesses of the room. "My name is Greg Carter, and I'm here from the FDA."

"What are *you* doing here?"

"LaviTech Labs makes it a point to be open and honest with all of their medical innovations. The drug your mother was placed on was technically no longer in trial, which made it significantly easier to get your mother approved for it. At the first sign that something was off, he gave me a call. The drug your mother received could change the way we treat patients, which is why I'm here. We need to know everything about why this is happening because there are a lot of people that could benefit from it."

As if I didn't feel guilty enough. Having the weight of thousands of sick people on my shoulders makes me want to crawl inside a sewer.

"Can I pull up a chair and sit with her?" I ask.

"Actually, you being allowed inside this room is a favor to Cassius," the doctor says. "There is no waiting area on this floor because it's for special cases. Like your mothers."

"Which floor should I go to?"

"I think it would be better if you went home," the doctor says.

"Home? While my mother—"

"She's in a medically induced coma. She can't wake on her own, and she's not in immediate risk of danger. The moment that changes, we'll give you a call."

"But I'm not going to be able to do anything knowing she's here all alone."

"She'll be in the best care, Cassius will see to that," Greg says. "But this isn't going to be quick. She'll probably be in this state for at least a week."

I look down at my mother and all the tubes coming out of her. "I'm so sorry, mom."

"I promise, she won't be alone," the nurse says. "I'll take good care of her."

I clear my throat. "I guess I'll go home. Please call me if there are any changes."

"Of course."

I exit the room in a daze, unsure if my legs will carry me where I need to go.

"Ari," Hunter says, but I can't even look at him.

I don't deserve his arms holding me, his kind words, or his shoulder to cry into. Not after I told my mother to sign on for a new treatment without so much as attending a doctor's visit with her.

Now, she's going to spend her final days being poked and prodded without her family here to comfort her.

I walk past Hunter and Cassius to the elevator at the end of the hall.

I'm done with Davies Corporation. I'm done with Hunter. I'm done with school. I'm done with whatever money he transferred into my account.

I don't deserve any of it.

I'll work the lunch shift at the diner down the street that's always hiring, and I'll do entry-level coding jobs at night. I'll make my life work without any of the comforts Hunter afforded me, and I'll do it alone.

Because now I know the price of happiness is not worth the cost.

Chapter TWENTY

Arinessa

It only took three days to destroy my nicely manicured nails. Between hand washing dishes, nail biting, and typing, they didn't stand a chance.

Disenrolling from college was bittersweet, but it had to be done. Luckily, I've been able to snag a few freelance jobs formatting manuscripts. They only pay twenty-five-dollars a script, but it takes me less than an hour to complete the work, so it's a good use of my time.

Looking over my bills, I know I'm going to need a roommate soon. Even though the apartment is only one bedroom, it shouldn't be too hard to find someone. I just hope they aren't obnoxious.

The microwave dings, and I grab my pizza rolls and settle into the couch, turning the television on to Hope and Frustration. The movie is twenty-eight years old, but it stars Ernestine Whitmore. A woman I've come to adore.

Every scene she's in captivates me, from when she's running in the rain, to her romantic embrace with Chet Inglewood, her co-star.

Hunter hasn't contacted me since I left the hospital. I'm sure he's relieved that he doesn't have to make up some lame excuse for sending me back home. I want to believe what we had was something special, but to him, I was just one of…I can only assume a lot.

To me, he was everything.

His money still sits in my bank account, but I've put in a request to have the transaction reversed. If only I could reverse the entire week, but there are no take-backs. It's one thing to have no idea what you're missing out on; it's another to know and crave it with every cell in your body.

My life is now torture.

A knock sounds on the door, and I drop a pizza roll on my twice-worn shirt.

Fuck! I hadn't wanted to change today. I blot the sauce stain with a napkin, but it's a battle I'm not going to win.

The knock sounds again, this time harder.

Part of me wants to hide and not face whoever has decided to pay me a visit.

But the very real possibility exists that it is the police at my door, telling me my mother has passed.

Each day the nurse calls, giving me updates on my

mother's condition. She's never better, never worse. The doctors don't want to wake her prematurely, but she can't go on as she is forever.

The knock comes again when I'm just a foot away.

"Hold your horses, will ya!" I shout.

I open the door to a flamboyant pixie of a woman holding several bags.

"Neon—Sam? Sorry."

"Oh, no worries! I love my new moniker. Hunter has taken to calling me it."

"What are you doing here?" I ask, unsure of what it is I'm feeling.

"Is that really how you greet guests? Can't you see my arms are full?"

Neon rushes past me without being invited in. I stand, gawking at her, wondering how she knows my address and what it is she's carrying.

She drops the bags on the couch and looks around the room, scrunching her nose. "Wow…not what I expected from Hunter's girlfriend."

"Not girlfriend. Not anymore," I say morosely. "Why are you here?"

"Hunter wanted to make sure you got your things. There's like a ba-zillion bags downstairs. Help me bring them up."

"No! I don't want them."

"I understand. Breakups are hard. But let's just get it all up here, so nothing is stolen."

I sigh, as though her presence exhausts me. "Fine."

It takes an hour for us to haul up the hundreds of bags Hunter sent with Neon.

"I can't believe he didn't just hire movers," Neon

says, plopping down on the couch.

"You should have just hauled it all to Goodwill."

"Ummm...these goods would make it to my apartment long before they made it to Goodwill."

"You're free to take them with you when you go," I say, staring brazenly at her, hoping she'll take the hint and leave.

Her eyes hone in on the paused movie I'm watching. "Oh, isn't this one of Ernestine's old films?"

"Yeah, it's available on most streaming services, if you're interested."

"Hit play! I want to see what she was like."

I exhale loudly, but she doesn't seem to sense my annoyance.

"You know, I have a lot of stuff to do." To emphasize how busy I am, I start throwing away old pizza boxes and paper plates.

Neon gives me a quizzical look. "But you were watching a movie?"

"Look, I've had a bad couple of days, and I need some time alone."

"Whenever I have a bad day, I like to binge-watch TV and eat Chunky Monkey ice cream."

"My mother is dying."

Neon's mouth falls open. "Shit, Hunter never told me that."

"I was with Hunter when she needed me most."

Neon's face softens, but she doesn't budge.

"I have to drop out of college. I have six figures' worth of debt and nothing to show for it. Pretty soon, I won't be able to afford this apartment."

Neon still doesn't move.

"Haven't I depressed you enough?" I gesture wildly in the air. "Why aren't you gone yet?"

She looks up slowly, locking gazes with me. "Because you need me."

"Huh?"

"Look, Hunter paid me well to haul all your shit over here, so I might as well make a day of it. Let's grab some ice cream, watch TV, and shoot the shit."

"But you barely know me, and I have nothing to offer you."

"A girl from a shit hole like this, who manages to bag Hunter Davies, dumps him, only to go back to said shit hole has got to be interesting."

"I didn't dump him," I say truthfully.

"Well, he certainly didn't dump you. I've never seen him so upset before."

I arc a brow. "Really?"

"Girl, he's a mess." She rises from the couch. "Now, let's go get some ice cream."

"I have chocolate in the freezer. Wanna order pizza?"

"From Marios! Deep dish."

We order pizza, and I settle in on the couch next to Neon.

It's not often that I have guests over, and by not often, I mean never.

I try not to mull on Hunter being upset with my absence. It could very well be because I couldn't find his aunt.

Of course, I feel terrible that I abandoned the search for Lucy, but I know I wouldn't have found her anyway.

Neon gives me an awkward look. "Can I ask you a personal question?"

"Ummm…sure."

"Was Hunter your first?"

My head snaps in her direction.

"Sorry. You just seem so innocent."

It's not often I confide in someone, but some good old fashion therapy might be what I need right now.

"When I was fifteen, I got charged with a federal crime. I basically hacked a bunch of shit in order to gain evidence on some rather vile human beings. I got off with a slap on the wrist, but I was kicked out of my private school and basically put on probation. Let's just say my teenage years were not typical."

"Wow…that's…impressive."

"But to answer your question: yes, Hunter was my first. And I fell for him. Hard."

"I don't blame you. If I wasn't so gay, I'd probably go after him."

I blink half a dozen times, trying to register what she just said. "You're gay?"

"A little."

"But Hunter told me—"

"About being in his bed? At the time, I was playing the field more. Figuring myself out. I have a girlfriend now, but probably not for long."

"Oh, congratulations."

"Let's watch Ernestine in action!" Neon enthuses.

I hit play. "Fine, but I'm not starting over."

Several minutes pass as Neon looks on, wide-eyed at her client on the screen.

"They don't make 'em like they used to," I say after an emotional scene.

"You can say that again. I guess the only modern

actress that could compete is Ali Kat Carter. No wonder Rand was so obsessed."

"Is so obsessed," I reply.

The movie draws to a close, the heroine finally taking control of her life and buying her freedom. Midway through the scene, as she's signing a check, I hit pause.

"Do you really need a bathroom break during the very last scene?" Neon snaps.

"Just give me a minute."

I replay the scene, thinking back to the many conversations I've had with Hunter. She bends to sign the check again, and I think about the file labeled: Rand.

A knock sounds on the door.

Neon jumps up from her seat. "The pizza's finally here!"

I continue staring at the screen.

The pizza box lands with a smack on the coffee table, and Neon wastes no time throwing the lid back and grabbing a slice.

My mind continues to work in circles, trying to piece together a puzzle with new pieces.

This isn't your problem anymore. Move on. Your life is in shambles.

"So, what now?" Neon says. "Another one of her movies?"

Let sleeping dogs lie.

"Actually, I was wondering if you could help me with something?"

"What's that?"

"Do you think you could teach me how to better handle my hair and makeup?"

Neon smiles. "That's what I like to hear! Moving up

and moving on! Though…I'm not entirely sure if you can move up from Hunter—shit! I didn't mean it like that."

"It's fine," I say with a shrug of my shoulders.

Neon grabs my hair. "We're going to have to start with this."

TWENTY-ONE

Hunter

"Whoever is behind this knows how to move around the internet unseen," Gabriel Icor says. "The emails could have come from Peru, or even inside the building."

I tap my fingers nervously on my desk, unable to relieve my frustration. As much as I wanted to be done with this mystery, it disallows me from sleeping at night.

"I could run this by Dallanger, but to be honest, I don't think he'll be able to pinpoint the origins either."

"No, there's no point. There isn't a person on the planet that can do more than what's been done. Thank you for your assistance."

Gabriel doesn't move, either not getting the hint or not caring.

"If you ever need anything, feel free to give me a call," I say, hoping that drives the point home.

"May I offer some advice?"

I suck in a breath, trying to remember my decorum. I want nothing more than to show him the door, but I'm the one that asked him for a favor, and it would be grossly inappropriate for me to be rude.

"And what would that be?"

"Talk to your father."

"Out of the question."

"You don't trust him, do you?"

I cast Gabriel a glare that tells him it's none of his business.

"Look, I'm not saying he's a bad guy, but we both know parents will go to extreme lengths to protect their children. You need to warn him if he has something to hide."

"My father is careful out of fear, not guilt. He had nothing to do with my aunt's death, of that, I promise you."

"I believe you. I'm actually jealous of your relationship with him. He seems like a good guy who loves his family. Mine was an absolute dog."

Guilt needles me, and I rethink being so defensive. Gabriel's father was notorious for his skirt-chasing ways, and it's said he left his son a mess when he passed.

"Every family has its skeletons, as does mine. It's just that I'm pretty sure kidnapping and murder isn't a part of my family's history."

As soon as the words leave my mouth, I chuckle

dryly.

Gabriel cocks a brow. "May I ask what is so funny?"

"Well, that was a lie. As of late, I've taken to kidnapping, though it was entirely accidental."

"You accidentally kidnapped someone?"

"There was a woman helping me find my aunt. When I hired her, I had a team of mercs go in to get her and bring her to me."

"Now that's a skeleton…"

"They dragged her into my family's estate with handcuffs and a bag over her head."

"That must have made for an awkward work environment."

"Once things settled, we worked well together. I let my mother think she was my girlfriend and she just about fell in love with her."

"You know, our mothers are a lot alike. Mine was over the moon when I introduced her to Remi."

"I'm such an asshole. My mother has been campaigning for me to settle down and provide her with grandkids for the last three years, and I led her to believe I'd found the one. It broke her heart when my fake relationship ran its course."

"Ironically, I too was in a fake relationship, but I did a direct transition to Remi, so there was no broken heart. Just a lot of confusion."

"Don't tell my mom that," I say, pointing an authoritative finger at him. "The last thing I need is comparisons."

"What my mother wouldn't give to rub it in your mother's face."

"What the hell happened between them?" I sit back in

my chair and run my fingers through my hair. "They literally have a legendary rivalry, but why?"

"After the movie Belles of Boston, they were constantly compared to one another, and it more or less led to a turf war," Gabriel says.

I chuckle. "My mother in a turf war?"

"Scarlet Primrose versus Ernestine Whitmore. Their legendary catfights landed more tabloid covers than almost anything in modern times. Both went on to marry tech giants, have dashingly handsome sons, and eventually leave Hollywood."

"Sons who have both engaged in fake relationships and workplace romances."

His mouth upticks into a smile. "So you and that girl —"

"Shut it!" I snap, casting him an aggressive glare.

"You know, with all the attention given to our mothers, it's easy to forget that our fathers were far bigger rivals," Gabriel says. "Though they competed for contracts."

"Let's not become them."

"Deal." Gabriel looks down at the file I gave him, thumbing through the papers. "I can continue to work on your case if you could provide me with copies—"

"Do you think I'm a fucking idiot?" I snap.

Gabriel's expression doesn't change. "We all have our secrets."

"And apparently you'd like to be privy to mine."

"I have a half brother that tried to sell out Icor Tech to a Chinese corporation two years ago."

My brow shoots upward in surprise.

"Family shit is never pleasant, and boy does it stink.

You had nothing to do with whatever it was your aunt was into, or still is into, though something tells me it's not her who's been in contact with you."

I soften my gaze, just shy of looking warm. Despite the fact that he's a corporate enemy, Gabriel has been helpful, and I don't think he's looking to make personal enemies out of me.

"I trust you, Icor, but I can't let these files leave my possession."

"I understand. I can try to hunt down the origins of those emails if you'd like."

"I'd appreciate that, but no involving Dallanger or anyone else. Just you."

"And my wife?"

"And Remi."

Gabriel nods. "That girl you were working on this with, I'd like to utilize her."

"Absolutely not."

"I'm not headhunting her. I'm trying to run a tight ship. An additional set of eyes is a boon, and you won't allow me to employ my own."

His logic checks out, and I could certainly make it worth it financially to Ari, but her mother is in a coma, and she's about to start school. It wouldn't be fair.

"Her life has taken a rather difficult turn, and she can't manage the additional stress."

"You know as well as I do that money can fix damn near anything, or at least make it better," Gabriel says.

"Her finances are taken care of."

Gabriel's eyes bore into mine, but I refuse to divert my gaze. Men like us are always dick-swinging, as they call it. Alphas of our packs. A clear, strong, dominant presence is essential to our success.

"You are a stubborn man, Davies. And so full of secrets."

My phone vibrates with a text from Sam, or as Arinessa would call her, Neon.

"This will take just a moment."

> **Sam:** *I did as you asked. She is NOT okay. She feels guilty over her mom and is about to drop out of school and take on like three jobs.*

> **Hunter:** *But I paid for her college and made sure she was taken care of. Why would she do that?*

> **Sam:** *She's not taking your money. This woman is a piece of work. She's not like any of my clients, and quite frankly, I'm glad. You were stupid to lose her.*

> **Hunter:** *There's nothing that can be done about that now, so it's best to move on.*

> **Sam:** *I did give her a mini-makeover. You'd be drooling.*

> **Hunter:** *Do me a favor and keep an eye on her over the next couple of weeks. I'll make it worth your while.*

> **Sam:** *Roger that!*

Arinessa is never going to make it on her own. She doesn't have connections and isn't cutthroat enough.

A notification in my email shows that she's reversed the cash transaction, and my guess is that it's only a matter of time before the tuition is returned as well.

God, Ari, why do you have to be so stubborn?

Gabriel sits patiently across from me. I loathe having to ask him for anything else, but I see no way around it.

"I need to ask you another favor."

Gabriel chuckles, taking a sip of his scotch. "Another one? What would it be?"

"That girl you wanted to assist you, her name is Arinessa. I want you to offer her a job, but you can't have her working on my stuff, and you can't let her know I had a hand in her getting hired."

He furrows his brow, mulling over my request. "Consider it done."

TWENTY-TWO

Arinessa

"You'll be working directly under me on a small team dedicated to analytics." Remi Icor hands me a badge with my face on it.

"But I don't understand. I came in for an interview. How do you already have this?" I hold up the badge. "I literally just told you I wanted the job."

"To be honest, we've been watching you for quite some time. When one of your professors told Gabriel that you would not be returning to campus, we assumed it was because someone recognized your talent and made you an offer. We figured we'd put together a competing bid to give you another option."

"You've been watching me?"

"Are you surprised? Talent like yours is hard to come by, and tech companies know they need to be quick to snatch it up or someone else will."

Everything she says makes sense, but it just feels too convenient.

Remi isn't an unfriendly woman, but she is firm and direct. Someone who would make a great mentor. Passing up this opportunity would be insane.

"Is there anything else we should know before we continue?"

Don't tell her. Let sleeping dogs lie.

"No."

"Good. The background check for your security clearance will include your criminal history, credit—"

"Excuse me, did you say security clearance?"

"At the level you'll be hired in at, it's standard to obtain one of the highest levels of clearance."

I hand her back my badge. "Then you should probably take this back."

Remi furrows her brow. "Why? What is it we will find?"

I clench my hands into fists, trying not to become emotional. "It's supposed to be expunged, but with your resources, you'll surely sniff it out."

"Sniff what out?"

"When I was fifteen, I hacked into a bunch of shit and gathered a bunch of evidence on some human traffickers. I forwarded the evidence, thinking I was being anonymous, but the FBI found out it was me, and…well…it landed me in trouble."

Remi sits back, a dumbfounded expression on her

face. "Huh?"

"There's no way I'm going to pass whatever clearance check you have going on."

She folds her arms across her chest, her brow narrowing. "You went after human traffickers?"

"Yeah, and I royally fucked up a case against them." I look down at my hands, trying to gather the courage to own my past. "I was fifteen. I didn't know."

Remi rises from her seat. "Stay here. I'll be back in a minute."

She leaves the room, allowing me to unleash the floodgate of tears I had been holding back.

For the thousandths time in two weeks, I'm bawling my eyes out, though this time, it's not at my apartment.

I check my phone to see if there's any word on my mother. I'm not too optimistic with her having spent ten days in a coma, but eventually, there has to be a new development. I just hope it's a turn for the better and not the worse.

The door opens again, and I quickly try to dry my tears and look as nonchalant as possible.

"Arinessa Sylvan," a male voice says, and I turn to see Gabriel Icor approaching.

My jaw drops, amazed by the tech juggernaut, a man who is known for both his technical genius and his debonair good looks.

But he doesn't hold a candle to Hunter.

"My name is—"

"Gabriel Icor," I finish without thinking.

He holds out his hand for me to shake, but I'm paralyzed, only able to stare up at him.

After a moment, he retracts his hand as though he's

used to bad manners like mine.

"Remi asked me to join in the meeting because of a unique situation."

All I can do is continue to stare back at him.

"Here, take this." He hands out a handkerchief.

It takes me almost a minute before I realize it's for me to dry my face, and I hurry to blot my eyes.

"That's better," Gabriel says with a stunning smile. "Now, I don't want you to feel upset or stressed in any way. I just want to know what happened with your case."

He takes a seat in the chair Remi was in, and Remi pulls up another chair for herself.

Finally, I find my manners. "I…got into a lot of trouble," I mumble.

"We're not going to judge you," Remi says. "Go on."

"When I was fifteen, I fucked up an FBI investigation," I start, throwing refinement to the wind. "I got upset when I learned what human trafficking was and hacked a bunch of shit, sending whatever evidence I could find to the police."

Gabriel blinks back at me, brow lifted, mouth gaping.

"I got a slap on the wrist, but it got me kicked out of school, and although it happened when I was a minor and my name was never released, my guess is that it's easy to find."

After a long moment, he says, "That's…impressive."

"Yeah? Tell that to my parents."

Gabriel eyes me curiously. "I'm sorry, but did you say you did that when you were fifteen?"

I nod my head.

"Remi, change of plans. She's not working for Icor Tech. She'll be hired on as household staff."

I furrow my brow in confusion.

"I'll get right on it," Remi says with a smile.

"I'm sorry," I reply. "But am I going to be like a maid?"

"You'll never make it past Icor Tech background checks, but to work for the Icors, you don't need one." Remi grins. "So Gabriel and I will hire you on to work for us. You'll be doing different things, but we'll make sure to start you out at the same salary as you would if you were starting with Icor Tech."

"No," Gabriel cuts in, "double it. I hate traffickers."

"Agreed," Remi says. "When can you start?"

"My mom is in the hospital."

"Oh, I'm sorry to hear that," Remi says.

"I mean, I want to start now, but I could be called away at any moment."

"It's a nonissue. I have a mother too. Scarlet Primrose," Gabriel says with a wink. "You may have heard of her."

"Of course. If my mom ever gets the chance to find out I'm working with Scarlet Primrose's son and have met *the* Ernestine Whitmore, she'd be floored."

"So you've met Ernestine?" Gabriel asks with a wry look on his face.

Shit...

"I...saw her at brunch a week ago. She was at a crêpe place."

"Well, if you see my mom around, try not to mention that. They were rivals back in the day."

"Understood."

"Whenever you're ready, I have your project," Remi says.

"And what's that?"

"I need you to, by any means necessary, hack into a server and download the data on it for me."

Why, oh, why does my first project have to sound illegal?

I exhale audibly. "Just point me to my workstation."

TWENTY-THREE

Hunter

"They've already expanded into an online app, and I'm one of their top influencers, or as they like to call them: Topless Influencers!" Sabrina holds out her phone displaying the centerfold she shot for the new magazine LaLa's. "I could earn seven figures!"

I force a smile. "That's wonderful."

"And then maybe I'll be taking you out for dinner." She winks at me, grabbing the collar of my work shirt and pulling my lips to hers.

My brain tells my lips what to do, but for some reason, the message doesn't come out right, and my lips strew against hers awkwardly.

"What is going on with you?" Sabrina giggles, pulling away and giving me a playful slap.

If she had done that the last time we had been together, I would have scooped her up into my arms, pressed her against the wall, and buried myself in her.

And that's exactly what I went to her apartment to do.

So…why am I just standing here?

Sabrina stretches her arms upward, revealing a hint of her taunt, tanned belly.

I force my hands to the gentle curve of her hip, pulling her close to me.

"I've missed you," she purrs, nipping at my chin playfully with her teeth.

My breath hitches in my throat. The last thing I want to do is make Sabrina feel bad, but I can't stand being in the same space as her. It's like I'm suffering some kind of allergic reaction.

She presses forward with her body. "Whaddaya say we take it on over to my bed…"

She snakes her hand into my pants, and at this point, I have to grab her by the wrist and pull her away.

Her face falls, her cheeks flushing pink.

"Sabrina, I'm—" My phone vibrates, and I breathe a sigh of relief.

"I just realized I have a meeting scheduled to start right now." I hold up my phone. "They're hunting me down as I speak."

Her mouth twitches in annoyance, but at least she's no longer embarrassed.

"A big deal is coming down the pipeline. I'll call you later." I cast her a smile, then exit her apartment, making my way down to my car.

Once the door closes behind me, I pull out my phone and open a text from Gabriel.

> **Gabriel:** *Arinessa was quite a catch. I should pay you to headhunt for me.*

My gut twists with jealousy, but I'm determined to keep it at bay.

> **Hunter:** *How has her first week been?*

> **Gabriel:** *Good, she's exceeded mine and Remi's expectations. She has a very interesting past.*

> **Hunter:** *And, might I add, an admirable one.*

> **Gabriel:** *Wish you would have told me first. Hiring her to work for Icor Tech isn't an option. So, I hired her onto my household staff to work on personal projects.*

> **Hunter:** *Thanks. Treat her well.*

> **Gabriel:** *If you don't mind me asking, why didn't you offer her a job?*

> **Hunter:** *I mind you asking.*

> **Gabriel:** *Noted.*

I shove my phone back into my pocket, trying not to fall into misery. It's been two and a half weeks since I last saw Ari, and there's not a day I don't feel her absence.

At least Arinessa is able to have a real start to her life, free of the strings of her past. And I had a part in that.

Cassius has been keeping me in the loop, assuring me that his team is working round the clock to figure out what's wrong with Ari's mother. No expense is being spared, and she couldn't be in better hands.

What more, Cassius has invited me out for drinks with the guys. With my history, I've always shied away from tight bonds, betrayal lurking around every corner, but his crew has been friends for over a decade with very little drama. Who's to say I wouldn't get along with them?

"Take me home," I tell the driver, closing the patrician between us.

For the hundredth time today, I close my eyes to see Arinessa's staring back at me, wanting me. I miss the weight of her in my arms, the gentle touch of her hand, her sweet scent.

Mother took our 'breakup' fairly well, giving me a tight smile and telling me, "Maybe next time." Father looked at me with pity.

To say I'm haunted is an understatement. Sabrina can't take my mind from her, and neither can throwing myself into my work. I've abandoned trying to figure out what's happened with my aunt.

Whatever happens, happens.

Instead of being productive, I spend entirely too

much time replaying every moment with Arinessa that's etched into my brain.

She's always going to be the one who got away.

I can't go on like this, but I also can't go back to the man I was before her. I can't travel alone in this world. Not anymore. I may not ever find love, but I can potentially forge lifelong connections.

I enter into Gabriel's text box because I'm in over my head, and I desperately need help.

> **Hunter:** *Your friend Cassius invited me out for drinks with his circle next weekend, which you are a part of. Would you mind if I accepted the invite?*

> **Gabriel:** *Not at all, but the hazing is brutal.*

> **Hunter:** *Hazing?*

> **Gabriel:** *It used to be we'd get shit-faced drunk and hop on a private jet to unknown lands and continue to get shit-faced drunk. Now, it's find a woman to fall head over heels for, somehow manage to fuck it up, and spend a considerable amount of time, money, and effort making things right.*

It hadn't occurred to me until now that their circle seems to be settling down. Cassius, Gabriel, and Zev are all either married or with serious partners.

The land of happy couples is a place I don't belong.

> **Hunter:** *Never mind. I would have precious little in common with your crew.*

> **Gabriel:** *Oh, I insist that you at least go to our newcomer orientation.*

> **Hunter:** *Nah, I'm good.*

> **Gabriel:** *You can't say no because you owe me. I'll text you the time and location as we get close.*

The last thing I want to do is surround myself with men in happy relationships, but as he said, I owe him. Big time.

> **Hunter:** *I can hardly wait.*

TWENTY-FOUR

Arinessa

I pick up the phone on the third ring.

>**Nurse:** *Hello, Arinessa, it's me, Nurse Agnes.*

>**Arinessa:** *Hello?*

My hand is trembling so violently I can barely hold the phone up to my ear.

>**Nurse:** *I'm calling to tell you that we've made a discovery regarding your mother's condition.*

Arinessa: *Oh my God—is she going to be okay?*

Nurse: *What we believe happened is this: your mother discontinued treatment some four months before she began the trial. During that time, she refused everything except palliative care. There were no tests and no monitoring done.*

Arinessa: *Oh-kay...*

Nurse: *Because of that, we believe she developed a comorbidity that went undetected. The good news is that LaviTech's treatment did exactly what we expected it to, and her primary condition is cured. The bad news is that she has a new and unrelated condition.*

This was one of the many theories passed around, so I shouldn't be surprised, but it still feels like a gut punch.

Arinessa: *She's already been in a coma for nearly three weeks. What's going to happen?*

Nurse: *We're confirming the diagnosis with a specialist. Once we do, we will pull her out of her coma and go over treatment options. The doctor thinks that will be*

Monday.

Arinessa: *Holy fuck—we're going through the same shit all over again, but with something new?*

Nurse: *Actually, the situation looks a lot more promising this time around. Cassius has ensured she will receive the best care, and the doctors suspect that this new ailment will be far easier to treat.*

A flicker of hope tries to ignite within me, but I know better than to kindle it.

Arinessa: *When can I see her?*

Nurse: *You can be here when we wake her. I'll give you a call shortly before we start the process.*

Arinessa: *Thank you.*

The phone goes dead, and I stand there, trying to process the information.

"You okay?" Remi asks.

"I don't know."

"Do you need some time off?"

"No. It's actually good that I'm here so I can keep busy."

"Do you want to share anything?"

"It's just that my mother's primary condition has

been fixed, but she may have a completely different condition that caused her new problem. It sounds horrible, but it might be easy to fix."

"That's great news...I think," Remi says with a confused look.

Tears spill down my cheek. "I feel like this is all my fault."

"Oh, honey—you had nothing to do with your mother's illness."

"It's not that..."

Remi pulls me over to a couch, forcing me to sit. "I want to hear everything."

Her concern touches me. Remi may be reticent, but she is kind and genuinely cares for her staff and friends.

"It's so stupid, but I met this guy, and I began working for him. He was able to get my mother on this new drug, and I made her agree to it. While she was receiving the treatment, I was elsewhere. I should have been by her side."

"Ari, you couldn't just stop life and sit at the hospital twenty-four-seven. You had an apartment, college—"

"I was fucking the guy that hired me! That night, as she was in pain and being put into a coma, I was...I was —"

"Shh-shh-shh, it's going to be okay," Remi whispers, pulling me to her shoulder.

"Obviously, I left the position, and before you guys poached me, I was seriously formatting ebooks and looking to go back to skip tracing."

"Well, it's lucky that we found you."

"And for once, I actually met a man I trusted. Now, I'm destined to be alone."

Remi pulls back. "Did the guy hurt you?"

"No…"

"Then what happened between you two?"

"Because I was with him while my mom was being put under, there's no way I can allow myself to continue it."

"I have a feeling your mother wouldn't want you beating yourself up like you are. You should give him a call."

I downcast my eyes. "I can't. I really let him down. He did so much to help me when I was supposed to be helping him. I left before the project we were working on was complete. He has every right to hate me."

Remi looks at me with sympathetic eyes. "One thing I've learned from my limited experience with men is that there is no real logic to their thought process when it comes to women. The only way for you to know how he feels is for you to ask him directly."

I snicker. "That's a tall order."

"It's better than wondering what could have been."

"Well, right now I need to focus all my attention on my mother and getting my life in order."

Remi frowns.

"You wouldn't understand."

"My friends and I are having a girls' night tomorrow. Why don't you come with?"

"A girls' night?" I exhale in distaste. "No, thank you."

"Ah, come on. It's a great group of women, and I think they'll like you."

"You do realize I have no real girlfriends, don't you?"

"That, I cannot understand." Remi smiles at me.

"What's not to love? You're smart, good at your job, and really likable, despite what you might think."

I have to admit, it's tempting being allowed into the exclusive places women go together, and certainly better than spending another evening alone. The friendships forged from shared life experiences are something I wasn't afforded in high school or college, and I do think my mother would want me to go.

It sounds terrifying, but maybe if I invite Neon, she'll be my courage. Someone like her is good in any social situation.

"Do you think I can invite an...acquaintance? Her name is Neon, or rather Sam. She's been there for me during my mother's hospitalization."

"Of course," Remi enthuses. "We'll start out at Madison's and see where the night takes us."

I pull out my phone to send a text to Neon, excited that I won't be spending another evening laid out on the couch, devouring quarts of ice cream.

> **Arinessa:** *Wanna go out tomorrow for girls' night? My boss invited me out, and I'd like it if you came along.*

> **Neon:** *Sure, but only if you let me do your hair and makeup first...and pick out your outfit.*

> **Arinessa:** *Seriously? You don't think I can dress myself?*

> **Neon:** *Honey, this isn't some hillbilly*

apocalypse you're going to. You're allowed to be cute.

Arinessa: *Fine.*

"Count me in with a plus one."

"Awesome. I'll add you to the reservation."

"Who else is going? College and high school friends of yours?"

"Fiona Fables Heartshire, Sadie Lavinius, Grace Anders might attend, though she's been busy, there's rumor Nadine Stry—"

"Holy shit! You can't be serious. Are you for real taking me on a girls' night with the world's elite?"

"Well, that's not what we call ourselves…but I suppose others do."

I shake my head. "There's no way—"

"You're going—that's the end of it."

I could fight her and spend every moment of the weekend waiting for a call from the hospital while thinking about Hunter Davies, but hanging out with a bunch of pretentious billionaires might actually be less torturous.

"Fine. Count me in."

TWENTY-FIVE

Arinessa

Trying to figure out what to wear with Neon is never what I would consider fun. She's rainbow neon everything, and I'm just trying to make sure everything is free of stains.

"I remember when I ordered this for you." Neon holds up a black corset. "It's perfect."

"Yeah, but I don't want to wear anything Hunter purchased."

"Then tell me what we're left with? Because over the last three weeks, I've seen you in pizza-stained tanks, Eeyore pajamas, dollar store sandals, and jorts. You seriously have jorts!"

"I bought a couple of new outfits for work." I open up the portable wardrobe I purchased and display the formal pantsuits."

"You're not wearing professional attire to girls' night!" Neon's voice is ripe with disdain. "You're wearing this teal, button-up floral shirt and the corset on top. We'll leave a few buttons undone to show a little cleavage."

When I try to speak up, she glares at me. "Zip it!"

Might as well wear the corset while I still can. It's not like it's going to fit in a few months anyway.

That thing they tell you about sex, you know, that warning that gets drilled into you from the moment you find out what sex is—the big ole pregnancy warning… well, it appears that I am determined to never learn from the mistakes of others.

That's right—I'm pregnant. Or, it's highly probable. My period is three days late, three weeks after having unprotected sex.

And if that wasn't enough confirmation, a pee stick confirmed it this morning.

"Fine, I'll wear it. But what skirt do I wear?"

"Oh, you're wearing these black booty shorts and a pair of thigh-high boots!"

"Neon!"

She chuckles. "I have all my friends calling me that now."

"It's fitting."

"Look, just let me do what I'm good at in life," she pleads.

I pout my lip out. "God, when did I become so weak-willed?"

Neon coaxes me out of my pajamas and helps me get dressed because there is no way I'd be able to figure out how to wear a corset on my own. Then she does my hair and makeup, turning me into the sexy siren I never knew I could be.

I look even more audacious than I did for the Davies' family dinner, which Hunter had assured me I looked tame at. I didn't feel tame, though, and now, I feel wild as I look in the mirror.

"God, you look so hot. Men will be begging for your number."

"Jokes on them because I'm the absolute last person they're going to want to date."

"Oh, really... you work for the fucking Icors and probably earn a shit ton of money. You're smart, low maintenance, have a killer rack, and you're hot. If you can't find a man, womankind has no hope."

I take a steady breath, bracing for what I'm about to tell her.

I've never confided much in other women, but Neon has been here for me when I really needed her, and I absolutely can't keep what I'm about to tell her to myself.

"Neon?" I say to the rainbow-colored pixie.

"Yes?"

"I'm pregnant."

She blinks her glitter eyelashes back at me. "Like, knocked up? You're going to have a baby?"

"Yeah."

It takes her a moment to process what I just said, and I don't much like the critical gaze she's giving me, but I might as well get used to it.

"Would it be insensitive for me to ask who the father is?"

My eyes grow round from shock. "Yes!"

"Just kidding! It's Hunter! I know it's Hunter."

"What do I do?"

"That's up to you."

"I mean, I know I'm going to keep it. But… everything else is a mystery."

"Whatever you decide, Hunter is going to take good care of you, and Ernestine will take even better care of you. I swear she's going to treat that baby like the second coming of Christ."

"He's going to hate me. He did so much for me, then I just…left. Without even a thank you."

"That's what people do when a relationship isn't working for them. He knows that."

"Yeah, but he trusted me," I say, careful not to let the true nature of our relationship come to light. "Hunter and I both have good reasons to distrust people. I guess I showed him he's right to be wary."

Neon's shoulders slump. "Oh, God…"

"What?"

She looks up at me with frantic eyes. "Please don't be mad!"

My heart rate doubles, knowing that I'm not going to like what I'm about to hear. "What would I have to be mad about?"

"Hunter asked me to tell him how you're doing."

My brow draws inward. "Huh?"

"He was worried about you. He wanted to make sure you were okay."

It takes me a full minute to understand what she's

said.

"For the first time in my life, I thought I had found a friend. Someone I could confide in."

"You did!"

"I trusted you! I told you my secrets!"

"It was a mistake—I see that now, but at the time, I thought I was doing a good thing."

"Everything is out of my control now—"

"That's not true! I promise I won't tell Hunter anything else."

I snicker. "And I'm supposed to trust you?"

"I know what I did was wrong, but the reason I told you is because I want to be your friend. Your real friend. I'll text Hunter right now, in front of you, and tell him I'm no longer giving him updates. You can tell him about the baby on your own terms."

"How much have you told him?"

"Just little things, how you're doing, that you like your job. You know, things."

It feels like ice is coursing through my veins, and it takes every ounce of restraint that I have not to throw something at the rainbow traitor.

I point toward the door. "Get out!"

"Can we talk about this?" she pleads.

"Absolutely not! Go!"

Her face falls, and a gleam shines in her eye. My heart softens.

"Look, maybe we can get over this. Maybe we can't," I say. "I just need time."

"I understand. I promise I won't tell Hunter about your pregnancy."

"Thank you."

"But you should tell him."

"I didn't ask for your advice."

"I know, but you're going to hear it. You and Hunter are fucked up in weird and similar ways. You both don't trust people and have yet to develop significant relationships outside of one another. You found each other like magnets, blindly pulled in each other's direction. Don't fuck this up."

Without another word, Neon exits my apartment, closing the door behind her.

I'm left reeling from her confession, something I should have suspected from the moment she knocked on my door. I guess I was so desperate for a friend, I threw logic out the window.

On the bright side, I look amazing, and I fully intend to meet up with Remi and her crew, even if I am going alone. Now that I know I didn't, in fact, kill my mom, I'm going to start living my life without any guilt or reservation.

And I'm going to do it one-hundred-percent on my own terms.

Fuck Hunter for buying me a friend, and fuck Neon for pretending to be my friend.

At least I was able to secure a job without his help.

I look at myself one more time before heading out for the night, excited for new possibilities.

TWENTY-SIX

Hunter

The last thing I expected was for New York City's elite to be hanging out in a dive bar such as Kent's, but here I am, walking through the rickety door to meet up with Cassius and his crew.

"Hey!" Gabriel holds his drink up, signaling for me to make my way over.

Just as Cassius suggested, I dressed down and no one gives me a second glance as I cross the room. My parents would have a heart attack if they knew I was in a place that didn't have their own security team, but I brought my own detail, and I wave my bodyguard over to sit with the others.

Alistair Whent, a man I've met and purchased a jet from, rises to meet me.

"I never expected your uptight ass to meet us here," he jests.

"I bought a large share of Lysol's stock in anticipation of this endeavor."

The table breaks out in boisterous laughter, and Gabriel calls the waitress over and orders me a beer.

Cassius stands to address his friends. "Everyone, this is the elusive Hunter Davies. Hunter, this is Gabe, Zev, Alistair, Sven, and Elric. Drake is supposed to be here, but something came up."

I wave to the crew, most of whom I recognize, then take a seat and join in the conversation.

Sven is angry his sister tried to get him disinherited, though tabloids show he's earned the title 'Train-Wreck,' so I'm not entirely sure his anger is well-placed. Elric has broken away from his family business and has started his own in communications, already launching a social media app and a magazine.

Each of them have so many shared experiences that I feel misplaced, though they do their best to welcome me while taking jabs where they can. I roll with the punches, but when the conversation shifts to my love life, my anxiety spikes.

"I much prefer that Hunter stay single," Gabriel says. "My mother would be livid if Ernestine were to become a grandmother before her."

"About that," Zev says wryly. "Fiona says Remi is drinking water."

Gabriel casts him a caustic look.

"Is Gabriel gonna be a daddy now?" Alistair says.

"The fatherly type, not the perverted kind."

"You guys are crazy!" Gabriel takes a long pull of his beer.

"Oh my God, are you not claiming your very own child!" Cassius cuts in.

Gabriel's eyes light in fury, but it doesn't stop Cassius from continuing.

"I tell everyone I knocked up Sadie because I never want anyone ever to say that I didn't claim my beloved child."

"For once, Cas—you disgust me!" Gabriel snaps.

"Is this seriously the first time Cassius has disgusted you?" Alistair says with a grin. "And quit dodging the question."

"Let me just say that if she was, both Remi and my mother would kill me if I were to tell you guys before they had a chance to announce it."

"Well, congratulations," I reply. "I really hope my mother doesn't look in the tabloids."

Cassius directs his attention toward me. "I thought you should know, Arinessa's mother is doing well. She'll be woken from her coma Monday."

"That's good…right?"

"She was under a lot longer than we had hoped, but we found out what was wrong. She should be fine."

"That's great!"

"Hey, no shop talk during boys' night out!" Alistair chastises.

"Oh, I was merely giving Hunter suggestions as to how to deal with his erectile dysfunction," Cassius japes, and again the table breaks out into laughter.

Gabriel orders me another beer once mine is drained,

and I listen to the antics of my contemporaries, getting in a smart remark every so often.

Elric elbows me. "You know, I remember when we were like seven, our parents got us together for a playdate. Your parents were so anal about everything, it's no wonder you turned out like you did."

This time, the table doesn't laugh.

"Elric, I think it's time you slow your roll," Zev suggests, pushing Elric's beer just out of his reach.

"No, it's fine. After my aunt's disappearance, which I'm sure you all know about, it kind of cast a shadow on our world. I don't want that to be the way you define me," I say quietly. "It's all anyone ever associates me with."

"Sorry, man," Elric says.

"Go ahead, ask me about it if you'd like."

After a long minute, Cassius asks, "How is your mother? It was said that they were close."

"She's had years to process it, and I think she has, but it changed her."

Cassius nods. "I imagine that it would have."

"In about an hour, we'll meet up with the girls," Gabriel says.

An alarm on Elric's phone sounds. "Looks like I have to cut out. Early flight."

"I think I'm going to cut out too," I say.

"Nonsense!" Sven says. "Soon, we'll be meeting up with the ladies. Meghan will be with them, and you're exactly her type."

Alistair snorts. "I hardly think you can say he's 'her type' when you barely know him."

"I knew it!" Sven shouts. "I knew you were hitting

it!"

"Just because I don't go making broad assumptions of who my friends should be seeing and hooking up with doesn't mean I'm 'hitting it,' as you suggest."

"Oh, he's hitting it," Cassius mumbles under his breath.

Gabriel settles the bill, then turns to me and says, "You're coming back to my place. It won't be a lovey-dovey couples' thing. I promise."

"Alright," I relent, figuring it would be better to keep my mind occupied.

My phone buzzes, and I look down to see a text from Neon.

> **Neon:** *You can keep those big bucks of yours. I'm no longer spying.*

Fuck! I need Neon to make sure Ari is okay.

> **Hunter:** *Why not? I need you.*

> **Neon:** *She knows, and she's pissed. You really need to talk to her.*

Fuck!

Arinessa

Going to girls' night has me feeling like an archeologist

of sorts, studying a completely different culture, only they're alive and right in front of me.

Each of them is devastatingly beautiful, even Sadie, who is enormously pregnant. They're all wearing sexy dresses that either show an abundance of cleavage or way too much leg than I'm comfortable with.

Well, I guess it's kind of hypocritical of me to say that when I'm wearing booty shorts and thigh-highs.

A redhead named Fiona is taking digs at a dark-haired beauty named Sari who refuses to drink out of the glass cups at Madison's and has very vocally deemed the place a 'public health hazard.' What a piece of work. Another woman named Meghan is signing autographs, so I can only assume she's some kind of celebrity, though I can't place her. And Remi is excitedly talking about analytics, which is very Remi.

"So, can you like hack into the Pentagon?" Sadie asks excitedly.

"Remi probably upsold my capabilities, but honestly, I'm not really sure. If I can't, I maybe could after some research."

"I think it's awesome what you did to those traffickers," she enthuses.

My head snaps in Remi's direction. "Did you really tell everyone what I did?"

Her cheeks flush pink. "I was just bragging about my new hire."

My hands begin to tremble as I remember my years of fear.

"That's deeply personal," I manage to get out, but as I look around the table, I don't see angry faces. I see looks of admiration.

"Honestly, I'd pay you a six-figure salary to do that all day, every day," Sari Heartshire says. "I may be a fucking bitch, but I'm not evil."

Fiona quirks a brow up. "Seriously, Sari…I'm not so sure you're qualified to make that statement, but I'm glad we've found some mutual ground to stand upon. I'd pay her six-figures too."

Meghan turns to me. "You're a real hero, and if you're ever willing, I'd love to do a docuseries on you."

I laugh so hard, I snort. "A docuseries on me?" I place my hand on my chest.

"Absolutely. You could raise awareness and really draw a crowd." She holds her hand out for me to shake. "And I may have been introduced as Meghan, but I go by Might Be Meghan, professional YouTuber who is now branching off into other methods of distribution."

I accept her hand, giving a professional shake. "Nice to meet you."

"We'll talk later," she says with a wink, then turns to Sari.

The loaded cheese fries are to die for, and I finish off a whole basket by myself. Remi's ordered so much food, I thought we'd surely only be able to eat half, but we absolutely destroy everything set on the table.

Fiona looks over at me, then spies my glass. "Did the waitress forget to take your drink order? What would you like? I have a big mouth, and I'm hard to ignore."

"Oh, I'm just sticking with water," I say, digging for another fry.

Fiona's brows knit together. "That's half of us drinking water on ladies' night. Interesting."

My anxiety spikes to astronomical levels, but luckily,

Fiona's eyes are trained on Remi, and I'm quickly forgotten.

"So, what does Remi have you working on?" Sadie asks.

"Ummm...boring things," I reply because the air-tight nondisclosure agreement I signed is not something I intend to break.

Sadie rolls her eyes. "You probably have the least boring job of all of us."

The truth is, I have no idea what I'm doing. Remi gave me all these instructions, and I've followed them to the letter, but I'm looping in and out of systems I'm completely unfamiliar with. The security is top-notch, beyond what even the Davies had, and they are world-renown for their anti-hacking platforms.

"I only hired her to keep her out of trouble," Remi says with a wink. "If I know what she's doing all day, she can't be hacking Icor Tech."

"Oh my gosh—guess who gets to be a bridesmaid?" Meghan exclaims as she eyes her phone.

All eyes turn towards her in anticipation.

"Ali Kat Carter has given me the honor!"

I blink, trying to register what she has just said.

Remi raises her glass in a toast-like fashion. "That's great!"

Still a little surprised, I ask, "Wait, you know Ali Kat Carter? The celebrity?"

"Look around, Ding Dong—we're all kind of a big deal," Sari says condescendingly.

"Hey—back off," Fiona threatens. "We want her here *waaaay* more than we want you."

"Holy Maiden Mother, would you two get your shit

together." Sadie exhales dramatically. "Why do you two even bother doing anything together if you're always going to fight?"

I listen to them ramble back and forth like an eavesdropper. I can barely follow what they're saying half the time, so I dig into a basket of fries, praying I'm not this ravenous throughout my entire pregnancy.

"Stop obsessing over Teagan!" Fiona's shrill voice draws my attention. "She's moved on, and you should too!"

"You think I actually want Teagan? I can get anyone I please." Her eyes scan the table falling on me. "Take her, for example. One smile, and she's all mine."

The heat of their gazes makes me incredibly uncomfortable. "Ummm....as great as that sounds, I think I'm gonna have to pass."

A look of shock crosses Sari's face.

"She is so obviously not a lesbian, so why did you expect differently?" Fiona says.

"I'm Sari Heartshire," Sari sneers. "Straight as fuck girls kneel to me."

I counter with, "Well, jokes on you, because even if I were so inclined, I wouldn't know what the hell to do."

At that, the whole table breaks out into laughter, and for the first time during the evening, Sari's face loses its dire and condescending expression as she silently chuckles into her hand.

And I can't help but kind of like the self-proclaimed bitch.

Remi's phone vibrates, and she looks at the screen. "The guys want to meet up now."

I dig into a wayward basket of fries while Remi

settles the bill and tell myself that this is a one-night thing, and I'll start eating salads for baby tomorrow.

And there it is again—my pregnancy. No matter how hard I try to push it from my thoughts, it's always there.

Exhausted from a long week, I grab my purse and turn to Remi. "Thanks for inviting me out. Your group is wonderful, all of them."

"Why don't you come back to the tower with us? I'll have a car take you home later."

The excitement I feel from being invited to hang out with her crew overcomes any tiredness I previously felt. After seeing how the group of friends interact, I'm dying for more of it. To be included in their special circle.

"Okay!"

TWENTY-SEVEN

Hunter

Lounging around Gabriel's penthouse, I can't help but notice how tame they are. Not long ago, they were making tabloid headlines for their antics. Now, they're tired after a night out.

"Ladies will be here shortly," Gabriel says, pouring a round of drinks.

My stomach twists in knots, but it's not from nervousness. I'm quite charming around women, and they tend to adore me. The problem is, there's only one I wish to see.

No one ever tells you the exact moment you're going to fall in love, so I had no warning. I so badly wanted to tell her, and almost did as my head laid on her thighs, but the phone rang, forever changing my relationship with Ari.

She didn't yell or scream. It would almost be easier if she had. Instead, she simply walked on past me, out of my life.

Afterward, she proceeded to erase all parts of me from her existence, returning the college tuition I had paid off and reversing the bank transaction. She tried to return all the gifts, but Neon convinced her to keep them.

Now, I get to hang out with Gabriel's crew, seeing them dote on the women in their lives, while I have none.

I accept a shot, drinking it down quickly.

"So, give it up." Zev glares at Gabriel. "You can't hide it forever."

"Whatever are you talking about?" Gabriel says with an arched brow.

"Remi isn't a huge drinker, but she always has a daiquiri or something fruity," Zev returns.

Gabriel glares at him. "Maybe she's eating 'clean' as they call it."

Zev takes a long pull of his drink. "Not with the cheese fries she was eating."

"Are you stalking my wife?"

"No, but my wife certainly is."

"Well, I suppose you can ask her about her diet when she gets here." The look Gabriel gives Zev tells me that there will indeed be an announcement made.

My mom's going to be pissed that Scarlet Primrose beat her to becoming a grandma. There'll be no end to the jabs and dejected looks.

Fuck me.

Gabriel glances down at his vibrating phone. "They've arrived."

Zev sighs. "Please, dear God, say that Sari isn't with them."

If there were a polite way to leave at this point, I would. The last thing I want is to be subjected to happy couples staring lovingly at each other, reminding me of what I can't have. Part of me is angry with my mother and father, but that's unfair. They may have made me this way, but it was out of love and their desire to protect me.

The door to the lounge opens, and a handful of chattering women come pouring through.

I recognize Remi instantly as she's been on numerous magazine covers. Fiona is easy to pick out as well with her bright red hair.

A blonde and brunette enter, chatting with each other in what sounds like snarky tones. Trailing behind them, I see Cassius's now-wife, Sadie, who is enormously pregnant but still light on her feet. My eyes don't linger on her, though, as it's the woman next to her that grabs my attention.

It's Arinessa.

Fuck Gabriel for not giving me a warning.

She's deep in conversation with Sadie, her hands animated and a smile on her face.

Her makeup is perfectly done, which means that Neon or someone else had to have helped her get ready. Her outfit is bolder than I would have thought, a black corset over a flowing blouse, topped off by booty shorts and thigh-highs. An absolute delight to behold, and I'm not the only one who notices.

Sven whistles loudly. "Hello, sexy lady." He saunters

up to Ari and Sadie, taking Ari by surprise.

"Oh, hi…" she replies.

I've never wanted to punch a guy so badly in my life.

"Name's Sven." He smiles obnoxiously. "And who might you be?"

If he were being honest, he would have introduced himself as Douche Bag, Extraordinaire.

"Uh, my name is Arinessa, but you can call me Ari."

He steps forward, invading her space, and I nearly jump to my feet to intercede. Thankfully, no one seems to notice how riled I am.

It's easy to see that Arinessa is taken aback by the domineering Sven, shrinking away until Sadie pulls her to safety.

My blood pressure continues to spike, however, as the hulking idiot doesn't seem to take the hint.

Luckily, Cassius is on top of the matter, and he damn near throws Sven across the room, onto a couch.

"I believe introductions are in order," Gabriel says, looking at each of us.

My eyes go back to Ari, begging her to see me, although I'm not quite sure that when she finally does, it will go as I hope. Will she show anger? Or perhaps joy?

The wait is excruciating.

Fuck, having real and true feelings for a woman is worse than I had ever imagined, and yet, it's the best thing that's ever happened to me.

Gabriel begins his introductions, but his words are lost on me. All I see is her. Everything else has fallen away.

When I'm announced, her gaze finds mine, and I have my answer. Her eyes grow round, her jaw falling open. She looks frantic, like she just remembered that she left the stove on.

My heart sinks.

I take another shot, a form of self-medication I'm not prone to, but I'm hoping it will do the trick.

"I just remembered that I'm tired. I mean, I just realized," Ari says to Remi. "I think I need to leave."

I want to tell her that she can stay and I'll gladly go, but there's no way to do that without it sounding terribly awkward.

"You have to stay!" Remi enthuses. "If only for a minute. There's something you have to be here for."

"And *what* would *that* be?" Fiona says with a smirk.

"Get yourself a drink and give it a minute," Remi says to her redheaded friend.

It's hard to force my gaze from Ari as she talks to Sadie. Her backside makes such a tantalizing visual in her booty shorts.

Zev plops down beside me. "You're like a real stick in the mud."

I realize what a dick I'm being, so I decide to soften my image a bit. "You and your friends are lucky to have each other, and I'm lucky to be here, hanging out with you all."

"Agreed, and if you play your cards right, you'll be invited back again."

I force a smile.

"Something tells me you don't want to come back."

"That's not it," I insist. "You caught me at a rather unexpected time in my life."

"You can relax with us. We all keep each other's secrets, and you're not the only latecomer to the squad."

"I'll keep that in mind."

Cassius catches Zev's eye. "Hey, Cass!" he calls. "Get your ass over here!"

The pharmaceutical giant veers in our direction, and Zev and I rise from the couch.

Again, I sneak a glance over at Ari.

"Sadie, you too!" Zev calls.

Sadie dons a sardonic look, walking over slowly. Ari tries to stay behind, but Sadie insists on her inclusion.

"I'm beginning to feel like a sales rep," Sadie jokes as she forces Ari into our circle, "trying to convince the new girl that she should join our cult."

"You're all just so nice," Ari mutters, clearly uncomfortable.

"Well, I'm still working on Hunter here," Zev claps a hand on my shoulder, "and I was going to get his thoughts on the big question at large."

"Jesus Christ," Sadie snaps. "Not this again!"

"We might as well suffer through it for the dozenth time," Cassius says with a chuckle. "They're never going to let it go."

"You see, Hunter, there's this ongoing question—"

"There is no question," Sadie interjects.

"Regarding who Cassius made come first: Sadie or her mother."

I remember Cassius telling me the story at the hospital, but I feign shock all the same.

Ari's face is paper white.

Sadie sighs. "You may have heard that during the trial for the O Go, there was a woman admitted to the hospital."

Ari nods.

"That was my mother. She found a bottle of the O Go lying around and thought they were heart pills."

Arinessa's eyes flutter open and shut a dozen times. "That was your mother?"

Zev is bright red from laughter, and even Cassius is wearing a comical grin.

Sadie, however, does not look pleased.

They begin talking amongst each other, and Ari slips away.

Unable to bear the tension any longer, I go after her, tapping a finger on her shoulder.

She turns, her brow shooting upward.

"You look great," I say awkwardly, which is completely unlike me. I'm pretty suave when it comes to women, but then again, none of the others have ever meant anything to me before.

"Same. For you. You look...dapper." Her voice wavers.

Men are supposed to love confident women, but the fact that Arinessa is unsure of herself doesn't turn me off at all. It makes me want to be the one to show her that she's worthy of being adored.

She's the only woman I want to be with.

I look around to make sure no one else is listening in. "I have a lot to apologize for."

Ari crosses her arms over her chest. "I can only think of one thing that requires your apology."

"I didn't know the trial—"

"That's not it."

I furrow my brow. "You're not mad at that? You left right after—"

"The trial isn't why she took a turn for the worse. If

anything, the trail saved her. I left because I felt guilty. She'll be coming out of her coma soon, and she may make a full recovery."

My face lights in elation. "That's great!"

"But I'm still mad, just not about that."

"Oh…so you must be mad about Neon?"

She nods, glaring me down.

"I'm sorry. I wanted to make sure you were okay."

"I'm a big girl. I can take care of myself."

"Forgive me for arguing, but you weren't doing a great job of that before I arrived on scene."

Her face contorts in angry rage. Of course, I had to say the stupidest thing one could to a woman who's trying to be independent.

"I didn't mean that! I was trying to be cute."

"Just don't ever try to deceive me like that again. I trusted her! If you ever lie to me again, I'll leave every room you enter."

"Understood."

"And I'll have you know, I'm not as helpless as you believe I am. I got a job with Gabriel Icor—all on my own."

My stomach twists with the knowledge that that is indeed a deception I've perpetuated.

"I'm going to have to tell you something…and you're probably going to want to be mad. Please, don't be."

"What?"

"I kind of asked Gabriel to hire you."

Her face falls. I swear to God, I'd rather be kicked in the nuts than see her looking so dejected.

"I'm sorry! I just needed to know that you were

going to be okay, and you're so damn stubborn."

She releases a shuddering breath. "How could I be mad at that?"

"You're one of the smartest women I know," I say honestly. "Don't let this get you down."

She gives a reticent smile.

"And might I add that you look amazing in the clothes Neon picked out for you?" I take a small step closer, so I'm a breath away. "I could barely take my eyes off of you tonight."

Her chest rises and falls like a piston. I can tell because so much of it is on display from the corset, blouse combo—thank you, Neon.

She bites her lower lip, and I have a feeling I've done a good job of winning her affection. All I have to do is break through the final barrier she has erected, and I can win my girl back.

"Can I have your attention, please!" Gabriel says, tinging his fork against a glass.

Dammit!

I look over to see Remi standing with Gabriel on one side and his mother, Scarlet Primrose, on the other.

"Oh, what ever could this announcement be?" Fiona says sarcastically.

"Thank you all for coming back to the tower tonight. It's always good to be around friends, old and new." He tips his head towards Ari and me. "Mother, I'm sure you'd like to do the honors."

Scarlet puts a protective arm around Remi, who looks like a hostage. "I am excited to announce that Remi Icor is carrying my first grandchild!"

It's the oddest pregnancy announcement I've ever

heard, but I'm fairly certain my mother would do no better.

"I knew it!" Fiona shouts. "You can't just show up at ladies' night when you have a driver and drink only water."

"It really was the lamest ladies' night I've ever been to," Sari Heartshire says. "Instead of going to a bar, we would have been better off going to tea time with Remi, Sadie, and that new girl." She waves her hand in Ari's direction.

What is that supposed to mean?

Ari's reaction tells me everything I need to know. At first, a deer in headlights look crosses her face, but it's quickly replaced with anger.

Ari doesn't trust people, so the last thing she'd want is people knowing her business, and right now, people are staring at her in curiosity.

I guess I'm going to be a father.

"When are you due?" Fiona asks Remi.

Remi chuckles. "Actually…we just found out. We haven't even seen the doctor yet. We only decided to tell you guys now because Scarlet would literally explode if she had to hold it in."

The room breaks out in laughter.

Arinessa looks down at her feet.

Don't fuck this up.

The girls descend upon Remi, except Ari, who is lost in her own world. Even Sari is congratulatory.

The guys are punching Gabriel in the arm, telling him 'nice aim' and 'girls just love a dad bod.' I say my own congratulations before turning to Ari.

Now I just need to figure out how to make everything

right between us.

Snapping out of her shock, Ari joins in the revelry, embracing Remi and giving her well wishes.

A tug on my arm averts my attention.

"Someone told me that you're Hunter Davies," says Scarlet Primrose.

Her beauty rivals my mother's, though I would never admit that to a soul. She's dripping in diamonds and gold, a bit too flashy for my mother's taste, but a stunning sight all the same.

"You've heard right," I say with a charming smile.

She moves to embrace me, but I put my hands up and back away.

"Hold up…my mother would never let me back into the house if she knew I consorted with *the* Scarlet Primrose."

More than one person is listening in on our interaction, chuckling at how she's looking at me up and down.

"I wouldn't mind taking you under my wing, if ya know what I mean." She gives me a sultry wink.

"Mother!" Gabriel says in horror. His face grows pale.

"Do you think I'd really pass up an opportunity to get under Ernestine's skin?" she says. "If she were here, she'd be laying it on thick for you too."

"But you haven't so much as dated since Father died."

Their interactions are comical, but all I can think of is Arinessa, who appears to be making the rounds, getting ready to leave.

I wait for the perfect moment before I approach, after

she's said her final goodbye.

This is your one shot. Don't fuck this up.

"Arinessa?"

She stops, pivoting on her feet to face me. "Yes?"

"If there's ever something you need, please let me know."

She looks me up and down, her face unreadable. I don't know if perhaps I've been too forward. After all, she essentially cut me out of her life.

Finally, I say, "I'll let you get on with your life now. Take care."

As I begin to turn, Ari clears her throat, and I return my attention to her.

"I can meet my own needs, thank you very much, but there are a few wants you could help me with," she says, biting her lower lip.

Stunned, it takes me a moment to find my words.

"Would you care to resume this conversation back at my place?"

She smiles, her eyes roving up and down my body. "I'd like that."

TWENTY-EIGHT

Arinessa

I'm done playing games.

From now on, I'm going for what I want.

We arrive at the Davies' estate, and on our way to Hunter's suite, we see Ernestine and Rand in the hall.

Ernestine's brow lifts in surprise. "Arinessa?"

Drunk on excitement, I rush toward her, taking her into a hug. "It's good to see you again."

She looks skeptically over at Rand. "It's good to see you too."

Hunter's hand finds the small of my back. "I have a feeling you'll be seeing a lot more of her going forward. I hope you're okay with that."

Ernestine smiles with her lips but questions with her eyes. "She's welcome here any time."

I remember watching her with Neon, bright and lively on the screen. A woman with bold ambitions and a fiery personality.

So little in common with the woman standing before me. But there's a reason for that, and I have a feeling we'll be addressing it soon.

As Hunter pulls me toward his suite, I look back over my shoulder and say, "We should do brunch again."

"I'd love to," she returns.

Hunter closes the door behind us, then presses me up against it, sealing his lips to mine.

God, I didn't realize how much I needed this.

His body presses against me, his cock hard against my thigh. There's an urgency to our coupling. We both feel it.

His tongue caresses mine hungrily. He tastes strongly of liquor, which somehow adds to his over-the-top sexiness.

His hand slides into the waistband of my shorts, maneuvering my panties to the side and rubbing lightly along my sex. I release a shuddering breath, anticipating his invasive touch.

"God, you're already so wet," he rasps. "I've been dreaming about this for the last three weeks."

I groan, spreading my legs, encouraging him to explore.

"Tell me how badly you want me, Ari."

"So fucking badly."

He takes his other hand and forces my chin up so that I'm gazing into his eyes. "Look at me when you say it."

"I want you, Hunter."

"Tell me exactly what you want."

He massages my clit, circling his fingers in a rhythm that makes my legs weak.

"Tell me!"

"I want you to make me come."

"That sounds so sexy," Hunter whispers, his other hand trailing from my chin, down my neck, over my breasts and corset, to my waistband.

He pulls my shorts and panties down, slipping them over my boots and off my body. Then, he drops to his knees, bringing his fingers up to trace the delicate folds of my sex.

His warm breath washes over me, a gentle tease. Impatient, I push my hips forward, and when he chuckles in response, I reach down and grab a hand full of hair and pull him to me.

He takes the hint, delving his tongue along my sensitive flesh.

Looking down at him on his knees, his shaggy hair falling over his face as he pleases me, is intoxicating. He isn't sweet and sensual like he was the first time we were together. Instead, he's hungry. Urgent. Demanding.

He forces my legs further apart, bringing a hand up to my core and sliding a finger inside me.

His tongue glides along my lips, honing in on my clit, drawing me closer and closer to my inevitable conclusion.

My body rushes toward releases, my hips bucking wildly upward, and as my passion spills, Hunter tightens his grip on me.

Oh, fuck...

As I come, I scream out in ecstasy, riding the heigh of my orgasm as Hunter works his magic, drawing out my pleasure.

Finally, my body calms, and he pulls away.

I'm panting, unable to speak, unable to even think. I nearly collapse, my body is so spent.

Hunter rises, taking me firmly by the arm and pulling me further into his suite.

I walk on shakes legs over to the table I worked at so diligently.

"Bend over." He guides me roughly, pressing me over the table.

He's never been forceful with me before, though when he made love to me, his urgency brought out a beast in him. Part of me is scared…another part, excited. Sure, it's nice being treated like a lady, but this is so much more interesting.

I hear the unzipping of jeans followed by the rustle of fabric. His foot pushes one of my legs further to the side, opening me for him and making me feel like I'm on display. His hips press against my ass, his cock against my leg. His hands snake up my body, reaching around to my breasts. After a quick fondle, he grabs the hem of my corset, ripping it open so my breasts spill out.

How can any man make me feel this good?

My heart races as Hunter teases my sensitive nipples. Then, he takes a hand and moves it between my legs, but instead of entering me, he squats and licks lightly across the folds of my pussy.

The sensations are so powerful, I can feel myself on the verge of exploding.

He thumbs my clit as his tongue stretches into me,

edging me closer to release. Everything is happening so fast, like an exhausting sprint. I'm panting, shaking, trembling, barely able to support myself.

I come hard, collapsing onto the table as my body quakes, and when I finally still, Hunter climbs up from the floor, and I know there's more to come.

He pulls me upward, repositioning me across the table. This time when I feel his cock against my thigh, I brace for impact.

His hands reach around, grabbing my breasts as he presses against my core.

"I love how wet you are for me," Hunter rasps.

He pushes into me, past my lips, plunging deep inside. I cry out from pleasure just as much as I do from pain.

He groans, his forehead pressing against my back, his lips kissing my spine.

"You're so fucking tight," he whispers, keeping one hand on my breast and bringing the other to my hip, pushing into me harder and faster until he fills me completely.

My passion builds, though how I have any left is beyond me. The steady rhythm of his cock pushing harder and faster into me ignites a spark, and I soon start spiraling wildly out of control.

"Oh, God, don't stop—I'm close."

"Fuck, Ari, you can't just say that," Hunter growls. "I'm trying my hardest to last longer than a fucking teenager."

I focus on the pressure building within me, the steady pulse emanating from my core, and as Hunter quickens, I feel my passion spill again.

My pussy clenches around his cock as another orgasm rips through me, coursing through my body like electricity, leaving me spent and unable to hold myself up.

Hunter stops pumping, his body slumping over onto mine.

"Fuck, you make me crazy," Hunter says, kissing my neck.

"Look what you've done to me?" I return.

After a groan, Hunter gets up, helps me right myself, and sits me atop the table.

"God, how did I get so lucky?" he says, his eyes roving my body.

I look like a hot mess in my thigh highs and the shredded remains of my corset and blouse still clinging to me, but Hunter doesn't seem to care.

His cock is glistening with a mixture of our fluids, still hard, reminding me of what we just did.

"I hope I wasn't too rough," he whispers. "Seeing you dressed like this brought out the beast within."

"It was…Jesus, I don't have words for it." My hands reach up and touch his chest. "I'm exhausted."

"Let's get you to bed…and I do mean the bed. I don't care if you don't like how high it is. I'm going to love watching your sexy ass as you climb up."

He bends to kiss me softly, sweetly, then gets to work removing my boots, corset, and blouse until I'm sitting completely naked for him to ogle.

"Can I ask you something?" he says hesitantly.

"What?"

"Are you pregnant?"

My breathing grows erratic. I hadn't expected to have

this discussion tonight, though I know I can't avoid it now.

"Hey, hey, there's nothing to get upset about," he assures.

"I didn't plan it."

"Neither did I," he says, his voice kind and caring.

"You're not mad?"

"Do I look mad?"

"I didn't know how you'd react. I was terrified."

"Oh, this is a huge relief. Can you imagine how my mother would react if she found out Scarlet Primrose was about to become a grandmother with no hope for her in sight?"

I smile back at him, remembering her words. Sure, she wants to be a grandmother, but it's more for her son than it is for her. She wants him to have someone in this world, and hopefully, me and the baby will fill the void that's cast such an obvious shadow over his life.

"She would have been insufferable," I agree, pressing my face against his chest.

"Thank you," he says, scooping me up in his arms. "Now, let's get you to bed."

TWENTY-NINE

Hunter

I wake with a joy I'm unfamiliar with. It's one part content, another part excited. I finally have something to look forward to, and a person to share my joys with.

After almost a month apart, I know with absolute certainty that I'm head over heels in love with Ari.

She stretches her body against mine, her eyes snapping open when she realizes she's not alone.

"It wasn't a dream!" she gasped.

"Thankfully, no," I reply, toying with the long strands of her hair.

"How long have you been awake?"

"About twenty minutes. It's calming watching you

sleep."

"I need a shower."

"That makes two of us."

I order up breakfast, have some clothes brought up for Ari, then escort her into the shower and proceed to lather every inch of her lush body.

"You do know I can wield a bar of soap myself, don't you?"

"With me, you'll never have to."

She pulls me to a wall, wrapping a leg around my body.

I grow hard from her desire for me. Following her lead, I plunge myself up and into her warmth as she moans out in satisfaction.

What a way to start a morning.

When we're done, I towel her dry, and we hurry to eat breakfast.

Ari giggles hysterically. "Now I can check fucking in a jungle off my sex bucket list."

"First, you have a sex bucket list? I would like a copy of that. Second, if you really want to fuck in a jungle, I can make that happen by evening."

Ari finishes a piece of bacon and says, "I'll have to take a raincheck. Today I need to get my life in order."

"Life in order? It seems to me like all I have to do is call some movers to bring your stuff here. Heck, if you want to leave it all behind, I'm fine with that."

"You really want me to just move right in? My mom is supposed to be moving in with me, ya know."

"We'll look at apartments for her close by. You won't have to worry about her."

"Hunter, I have a life and a job. I can't just

disappear."

"You won't disappear. If you'd like, you can go to college and finish your degree. Or, nepotism could provide you with a job here. Or you could just care for our child."

She shrugs. "If you don't mind, I'd like to finish up what I'm doing with the Icors. I feel bad about up and leaving with no notice."

"That's understandable. You can discuss it with them on Monday, but today, you are mine."

"Actually, I'd really like to get my things situated at the apartments. I have mine and my mother's to contend with."

"Nonsense. I'll send over a team to do that for you."

"Hunter, one was my home for most of my life. This is my way of saying goodbye."

"Okay," I relent. "I'll have my people escort you."

"You don't get it, do you?"

I arc a brow.

"I don't want some muscley dude standing there as I'm sobbing over the shit I'm going to throw away."

"Understood, but I still want—"

"I'm not bringing a security detail," she insists. "Let me get the two apartments situated and packed. Tomorrow, you can have your people come and load whatever I'm taking here."

I have to respect her wishes, as much as I'd rather not.

"Fine, but I will see you tomorrow, won't I?"

"Tomorrow is when my mother is being woken from her coma."

"Am I invited to join?"

"I'd love to have you."

Arinessa

After giving Hunter one last kiss, I leave his suite and make my way toward the exit. On the way to the elevator, I see Ernestine.

My mind goes to her movies. To all her secrets I've puzzled together.

She slinks on over to me, a suspicious look on her face. "Funny seeing you here."

"Yeah…about that—"

"So, you told him how you felt?"

"Yeah, and as it turns out, we both kind of suck at this sort of thing."

Ernestine smiles. "It gets easier. Once the love is established, it grows, multiples, and eventually, there's three."

I smile, excited to tell her about her first grandchild.

"I have some matters to attend to, but I look forward to seeing you again," I say.

"Same."

My mind goes to the emails Hunter has been receiving, but this isn't just a threat to his family now, not when I'm carrying his child.

I have to see what I can do to help Hunter, whether he wants me to or not. And this woman is my best chance at getting to the bottom of this.

"You remember what I was researching?" I ask.

She exhales a sharp breath. "Yes."

"I made a break in the case. A biiiiig break."

Her brow shoots up in surprise. "Oh?"

"The kind of break that blows the whole thing wide open."

She blinks back at me, mulling over my words.

"Fortunately, we'll have plenty of time to discuss my findings," I say. "Just the two of us." I give her a wink.

The unmistakable look of fear lights her eyes. "I look forward to it."

My heart races as I walk past her toward the elevator.

In no way did I want to come across as abrasive, but if anyone can help me figure out who's been sending the emails, it's her. And now that I have a good idea of what might have happened to Lucy, I might be able to help Hunter.

I catch a bus to my apartment, arriving home just before noon. Luckily, I still have the boxes from my move, and all I have to do is pack the important things I intend to bring with me."

I wonder what my mom is going to think, waking up from her coma to not only me having a boyfriend but a baby on the way.

Of course, she'll want me to finish college. I don't know if I want to, though.

Remnants of Neon scattered around the room needle me with guilt. After I've settled in with Hunter, I'm going to have to fix what I truly believe was our budding friendship. It's not that I didn't have the right to be mad, but I should have seen things from her perspective.

I go into the bedroom to start in on my wardrobe and flicker on the light. I know Hunter would very well buy me anything my little heart desires, but I hate being wasteful, so I start separating the piles into the takes and the take-nots.

A rustling sound alerts me to a presence.

"Did Hunter send you?" I sigh, turning to see a black figure rushing toward me.

"Hey—"

A cloth bag is shoved over my face. I struggle to free myself, but all I succeed in doing is falling to the floor. Something presses against my mouth. I scream, claw, kick upward into a solid mass, but my efforts prove futile, and I fall into blackness.

THIRTY

Hunter

With Arinessa away, it's impossible for me to get anything done, so I head to the family gym to sweat away my stress.

After five miles on a treadmill, I head over to the punching bags to work on my arms.

As I'm pulling on my gloves, my phone chimes with an alarm I've set for whenever I receive an email from my supposed aunt.

Not this again…

I exhale, annoyed. After weeks, things finally begin to go my way, and of course, there's a storm cloud waiting to rain down on my life.

It can't be that bad, I reason. If they really had something on my family, they'd have gone to my father, not me. They're only approaching me because they think I'll be easily scared.

I click into the message, and an image fills my screen. It's a video. I push play and see a woman slumped in the back of a car, groggy.

It's Ari.

My heart damn near stops in my chest and I struggle to take my next breath.

She looks disoriented, like she's just woken up. A gag is being shoved into her mouth.

All I can do is watch for thirty-five agonizing seconds, then the screen fades to black. It's then that I notice a line of text below.

"Are you going to start listening?"

With no better recourse, I call Gabriel Icor.

Hunter

"We have to go to the FBI," Gabriel insists.

We've been working in my suite for the last four hours, but the combined intelligence of myself, Gabriel, and his wife Remi has gotten us nowhere.

And as each minute passes, I feel like we're running out of time.

I shake my head, refusing to give in. "Once they're on the case, we'll have to follow rules, and it closes doors for us, taking away our options."

"I get it," Gabriel assures me. "But maybe—"

"I don't think you do," I say with an edge. "The FBI isn't going to care if she's returned alive."

"I understand how much she means to you," Remi says, "But Ari was the hacker and infiltrator. I know my way around programs, but not like she did. There's precious little the three of us can do."

"Can you get that friend of yours…Dallanger?"

"He's away," Gabriel says. "If we gave him remote access to your system—"

"That would alert my father."

"We probably need to do that anyway. He has access to some of the brightest minds in the tech world. We need to get him on the case."

I draw in a frustrated breath, angry that I let this happen.

"You're not in this alone," Remi says. "I adore Ari. I don't think I've ever felt more comfortable around someone."

"She's pregnant," I confess.

"Oh…" Gabriel replies.

"I didn't know until last night. We made up and were talking about a future together. "

"We have to get her back," Remi insists. "But first, you need to tell your father."

As much as I loathe the idea of going to my father for help, I see no other way around it.

"Fine. Let's get this over with."

Hunter

"How could you let it get this far?" my father shouts, reading through the emails from my supposed aunt. "You should have come to me immediately! What in the world did you hope to achieve?"

Sitting on the opposite side of my father's desk with Remi and Gabriel, I'm too angry to feel apologetic. If anything, my father owns a share of the blame. It may be my fault that Ari is involved in this mess, but it would have never gotten this far without his secrecy.

"That poor girl," Father mutters, shaking his head in anger. "Fuck!"

"Whatever secrets you have are coming out now!" I warn.

"Who are you to tell me—"

"Who am I? You know everything about me, but I know very little about you. What is ScryptX, and those other programs I've seen remnants of? Why weren't they on the books? What were they for? Why is it that almost every piece of information on them has been redacted or deleted?"

"We are not talking about this with Gabriel Fucking Icor here!" Father shouts.

"You will tell me, and you will tell me right this fucking second! The woman I love—who is carrying my child—has been kidnapped by someone claiming to be my aunt. And you better believe I will do anything to get

Ari back."

My father leans back in his chair, stunned. "Holy shit. She's pregnant?"

Gabriel leans forward to address my father. "Mr. Davies, we don't need your company secrets. Right now, we're in two completely different areas of technology, and I see no reason to make enemies. Ari's kidnapping isn't just a concern of yours. She's been working for me for the last several weeks, and I'm afraid of what she might say under duress. This might be hard to believe, but I am on your side."

Father slams his fist down onto his desk. "Fuck—my own fucking son, right under my nose!"

My father has always been a mild-mannered man, a level-headed guy to a fault. I've never seen him this furious.

But I'm angry too.

"What the hell is that program you were working on?" I demand. "And why does Ari's captor care so much about it?"

"I can't tell you," Father insists through gritted teeth.

"You have to!"

"It's top-secret, classified at a level so high, that if the information fell into anyone's hands…well, let's just say I'd fear for their lives."

I blink back at my father, confused. "But all our government contracts are—"

"Not all on the books, as you saw," he says grimly. "Son, back in the day, there was a whole department we called: Black Tech."

"Was?"

"It was stuff we couldn't do in the light of day. Stuff

people didn't want others knowing about. After what happened with your aunt, we finished up what we had on our plate and pulled out of that line of work."

"Jesus Christ."

"We can discuss it later," he says. "When we're alone."

"No—we're going to discuss it now. Even with Gabriel Icor in the room."

"I always knew this would come back to haunt me. I can't tell you how many nights I laid in bed, awake, worried that everything was going to fall apart. I had just started to let down my guard. I thought, after all this time, surely we'd be in the clear. Some things just don't stay buried."

"Do you know who took Ari?" I ask.

"No."

"Do you know how to find her?"

"No, but I have some ideas, and someone who could help."

"Then you need to get them here, right now."

Father pulls out his phone, dials a number, and says into the receiver, "Black Tech has been compromised. I'm going into the tank. Await instructions."

THIRTY-ONE

Hunter

G abriel, Remi, and I follow my father to an elevator I didn't even know existed. He triggers it with a handprint and a retinal scan, and after a green light flickers, the doors open.

After we are inside, Father says, "I really am sorry about this."

"I don't care much for apologies," I reply. "I want this to be made right."

"Understood."

"What if Lucy has already—"

"Your aunt isn't the one keeping her."

"How can you be so sure?"

Father's eyes grow dark. "You'll find that soon, though I'm not sure if you're going to like what you learn. Right now, we need to focus on getting Ari back."

The door slides open, revealing a long hallway. My father leads us down a maze of tunnels, eventually opening into a room filled with workstations and computer monitors.

"These terminals contain all of our covert ops, the programs you only found remnants of. Not even the government knows we still have copies in their base form."

It's an impressive setup, and by the looks of it, it hasn't been touched in years.

"So this is what Ari was taken for…what Aunt Lucy may have gone missing over…"

"We were contracted to work on military systems and platforms, but also some standardization of necessary industries. Banking, for example. They didn't want the name of who worked on the banking platform to get out, lest they know who to torture for information."

"Is it what Aunt Lucy was working on."

"Yes."

"And ScryptX?"

"Is the base program banks use today. Earlier this year, it was announced that they will be going through a complete system overhaul, swapping out every component of ScryptX for some new design."

"Which means that whatever access could be granted with system knowledge of ScryptX will no longer work," Gabriel cuts in.

"Exactly. Whoever took Ari knew we had it all along, but I suppose they may have forgotten about it until the announcement was made. This is their Hail Mary pass, if you will."

I run my fingers through my hair, trying to make sense of everything. "If they gain access to ScryptX, it could get messy."

"They could be King Makers," Father says. "They could bring about the financial collapse of sixty-percent of global banking, though I doubt that's their end game. They're probably looking to take as much as possible and screw over a few competitors without triggering a meltdown."

"And you're sure it's not Aunt Lucy?"

Father exhales, a reticent look on his face. "She's dead, but I'd rather not get into that now."

It takes me a moment to fully process what my father just told me, and when it finally clicks, I decide it's not worth discussing. Yet.

"We have to save Ari," I insist.

"I know, but we can't just give them what they want. Or at least not the way that they want it."

"Father, I don't think you understand what this woman means to me. We have to do something."

"I have some tricks up my sleeves, but it's just gonna take some time."

My phone buzzes, and I reach into my pocket and pull it out. It's an email from the person that's been posing as my aunt. There's an attachment.

Please let Ari be okay.

I open it, and my heart damn near explodes in my chest.

Fuck!

Arinessa

The light hurts my eyes as I try to force them open. I'm pretty sure I'm not hungover, but my memories of last night are hazy.

I twist, quickly realizing I'm not in my own bed.

"There's water on the nightstand," a man says.

Slowly, I turn towards the voice, blinking my eyes a dozen times, trying to bring the room into focus.

"Where am I?" I croak out, my throat raw and painful.

"You are safe. For now."

The nightstand barely comes to focus. A tall glass of water is exactly what I need right now. I reach out, misjudging its distance and knocking it over.

The man grabs the cup and disappears from the room only to return a moment later, take my hand, and press the glass into it.

"Drink."

I obey, tipping back my head and letting the cool liquid run down my sore throat.

"What are you doing for Hunter Davies?" the voice asks.

"Huh?"

"What are you doing for Hunter Davies?" he says again.

"Nothing."

"What does he want from you?"

"He didn't want anything—"

"Bullshit."

The shape of the person begins to take form. Slender body. Dark clothes.

A black blur whips out in front of me, knocking the glass from my hand. It crashes against the wall, shattering glass on top of me.

"What the fuck does Hunter have you doing?"

Say something—anything.

But I can't.

I exhaled a raspy breath and rub my eyes, trying to force clarity into them.

I'm in a small, windowless room; a bed, chair, and nightstand are the only furnishings. There's another room attached to this one, but I can't make out what's inside it. Everything is so hazy.

Then I remember Hunter and our night together. I'm still wearing the clothes he got for me, a pair of fashionable sweats.

"Help," I cry out, though the words are breathless, and there's no one to hear me except my captor.

"Fuck!" the man says, getting up and leaving the room.

Someone kidnapped me, though why, I cannot say. Very few people know of my acquaintance with Hunter, which means someone's been following me.

I recall hearing the voice before, though I can't say where.

A vein in my head pulses, throbbing with anger. I lay back down, but the motion makes me dizzy.

I'm pregnant.

God, what have I gotten myself into?

Then I remember the secret I hinted at in the hallway. Was the Davies matriarch so scared that she had hired someone to kidnap me? Maybe I misjudged her.

The door opens, and the man steps into the room again. I can see better now, what little good it does me. He's tall, well-built, with very little fat. He's wearing a mask and gloves, but I can tell he's white by looking at the holes for his eyes.

In one hand, he carries a laptop; in the other, a bag of McDonald's.

He tosses the bag onto the bed. "Eat."

As queasy as I feel, I open it and eat some fries, not knowing when I'll get my next meal.

What if the last food I ever get to eat is McDonald's?

"If you want to get out of here alive, you're going to do everything I say," he rasps through the mask.

"You have a funny hiring process."

He sets the laptop on the nightstand and takes a seat in the lone chair.

I grab a nugget from the bag and chow down. Thankfully, the food helps to settle my stomach.

"What were you doing for Hunter?"

"Dating."

"Why did he hire you?"

He's not buying it, and you're only making him mad.

"I am a computer science major, in case you didn't know, and he is heir to a tech corporation."

He stares at me.

"Look, I was basically interning. Not doing anything super special."

"How well are you acquainted with Hunter Davies?"

"Well enough to be considered for a job."

The man shoves a hand in his pocket, takes something out, and tosses it on the bed.

It's my pregnancy test.

"Who is the father?"

"That's none of your business."

"I know you're a hacker. A quick twenty-five dollar background check told me that. It also told me that you're in quite a bit of debt."

I respond with silence.

"What were you hacking?"

"Was I hacking? Or was I getting knocked up?" I reply sarcastically. "You seem to be confused."

"I have no intention of hurting you, but if you don't give me what I want, I make no promises."

After a long minute of deliberation, I decide to respond with the obvious.

"I was looking for Hunter's aunt, and in case you're wondering, I have no idea what happened to her, but I managed to clear her personal trainers."

It's a lie that I pray he buys.

"How much luck did you have with the program?"

My brow draws inward. "Program?"

"ScryptX. What do you know of it?"

"He said something about a program, but all he cared about was me locating his aunt. I used facial recognition software and tapped into various computers around the world, looking for evidence of her. "

My heart races as the man fixes his intense gaze on me.

"Look, I have no reason to lie to you."

"You're going to hack into Davies Corporation and retrieve all files related to ScryptX."

"What makes you think I can do that? The Davies' systems are known to be some of the most secure in the world. There's no way I can hack that."

"Then you better learn how."

"Are you insane?"

"One wrong keystroke, and you'll become just as much of a cold case as Hunter's aunt," the man threatens. "Clock's ticking."

He gets up from his seat, and without saying another word, exits the room, leaving me with the laptop.

I stand, my legs shaking from strain, and make my way over to the adjoining room, finding a toilet and sink.

Thank God for small dignities.

After finishing up in the bathroom, I go back to the bed, take the laptop from the nightstand, and turn it on.

It's custom made and lightning-fast. One that could easily rival any I've worked on before.

Which means whoever's taken me has connections.

The desktop is being watched, recording my every click, so there's no way I can get communication out to anyone.

Or at least it won't be easy.

The laptop is loaded with standard hacking programs that assist with password cracking and back door infiltration. I get straight to work, cycling through the programs.

The high-tech software allows me to slip in easily, though gaining access to certain programs proves a challenge. I have to avoid drawing attention to myself until the right moment when an opportunity presents itself.

I start by looking for ScryptX, which ultimately

proves to be a fruitless venture, until I look at accounting records.

There's a small note made on an account going back twenty-five years that reads: ScryptX.

It appears that twenty-five-million-dollars was transferred from their main account to another. What more, the note that read ScryptX was later changed to show: NonProfit technical arts, which means the person that made the initial deposit made a mistake and had to rename it.

What was Rand Davies up to?

THIRTY-TWO

Hunter

M y father looks over the company's older contracts while Gabriel, Remi, and I try to locate where the emails are coming from.

We have a small team of trusted professionals working on the case, though I doubt they'll get much further than we will.

Fire pumps through my veins, pushing me to work at lightning-fast speed. I'm angry at what's happened to Ari and that my father had a hand in it, though I admit it was not purposeful. He should have known that taking on such programs came with risks, and now, I have to pay the price—Ari has to pay the price.

But the moments I'm being honest with myself, I know full well that I had just as much of a hand in it as he did. If not more. I'm the one that hired Ari, and I'm the one that allowed her to leave without a security detail. I'm the reason Ari's life is in danger.

I open up the last email sent to me. The one that contains a picture of her pregnancy test.

I'm terrified that whoever took her will keep her now, thinking they can get a handsome ransom from Arinessa's baby.

From my baby.

Father had me send a reply, pretending to obey. I told them I was working on getting a copy of the program, but things have escalated so quickly, it's impossible to say how much time we have left.

"Do you think they'll accept a bribe?" I ask.

Father's shoulders slump. "That won't work. This isn't just about acquiring money. If it was, they'd have it in spades with their capabilities. My guess is they're gunning to bankrupt a few corporations, take down some competition, manipulate markets. The power they'll have is incalculable."

"Surely that will alert the authorities or some governing body," Remi interjects.

"That's why they want the base program," Father replies. "Working from the source will help them hide their actions. They'll have months to wreak havoc, but they'll do it subtly, so no one understands the gravity of what's going on."

"Jesus, this feels like Dallanger all over again, except this time there's no risk of nukes," Gabriel says.

My father chuckles dryly. "I wouldn't be so sure of

that. If government accounts get hacked, and they don't know who to blame, they'll look to each other. Russia, China, India, Ukraine, Korea—all suspects."

Gabriel spins his chair around, brow furrowed. "Then, we need to contact the FBI."

"Not with Ari being held hostage!" I snap.

"We're walking a fine line," my father says. "If we tell the authorities, the government will cease our efforts, and Ari is as good as dead. We'll also never know who was after ScryptX. If we give them what they want, there is no guarantee they'll release, Ari and the world will suffer. I have a way we can 'flip the script' so to speak."

"I'd sure as hell would like to know what you're going to do," I say with an edge.

My father looks uncomfortable but doesn't brush me off. "Fortunately, I have the original program architect on the case. They're helping me change ScryptX as we speak, and each transaction done by the culprit will have a fingerprint attached, but that's not all. It has a GPS tracker that will allow us to tell the location of all the terminals that access the program."

My jaw drops. "So…we're just going to give them the program?"

"A form of it. I'm blocking some of the functions, but it will take them time to figure that out. The danger is minimal."

My heart sinks. "But that means the authorities are going to know—you could go to jail."

"I will go to jail, of that I have no doubt," my father says, his eyes never leaving his screen. "But it will be worth it to get Ari back to you and to capture whoever is behind this."

I'm rendered speechless, and although fury still rages within me, it has slightly less of an edge.

My father's phone blares an alarm. He picks it up, looking at his screen in confusion.

My eyes narrow. "What is it?"

"Someone's trying to hack our in-house hacking programs. They input something weird when trying to get into one of the platforms. Something that makes no sense."

"What?" Remi says.

"ChickenDinner," Father replies.

"That's Ari!"

"It looks like she attempted to access the program a second time, and she was successful."

"She's leaving a trail of breadcrumbs," Gabriel says. "Smart girl."

For once, Father looks hopeful. "Whoever took her must know that she's a hacker. They're trying to get her to find the program."

"How can we use that to our advantage?" Remi says.

Father's fingers fly over his keyboard again. "Give me a minute."

I wait with bated breath as my father works his magic, and after a long minute, he breathes out a heavy breath.

"We need to leave this blank file where she can easily find it. It looks innocent enough, but it has a GPS locator woven into it, one that's hard to detect. All she has to do is open it, and it will alert us to her location."

"Brilliant!" Gabriel enthuses.

"Label the file Winner," I say. "She'll know what that means."

"Done," Father says. "Now to place the file."

After a couple taps of the keyboard, he turns to look at me. "I've already put in a request to Snake. He and his men are on the roof, waiting for orders. Once Ari opens the file, they'll go straight to her location."

"I'm going too!" I insist.

"Fine, just give me a few minutes," he says as he returns to his keyboard. "When you're close, I'm going to forward the program I'm working on to her captor. Hopefully, they'll open the file right away and forward it on to whoever they're working with, and you'll never be bothered again."

My heart aches for my father, but this was his choice, and I'm glad it's one he's willing to make. Ari is innocent, as is our child. She deserves to live her life free from fear and harm.

"I'm contacting a friend at the FBI," Gabriel says. "When this comes to light, you're going to need people on your side, and this man can pull some strings."

"Fine," Father says, then looks to me. "Do you have a picture of Ari I can send to Snake? He needs to know who he's going in for?"

"Just tell him it's the same woman he collected for me nearly a month ago."

Father blinks, clearly confused.

"Unfortunately, this isn't the first time I've gotten Ari kidnapped, but she's forgiven me for the first."

"Jesus fucking Christ—tell me you're joking," Father says in disbelief.

"Afraid not."

He shakes his head. "Just sit tight. I'll have the program ready shortly."

Arinessa

I race through the Davies system, looking at the many files and folders I'm already familiar with to buy myself time.

Because Hunter told me that certain systems would trigger alarms, I made the rounds, basically being as sloppy as possible, going so far as to include the words *Chicken Dinner* in one of the logins, which was Hunter's handle when we initially spoke.

A file appears where there was none before with a simple label of: Winner, and I know I've hit the jackpot.

I go into the program and download a file, but nothing happens.

"Time's running out," a voice booms from unseen speakers. "Better hurry."

Please, don't let it end like this….

Hunter

Father's face lifts with surprise. "I have the coordinates."

I rush to him and see a map on his screen, a blip flashing on a corner near a marina.

"Get to the roof," Father instructs. "I'll send the file

to her captors when you're a minute out. It will give them enough time to forward it, but not enough to put Ari at additional risk."

I'm almost out the door when I look back and hesitate.

My father is back behind his screen, doing things to help me right the wrong I helped create.

And he's going to pay a pretty big price.

If only I had told him sooner, maybe then we could have avoided this.

I jog back to the terminals and wrap my arms around him. "Thanks, Dad."

His hand comes up and pats my forearm. "For you, anything."

THIRTY-THREE

Arinessa

After hours of searching through various programs, the door opens, and the guy who's been holding me walks through, gun in hand.

My heart sinks to the pit of my stomach, knowing what comes next.

"I'll try harder," I plead. "I just need more time."

"They're giving me the file," he says. "It's uploading now."

"Then ransom me! The baby belongs to Hunter Davies, and believe me when I say he'd pay a steep price to get me back alive."

"I wish this was just about money," the man says. "I

don't want to do this, but I have to."

"You don't have to do anything!"

He pulls off his mask, and I find myself looking in the eyes of Chet Inglewood.

"Chet?"

"I'm sorry. I didn't want this."

"But you're friends with Ernestine."

Chet chuckles dryly. "Friends? I barely know her now, she's so depressed. I stayed close to the family and feigned concern in case they had new information. Now, I'm cleaning things up."

"At least tell me who hired you."

He snickers. "Hired? As if I'm getting paid. I got roped into this over twenty years ago, when Lucy dragged me into it."

"Lucy? Did you know her?"

"I was in New York a lot, and sometime after Ernestine got with Rand, Lucy contacted me, asking to go out…quietly. I told her I was game, and we hooked up a few times. Then, she brought me to a sex club. I thought it was super sexy that Ernestine's quiet sister was a fucking sex maniac…then I found out she was videotaping things. Things that could get me into a lot of trouble."

"So she blackmailed you…"

Chet's nostrils flare with anger. "That bitch got what was coming to her."

"What did you do?"

"She was asking me for things—favors. Information from people I was connected to. We were at her apartment, and she played a video of me doing lines of coke with…questionable people. It would have destroyed my career."

"So…you killed her?"

"We went out to lunch, and I slipped some hemlock into her food. Shortly after, I went to the bathroom and slipped away, standing in an alley to watch the scene unfold."

"But she didn't die at a restaurant…"

"She was picked up by authorities. I knew she'd die in custody. I rushed to her apartment to find any evidence she had against me and found a trove of files she had from people she'd been blackmailing and various groups she was conducting business with. I left out files from foreign groups, so they wouldn't look close to home. I even stole her computer. Then I called the cops and told them to check on the apartment, that it was giving off a suspicious odor, knowing the FBI wouldn't be able to sweep it under the rug if local cops broke the case. I guess I wanted to hurt Rand and Ernestine."

"But…that doesn't make sense. Why didn't they report Lucy's death?"

"It's the fucking FBI. They play by their own rules."

"Why are you here now? Kidnapping me."

"Two months ago, someone sent me videos of my time at the club and told me that if I didn't do everything asked of me, they'd release it. They gave me all the things I needed and said there'd even be a reward in it for me."

"So, you've been behind all the emails to Hunter?"

"Yeah. They helped me prove I was her by providing code."

"You may think you'll be able to sleep after what you do to me, but what do you think they'll have you do next? You're never going to be free from whatever master you've taken."

He pauses. I can tell I've rattled him.

His phone buzzes, and he looks down. "Download's complete, and now it's on to the bosses."

"Masters," I say.

He puts down his phone and raises his gun, and I prepare to launch myself into the bathroom.

Crack!

Chet falls forward, the gun falling to the floor.

It takes me a moment to realize the bullet hit a wall and not my body. Relieved, I look up to see one of the men who took me captive at Hunter's behest standing over Chet who is crumpled on the floor.

The hired muscle looks up at me. "Am I gonna hafta put a bag over your head this time, miss?"

Armed men flood the room, restraining Chet and taking his personal belongings.

A muscular man grabs me by the arm, pulling me from the bed. "Name's Snake, and I'm gonna get you to safety."

"Move aside! Move aside!" someone shouts from the hall, and I look up to see Hunter.

"Let me through!" he says, hurrying to me.

His face is wrought with worry, his eyes scanning my body to make sure I'm not hurt.

"You're okay," he whispers.

"I'm fine."

He exhales a sigh of relief and scoops me up into his arms.

"Target has been obtained, sir," Snake says.

"What have I told you about calling her a target!"

Snake chuckles.

Hunter looks down to see Chet, his face contorting in surprise.

"I'm so sorry," I say.

"It's fine. I guess it makes sense."

Snake binds Chet's hands behind his back. "Why don't you leave this scene to us?"

"FBI will be here soon, so you're going to have to work with them," Hunter says.

"Roger that."

"I can walk on my own," I tell Hunter once we've left the room.

"It's so good to see you!" He sets me down and covers my face with kisses. "I was so worried."

"I'm fine."

"I know you're probably exhausted and eager for sleep, but I'm afraid we're going to have to meet up with the FBI at Icor Tower."

I exhale a nervous breath, knowing that what'll come out in this conversation will forever change how Hunter sees me, because Chet only had part of the story.

And the rest is terrible.

"It's okay. I'm tired, but I can get through it."

He gives me one last kiss. "Good, now let's get to the chopper."

THIRTY-FOUR

Arinessa

The mood going back to Icor Towers is somber. Probably because we have no idea what's going to happen.

The helicopter lands and Hunter does his best to give me a warm smile, but his worried eyes tell me he's in pain.

"I'm sorry about what you're going through," I say.

His brow draws inward. "You're the last person who should be sorry. I got you kidnapped."

"Guided," I return, and we both smile.

I don't think he's going to be as forgiving once he hears what I have to say, however.

We're escorted by Gabriel down to a boardroom.

"This is where I first met my wife," he says.

"Oh?" Hunter replies.

"Yeah, and I didn't have to bring her here by force."

As funny as it is, I can't bring myself to laugh. Not when so much is at stake.

"This is the FBI contact I was telling you about," Gabriel says, gesturing to a burly man at a long table.

The man rises, holding out his hand. "The name's Jim."

Hunter shakes his hand, then takes a seat at the table where Ernestine, Rand, and Remi are already seated. Gabriel and I follow suit.

"The first thing I want to say," Jim starts, "is that you must tell me the truth. With everything that's at stake, I'm going to do whatever I can to bury this, but I can't risk things coming back to bite me. And you can't either."

"Understood," Rand says, and Ernestine nods her head in agreement.

"Now, family matters should remain family matters, so if you could be so kind, Gabriel, Remi, and Arinessa, I'd like some words alone with the Davies family."

"Arinessa's staying," Hunter says.

The Icors leave the room, and Jim's face grows dour. "I've already been spun up on what happened twenty-four years ago by my superiors, but I believe some new information has come to light. Ari, you go first."

I look around the table, unsure of what to say. I believe him when he says he wants to bury this, but some skeletons refuse to stay hidden.

"I was hired by Hunter to find Lucy Whitmore," I

finally reply. "She already knows that, though." I nod to Hunter's mother. "She told me during our brunch."

She looks down morosely.

Jim follows up with, "And did you find anything?"

I want to lie. I want to bury it. But I can't."

I start with. "Chet has been posing as Lucy Whitmore. He's the one who kidnapped me at the behest of others who have not been identified."

"Chet?" Rand says in disbelief.

"What about Lucy?" Hunter cuts in.

Why does it have to be me that hurts him?

I exhale a long breath. "I found Lucy Whitmore."

Hunter's head snaps in my direction, but no one else seems surprised.

"Lucy Whitmore never went missing. Ernestine Whitmore did. I didn't know that until after I returned back home. I was watching one of Ernestine's old movies and noticed that she was right-handed. Lucy, as shown in her journals, was left-handed. The woman I brunched with, who signed a fan's autograph, was also left-handed."

Again, the only person that looks at all surprised by my revelation is Hunter.

Poor Hunter.

I continue with, "Chet Inglewood poisoned her before she was taken into FBI custody, and that is where I believe she died."

"That can't be right," Hunter finally says, shaking his head forcefully. "My mother is right here…"

Rand places a hand on the lap of the woman who had been posing as his wife. "It is and I'm sorry."

"But…I don't understand," Hunter mutters in a daze.

"Let me set the stage for you," Jim says. "Twenty-four years ago, Ernestine Whitmore perished in FBI custody, though at the time we believed her to be Lucy. She was being held for questioning, but she barely made it through the door before getting sick and eventually dying. It was believed she was poisoned during lunch, but we could never figure out who she had lunch with."

Hunter's eyes train on the woman who had raised him for the last twenty-four years. "But-but…you're my mother…"

"I am," the Ernestine imposture says, a morose look on her face, "but I wasn't always. Once upon a time, I was your aunt."

Hunter's face goes pale, and I see a single tear in the corner of his eye.

"Hunter," Rand says, "give us a chance to explain."

Hunter

Staring at the woman who I thought was my mother fills me with profound sorrow. Part of me wants to strangle her; another part wants to hug her close to me.

Lucy looks down at her lap, a tear sliding down her cheek. "I loved your father so much. With all of my heart…but I never had the courage to tell him. Or at least, I didn't until it was too late. Ernestine had come to visit, and she read my journals. She demanded to know who I had a crush on, and I told her. She insisted I act on in. We had been drinking, and she had me send Rand a text telling him everything, and then…I passed out."

My father looks down guiltily. "Lucy wasn't the only one who was a coward with their love, so when I received the text, I felt a mixture of relief and joy. I told her I wanted to discuss it in person, and she offered to meet me at a hotel. We met up, but she wasn't interested in talking. I'll spare you the details, but that night was significant in that it's when you were conceived."

"You can't be serious," I say, my eyes darting between Lucy and my father. "Please tell me this is some kind of sick, twisted joke?"

"Afraid not," Lucy says, "and I'm sorry you had to find out this way."

Every part of me wants to scream with rage, but there's more to the tale, and unfortunately, I'm in too deep to turn back now.

Father clears his throat. "When I found out Ernestine had played a trick on me, I was crushed. I told her it was a one-time thing, and I never wanted to see her again. Then, three weeks later, she told me she was pregnant. I decided I had to do what was right. At that time, I still didn't know Lucy had feelings for me. I thought that was part of Ernestine's con. Then, we told her about the pregnancy." Father exhales a heavy breath. "The pain in her eyes was palpable."

I look to Lucy with scorn. "So…my conception marks one of the worst moments of your life. Great."

"I think you should look at it this way," Lucy says. "Your birth is the day I got to meet one of my favorite people."

I'm too angry to consider her words, let alone fully process them.

"Lucy buried herself in the government projects we had going on," Father says. "And I played house with Ernestine. We didn't have much in common, and she went out shopping all day, leaving you with nannies. Or at least I thought she was shopping."

"For whatever reason, Ernestine became obsessed with pretending to be me," Lucy says. "Sometime during our teenage years, Ernestine and I drifted apart. She went into acting; I went into computers. While she was on location overseas, she attracted a rather unsavory crowd. She liked the element of danger. She never introduced herself as Ernestine, though. She would tell people that she was me, visiting Ernestine while she was on location."

"But that doesn't make any sense," I reply. "Why would she do that?"

"At first, it was to cover her own ass and save her reputation," Lucy says, "but then she realized that Lucy's proximity to the Davies family gained her access to people and money she wouldn't have had otherwise. She began calling me, asking me about my work. I didn't think anything of it and chalked it up to sisterly camaraderie, but she was using our daily talks to subtly figure out things I might be working on. Eventually, she decided to relocate close to me, so she could seduce Rand. I guess she figured she could still act while continuing her side gig."

"But why would she do that?" I demand. "She was a famous actress with more than enough money!"

"Because it was exciting," Lucy says. "She didn't want to act in a movie; she wanted to be in a movie. She made her life into a spy thriller."

"What the actual fuck!" I shout.

"I know this is hard," Lucy says.

I glare at Jim. "Why the fuck did the FBI cover up her death? Why wasn't anyone charged?"

"From what I can gather, they thought they had Lucy. They found communications from her with an unsavory organization and took her in for questioning. Then, she died unexpectedly, and they went to her apartment. The cops were already there, finding a mountain of evidence against her, and unfortunately, someone called a reporter. If there's one thing the FBI likes, it's control, and at that point, they had lost it. They booked it to Davies Corporation to give Rand a head up before he heard it from the news."

"Jesus," I mutter.

Father continues with, "The FBI told me they had taken Lucy into custody, and she'd perished shortly thereafter. I thought they were crazy because I knew full well that Lucy was working in the secret workstations you saw earlier today. Then…it just kind of clicked, and things began to unravel quickly after that."

"My life was ruined," Lucy says bitterly, "but what had happened was far bigger than any one life. The bureau asked me to pose as your mother to see if anyone would try to contact her, and I couldn't refuse them. I played the role of Ernestine for months, but in the end, she didn't seem to have any contacts as Ernestine."

"Wouldn't she have had more contacts as Lucy?" I ask. "Why didn't you just go on being yourself?"

"Because someone had poisoned Lucy," Jim says. "So they'd know something was up."

"Months went by with no contact. Eventually, they

called the mission a bust," Father said. "They offered to reinstate Lucy's identity," Father looks to Lucy adoringly.

"But I didn't want to go back," Lucy finishes. "I loved your father."

"So you just decided to make a go of it?" I say.

Lucy's face grows pained. "I know it must sound terrible, but my life was ruined. If whoever poisoned Ernestine believed I was alive, they could have tried to finish the job."

After a long minute of silence, I reply with, "I can't say I'll ever get over this, but for what it's worth, I can see why you did it."

"I'm sorry you had to find out about your mother this way," Lucy says with eyes full of apology.

And then it clicks. I'm upset, but I'm not mad. I was raised by two loving parents. I'm lucky.

"I'm pretty sure my mother is sitting across the table from me."

Tears flood Lucy's eyes, and Father pulls her tight.

"Why did Chet poison my mother?" I ask in a daze.

"She threatened him with blackmail," Ari says. "Fake Lucy had dirt on him, and he was desperate to make it disappear."

I turn my attention to Jim. "How come a death was never reported?"

"Everything happened so fast, and eventually directives came down the chain telling us it would be safer to label her a missing person rather than deceased. Basically, they were trying to bait out information, and it just stretched too long, and there would have been too many questions."

"Where is she now?" I ask.

"Buried on one of our estates," Father says. "We've picnicked at the spot from time to time."

I look to Lucy. "There's a file on the system addressed to Rand. What's in it?"

Lucy snickers. "It was my first love letter to Rand. I showed it to him after we eventually got together, and he insisted it always stay there."

"As a reminder not to be a coward," Father adds.

I know I should be angry. I should hate him and Lucy. But…I can't find it in myself to harden my heart toward them. This disaster wasn't their fault, even if they did perpetuate it.

"So, what are you going to do with us?" Father asks Jim.

"With the program you gave them, we've already been able to locate five militia bases, and we're preparing to move in on them now. So, maybe give you a medal."

Father looks surprised. "So, we're good?"

"Oh, the superiors are pissed, but they're coming around." Jim winks.

Lucy brings a hand to her chest. "Thank God."

My parents fall into each other, exhaling in relief. I know I should be absolutely devastated about the revelations made today, but I'm not.

Jim smiles as he looks down at his phone. "Looks like they've made Chet crack."

"What's going to happen with him?" I ask. "He killed my mother."

"We may not be able to get him for poisoning Ernestine, but he's up against treason and kidnapping charges. He'll never see the light of day again."

"I get it," I reply. "I think I'm going to need a minute alone with Ari if that's okay with everyone."

"Sure thing, kid." Jim turns to Arinessa. "If you ever find yourself in need of a job, I know several government agencies that would fight tooth and nail over you."

Ari smiles. "I'll keep that in mind."

Father rises from his seat and approaches hesitantly. "Son, I've always tried to do right by you."

I embrace him. "I know."

Lucy casts me a timid gaze, and I smile back, letting her know everything is fine between us.

After Jim and my parents leave, I turn to Ari and say, "Finally."

THIRTY-FIVE

Arinessa

Hunter's hand brushes against my cheek, a look of relief on his face. "I'm so sorry you were dragged into this."

I cock a brow. "You realize that's the second time I've been kidnapped in one month?"

"Guided," he insists.

I punch his arm. "Bullshit!"

His lips cover mine with an eager kiss, which I return with fervor. How could I have been stupid enough to believe I could stay away from this man that is so obviously a drug to me?

We break apart but still cling to each other. It's then

that I see a shadow of pain in his eyes.

"I'm sorry about how everything turned out," I say in earnest.

"You know, they say everything happens for a reason, and we would have never met otherwise. I know this is going to be a bit difficult, but in the end, there is no other way I'd rather it have gone." He leans down, planting a kiss on my forehead.

"I have to admit, I'm excited to meet *the* Lucy Whitmore."

"Now she has a contender for the title: Smartest Person in Every Room."

"Oh, there is no contender—she's earned that title."

His face grows serious...curious. "So, are we really doing this? You...me...baby?"

"Makes three," I finish.

Hunter chuckles. "It'll hardly be three with how clingy my mother's about to get."

I nod my head in approval. "I'm okay with doting grandmas."

He pulls me closer, his hand roving my hip. "Why don't we go back to my place, or shall I say, our place, and celebrate."

"As much as I'd love to, I want to see how my mother is doing."

Surprise flashes in Hunter's eyes. "I forgot about that. The helicopter should still be on the rooftop. Why don't I take you there right now?"

Arinessa

At Cassius's request, the doctors agree to wake my mother twelve hours early as it would have no ill effects on her health.

They've assured me that she should be fine, but there's no way I'm going to fully believe them until she's awake and tells me herself.

Hunter has been ever attentive, bringing me food and water as I sit holding her hand. The process isn't as quick as I had hoped, not that I'm complaining. I get to see my mom again.

"Ah, she's beginning to stir," Cassius says, and a doctor rushes to her side to check her vitals.

She groans, her eyes fluttering slightly.

My heart races and my grip strengthens around Hunter's hand.

"It's going to be okay," he whispers into my ear.

The minutes it takes for my mother to gain consciousness are the slowest I've ever experienced, and that says a lot seeing as how I've been kidnapped twice.

When it looks like my mother has some awareness, the doctor says, "Mrs. Sylvan, can you hear me?"

"Where am I?" she rasps.

"Mrs. Sylvan, my name is Doctor Ryan, and you're at the hospital. How are you feeling?"

"Like shit."

He continues with, "Three weeks ago, you were placed in a medically induced coma."

The unmistakable look of fear flashes in her eyes. "Oh, dear…"

Cassius steps in and says, "If I were you, I wouldn't worry. You're better than you've been in a long time, thanks to your daughter."

A nurse puts a damp sponge in her mouth to help with the dryness.

"I'm going to give you a few minutes alone with your daughter," Doctor Ryan says, "then we'll meet privately to discuss your medical care."

They leave the room to afford us some privacy, and I prepare to introduce my mother to my first actual boyfriend. Or rather, the man that knocked me up.

"Mom, I'm so glad you're okay!" I enthuse.

Her face is confused and scared. "Am I, though?"

"Yes, you're going to be fine."

Her eyes scan the room, falling on Hunter.

I pull him to my side. "This is Hunter Davies."

"Hunter, who?"

"He basically got you recommended for the new treatment," I say. "And…he's my boyfriend."

Her eyes grow round. "You couldn't have introduced us under better circumstances?"

"No! Because I can't wait to tell you something else, and it's important that he's here."

"What is it?"

"I'm pregnant!"

Her face grows serious. "But your school?"

"She can attend any school she'd like," Hunter says.

If she gets to cheat death, then I feel like I'm allowed to realign my priorities.

"I don't care about school, mom. Right now, I can get a job in my field, and I don't want to waste a year of my life getting a piece of paper that can literally do nothing for me now."

"But you need—"

"A lot has happened since you've been put under," I say. "I've been working for Gabriel and Remi Icor. I've been offered a position with the FBI. The Davies family, you know, the super-secret tech family, will hire me in a heartbeat. I just want to live my life."

Mother's face relaxes. "Good for you."

I plant a kiss on her forehead. "I'm so happy you're awake."

"Ari, I don't know if you're aware, but this is a lot to take in. Medically induced coma? Boyfriend? Baby? Dropping out of school?"

"Everything is going to be fine, mom—better than fine. I promise."

Mother sighs. "I sure hope."

"Oh, and we're moving you close to Hunter's estate."

Mother's eyes flutter. "Okay, I'm pretty sure I'm still under, and this is all a dream. I just thought I heard the word estate coming out of your mouth."

"I think I've overwhelmed you. I'm going to call in the doctor, and he can at least help you make sense of your hospital stay."

"Please do," mom replies.

We leave the room, and Doctor Ryan goes back in to talk with her.

"See, she's going to be fine, and you running off on me like you did was a big overreaction," Hunter chides. "We'll call it a pregnancy hormone surge."

I lob my fist into his shoulder, and he feigns pain.

"It's going to be so weird going back to the estate," Hunter says. "I don't even know how to address Lucy."

"She's still the same person," I reason. "She did what she had to do, and she loved you while doing it."

"I suppose you're right."

"How do you feel about her?"

"I'm actually mad at myself for loving her so much."

"That's nothing to be mad about. That woman would die for you, and your father would die for her."

"Ari, I just want you to know that I love you with all of my heart and every ounce of my soul."

"Then I should probably tell you that I love you too."

I stand on my tippy toes, tilting my chin up as he bends to plant a kiss on my lips.

And I know for sure, from the bottom of my heart, that I can trust him.

And that he trusts me.

Arinessa

EPILOGUE - SIX MONTHS LATER

"And then I was dragged into an elevator, bag over my head, thinking I was about to be sex trafficked."

"I know it's horrible, but it sounds terribly romantic," Sadie says with dreamy eyes.

Cassius sneers, looking around the room in disgust. "Are we really romanticizing this woman's Stockholm syndrome?"

An animated Neon can't help herself and butts in with, "I got to see her while she was being held captive!"

Hunter rolls his eyes. "She was *guided* to my office—

guided!"

"Guided with firearms," I interject.

Hunter drains his scotch and offers to get me another drink as he gets his own, then remembers I'm nursing a water.

"This whole thing is exhausting," Cassius says. "Just wait until the babies come. I'm dead on my feet and it's only seven. I can't remember the last time I saw the gym."

"As if you don't have help," Gabriel says. "How many nannies do you have?"

"We have two," Sadies replies, "but Cassius doesn't want them touching the little nugget and does most things himself. It was like pulling teeth getting him to come out tonight."

It's been seven months since I first met Hunter, and my life has yet to calm and reach a semblance of normalcy.

He's not the only new person in my life, though. We've assimilated into Gabriel's group of friends, and barely an hour goes by without someone entering our group chat with some kind of hilarious emergency.

Neon's been allowed into the circle, sharing in our secrets and adding to the outrageousness. In perhaps the craziest twist of events, she's been on more than one date with Sari, and even though they are opposites in every way, they seem to get along well enough.

A knock sounds on the door, and Gabriel dashes to get it.

It's Jim from the FBI, accompanied by Rand and Lucy. Scarlet embraces her one-time rival in a hug, my mother joining them.

Interestingly enough, Scarlet and Lucy have become fast friends, bonding over baby clothes and poor life decisions. It didn't happen overnight, but when Scarlet heard that 'Ernestine' was expecting her first grandchild, tantrums were thrown, and a big bouquet of flowers was sent to the Davies' residence. Flowers that Ernestine Whitmore is well known to be allergic to.

Their Hollywood rivalry really was vicious.

Lucy invited Scarlet out, and wouldn't you know it, they clicked, and eventually, Scarlet was let in on the secret of her identity.

Now, the whole group knows, each of them vowing never to tell a soul.

"We have news," Jim says.

My stomach twists in knots, hoping the news is good.

"Chet took a plea deal, and he's going away for life," Jim says, "I'd love for him to do time at the worst of the worst, but it's the best we could bargain for."

I breathe out a sigh of relief. "And the people he forwarded the program to?"

"We were able to raid five sites, and seventeen people are awaiting trial."

Hunter looks solemn, and I can't help but hurt for him with what happened to his mother. "Thanks, Jim. For everything."

"Don't mention it." Jim gives me a peculiar look. "Ya know, Gabriel and I have been talking, and we were kind of hoping you'd sign on for a project we have going on with Dallanger."

Hunter gives Jim a double-take. "Absolutely not! Not with what we've been through."

"I get it! I get it!" Jim says, holding up his hands

defensively. "But it is up to the lady." He looks to me.

"I-I don't know. I hardly think I could contribute much to the project," I reply.

"You do realize you've already worked on it," Gabriel says.

I cock a brow. "Pardon?"

"That system I had you trying to crack, it was to see if you could gain access to Dallanger's AI. Find any weaknesses."

"No!"

"Yes."

"I have to get in on this!" I enthuse.

"I thought you had your heart set on hunting criminals," Hunter says. "I don't want anything derailing your interests. I want you to do something you love."

Remi quirks a brow. "Hunting criminals?"

"Remember what I got busted for?" I say sheepishly. "Well, I kind of want to take that to the next level."

"And with my help, you can," Jim interjects. "Legally."

"So I can do both?"

"Let's not overwhelm yourself," Hunter says, glaring at Jim. "You are several months pregnant."

"She can set her own hours," Jim insists. "Any amount of time she can spare would be valuable to the cause."

Hunter looks hesitantly. "What do you say?"

"I can't wait!"

"Well, there is just one minor, incy wincy thing you have to do first," Jim says.

"And what is that?" I ask with an arched brow.

"Oh, it's nothing. Really. Just a small test that I need

you to pass in order to get you in."

"And if I fail, am I off the project?"

"Yep," Jim says.

"Just tell me where and when the test is, and I'll be there."

Jim pulls a laptop from his briefcase. "It's here and now."

I look around at the room full of people, all interested in what I'm doing.

"I'd like some privacy."

"You work better without people around?" Jim says, and before I can answer, he continues with, "Let's see how you work under a bit of stress then."

The room grows smaller as the crowd gathers even tighter around me.

Annoyed, I log into the mainframe. "Where do I find this little test?"

Jim hands me a piece of paper that gives me coordinates to begin.

It doesn't take long for me to locate a folder that reveals my next stop, and for the next thirty minutes, I'm maneuvering in and out of highly-secured sites. The world around me falls away. I could be alone or in a room with a thousand people; it matters not. All that exists is the screen.

Finally, I reach the final portion of the test—one last folder titled: Arinessa.

I click on it, and a box comes up asking for a password with one clue: Winner Winner!

What do we have here?

I type in: ChickenDinner, and click enter. The file opens, and inside is a single word document. I open it, finding one line of text:

Arinessa, will you marry me?

I look up to see the same room full of people looking down at me with glistening eyes, and to my left, Hunter is down on one knee, ring box in hand.

My arms fly out and wrap around his neck, completely disregarding the ring box.

"Yes! Yes!" I cry out. "Of course, I will!"

"Oh, my God!" Neon screeches. "I call dibs on hair and makeup!"

"A toast!" Cassius cries out, and flutes of champagne and water are passed around.

I stand, allowing Hunter to slip the ring on my finger, then Cassius weasels his way between us, lifting his glass to toast us:

> *"May thy life be long and joyful,*
> *Thy friends be tried and true;*
> *And your journeys together be a great adventure,*
> *As your love grows strong like superglue."*

The room cries out, "Cheers!" and glasses are raised and sipped.

Hunter pushes Cassius aside, snaking an arm around my waist and bringing his lips to mine for a gentle kiss.

"I love you, Ari, with all of my heart."

Without hesitation, I reply back, "And I love you!"

The End

Also By Lark Anderson

The Beguiling a Billionaire Series

The Billionaire's Board
The Billionaire's Fixer Upper
The Billionaire's Funding
The Bad Girl
The Dis-Graced
The Trainwreck
Hacking His Code

Reckless in Love
eBook Only

Love you…not!!!
Trust you…not!!!
Tempt you…not!!!

Savage in Love

Savage in the Sheets
Savage in the Streets

The Glow Girlz Series

Stacey's Seduction
Tempting Teysa
Desiree's Delight

If you'd like to become an ARC reviewer for Lark, please email her at:
mims@mimsthewords.com.

About the Author - Lark

Lark Anderson was raised near Syracuse, New York. She joined the USAF at 19 as a Flight Manager and eventually discharged in pursuit of a college degree. Her passion for writing manifested in elementary school, but she waited until she was in her 20's to pursue her dream. Now, she not only writes contemporary romance and fantasy, but she also writes for a sitcom!

Twitters: @mims_words / @lark_anderson
Goodreads: @Lark_Anderson
Instagram: @mimsthewords
Facebook: @LarkAndersonAuthor
Website: www.larkandersonbooks.net
BookBub: @mims8
Facebook Readers' Group: https://www.facebook.com/groups/larkers
Newsletter Signup: https://larkandersonbooks.net/subscribe/

A SNEAK PEEK AT.....

Savage in Love
Book 1

Savage
In the
Sheets

Jenna

"I hate you!"

"Again, I don't see how I had anything to do with Arnold's pick—"

"You liked that trashy bimbo with the big, blonde hair and fake boobs!"

"I did enjoy some of her segments—"

"And because of people like you, Ryanne is being sent home. She's an executive at only twenty-six—TWENTY-SIX!!!"

"You do realize this wasn't a viewer vote sendoff," Wes says, way too logically for my liking. "Arnold picked—"

"Which one, Wes!" I gesture wildly to the screen. "Which one would you rather fuck?"

Weston blinks, his mouth falling ajar. My cheeks turn red as I suddenly realize just how childish I'm being, but at this point, it's a hill I might as well die on.

"Which one?" I emphasize the words pointedly.

Weston looks down guilty. "Bianca…"

I launch a pillow at his face. "I knew it—I knew it!"

He holds up his hands in fake surrender. "To be honest, I don't even like her fake boobs. She just seems easygoing."

"Easygoing?"

"Yeah. She's the kind of girl that when eleven o'clock rolls around, she dares you to take one more shot. Ryanne…well, I'm pretty sure she's in bed by nine."

"Because she makes good life decisions!"

"Yes, because she has her shit together." Weston rakes his long fingers through his shaggy, dark hair. "I'm willing to bet Arnold isn't looking to settle down. Look at him." He points to the television. "He's twenty-three and obviously works out several times a week. The show is called Tempt Me, not Date Me, not Marry Me—Tempt Me. Bianca is both tempting and perfect for a week-long fling."

"We are *never* watching this together again," I insist, folding my arms over my chest.

"That's fine by me," he says smugly. "We can go back to that garage makeover show."

I frown. "That was boring."

Weston turns off the television. "Then we watch, nothing and just sit around, enjoying each other's company."

Feeling foolish, I give him my most pathetic puppy-dog eyes. "Sorry about my outburst."

"It's okay. To tell you the truth, this was way better than the whole Kate-Juliet argument we had when we binge-watched Lost."

I chuckle. "Why would anyone want Kate over Juliet—she's terrible!"

Weston rolls his eyes. "Want me to get you another beer?"

"Sure."

As he goes to the kitchen, I'm left alone with my thoughts.

From the outside looking in, it may seems rather silly that I'm ranting about a reality show that certainly has no basis in reality.

But the thing is, this is very much *my* reality.

I've always been a too-smart-for-my-own-good go-getter. An overachiever to an obnoxious degree. Valedictorian. Bar exam acer.

Everything seems to come easy for me.

Except love.

"Here ya go." Weston hands me a Bud Light Lime.

I take a sip, mulling over my many unfortunate relationships. If you could even call them that.

Things start off great. They're impressed with my accomplishments and happy to take me on date number two. And three. Then, we make it into the bedroom... maybe two times.

I have to know what's wrong with me. Why guys ditch me when everything seems to be going so smoothly. And who better to help than Wes, my bestie who's been with me through thick and thin the last eight years.

"Wes?" I say anxiously, not sure if I really want to know the answer to what I'm about to ask.

His face shows concern. "What's up?"

"I need to know what's wrong with me."

His brow draws together. "Wrong with you? You seem to be doing alright."

I take a sip of my beer, then dig in deep.

"I'm twenty-five, and I've never been in a real, committed relationship. There was a guy in high school I *'dated'* for two years, but we never did more than kiss. Every time I meet a man, things seem to be going good. We talk, and there are no awkward silences. We…make it into the bedroom…all the things men would expect." I waggle my brow to get my point across. "But then… nothing. They just tell me they're not looking for commitment, or they stop calling altogether."

"Uh-huh—"

"Which is bullshit. A month after one guy broke up with me, he was claiming some woman on Facebook. I couldn't help but think, why not me?"

Weston downcasts his eyes.

"Wes, do you know something?"

"It's nothing—"

"Oh, it is most certainly something. Now you better tell me—"

"You're reading too much into this."

"Don't act like I don't know you. If you know something that could help me, just tell me. I would do the same for you."

Wes swallows hard, and I know I'm in for a bumpy ride. I take another swig of beer and brace for impact.

"Remember a month ago when I got into that fight with Ashton…" Weston starts.

Ashton Penrose, the charming architect that shagged me three whole times before calling it quits.

"Yeah, you were at that new bar, and he was trying to hit on the girl you were with."

He clears his throat and licks his lips as if he's anxious.

Why would he be anxious?

"He wasn't hitting on your girl, was he?"

"No…I was there with some friends, and I said hi. He said, "You're friends with that smart, nerdy girl, aren't you?" I had to agree with him, because it was true but what he said next was something I couldn't tolerate."

"What did he say?"

"Just that…you were very mechanical."

I blink, trying to process what my best friend just said. "Mechanical?"

"He called you Rosie from the Jetsons, you know, the robot. She has those little metal hands shaped like this," he makes his hand into a claw. "Then, he demonstrated a weirdly mechanical hand job." Wes makes a mechanical jacking motion with his hand while simultaneously making a squeaky grinding sound to add to the effect.

"Stop!" I cover my eyes, too embarrassed to look on.

"I defended your honor! Damn near broke his jaw."

I reach over and hold a finger up to his lips. "Not another word."

My worst fears have been confirmed. I'm a bad lay. That may sound dramatic, but it's a pretty valid fear. Men are known to fall for complete and utter train-wrecks that can't get their shit together. Even looks can be overlooked. What's ugly to some is extremely attractive to another. But bad in bed—that's a hard flaw to overcome.

After the longest minute imaginable, Wes says, "Look, it's not that big a deal. To some people, a warm body is a warm body."

I stare in shock at him, mouth gaping in offense.

"Oh, shit. I guess maybe you didn't want to hear that."

He's the last person I should be mad at because he's the only guy with balls enough to tell me the truth.

I give him a meek smile. "Thanks, Wes, for shooting it to me straight."

A friendship like ours isn't the norm, but we didn't exactly have a typical start to it.

During his years at a local community college, he needed a tutor, so he picked up a third job in order to afford one. He hired me, who was two years his junior but attending an Ivy League school.

He was the first person in his family to attend college, and due to having to work since the age of thirteen to help keep his family afloat, he wasn't always able to give his schoolwork proper attention, and it showed in his grades.

As it turned out, he was plenty smart; he just never got any sleep and had a million stressors on his mind. When I found out he took on a third job in order to afford me, I made him quit on the spot. I sat next to him as he gave his two-week notice. Then, we made a plan on how best to get him through school while keeping his debt minimal.

After that, we became best friends. I went on to graduate law school, and he eventually went on to university, graduated with honors, and now works in contract management for some big-shot tech company. Both of us in prime positions for our 'happily ever after.'

Wes looks guiltily down at his drink. "I wish I had handled the situation more delicately. With finesse. I didn't mean to embarrass you."

"I don't." I chuckle. "This was fucking hilarious." I make the Rosie hand job motion.

We break out into laughter, and I scoot over to him, resting my head on his shoulder.

"Wes…"

"Yeah?"

"When we first met, you said that you needed me. But more and more often, now, I'm the one that needs you."

"It's give and take with us." Wes grabs the remote. "Oh! I remember hearing something about a chicken beauty pageant on YouTube."

"This, I gotta see!"

Weston

I can't remember a time that I've felt more terrible than when I saw the hurt in Jenna's eyes. All because I was careless with my words.

If there ever was a person in this world I owed an incalculable debt to, it would be Jenna Savage.

Without her, I would have never graduated from college. Jenna saw past my good looks that normally strike a woman and my deficient math skills, and somehow saw the person I was meant to become. I was all but on the brink of dropping out of college before she came along. She was my Hail Mary pass.

And knowing that I've caused her pain has kept me up all night.

Jenna is as smart as they come, logical with everything she does, with an analytical brain that I'm entirely sure could aspire to world domination.

But she is not easy going, she does not suffer stupidity, and she doesn't need a man. Not like other women do. She's not a person that makes you forget your worries. She's the person that tries to fix them, which is great, but it's not a quality a guy looks for in a date.

Maybe, for once in her life, Jenna needs someone to solve her problem. Instead of coming to someone else's rescue, someone needs to come to hers.

And what better person than me, her very best friend who would do anything to help her and who owes her literally everything.

But how would I help her? I don't want to make her feel like she has to change who she is. I just want to teach her to cut loose a little and not take everything so seriously. We could start with movies, rom-coms that show a woman at ease like There's Something About Mary. That Cameron Diaz chick was one cool cucumber.

But it has to extend outside of watching movies. We're going to have to analyze her dates, her conversations…her love life.

Looking at Jenna, you'd never guess that she would be anything less than a ten in the sack. Five-foot-seven, cascading red hair, shapely breasts, heart-shaped face, intense green eyes, pouty lips, and curvy hips—she's the very definition of aphrodisiac. I reckon the only reason I'm immune to her is because when we met, I was in such dire straits the last thing on my mind was meeting a woman.

I grab my phone to text her.

Weston: *how you feelin'*

Jenna: *Like shit.*

Weston: *you shouldn't*

Jenna: *You told me I'm a Rosie Jetson in the sheets...*

Weston: *First, those weren't my words. Second, that guy was an asshole.*

Jenna: *Just because he's an asshole doesn't make it not true.*

Weston: *you're in luck*

Jenna: *How so?*

Weston: *Because I'm gonna be your new wingman. With my help, you're going to transition from Rosie Jetson to Wilma Flintstone.*

Jenna: *Wilma Flintstone?*

Weston: *She's a cute redhead in a short skirt...and wears a pearl necklace...*

Jenna: *To be honest, I don't know what you're getting at, Wes. Are you going to just give me advice?*

Weston: *Let me put it this way—I'm gonna make you a Savage in the sheets...*

Jenna: *Ummm...could you be a little more clear?*

Weston: *Get yourself ready because I'm swinging by in an hour.*

Jenna

I reread the texts from Weston for the hundredth time, trying to figure out what the hell his intentions are.

By the sound of it, he's coming over to teach me how to have sex. Which would involve...having sex?

Which would be the stupidest thing we could possibly do because we're friends. No, not just friends—best friends with an unbreakable bond.

But I guess an unbreakable bond suggests we could cross that line and come out the other side unscathed.

As crazy as it sounds.

After going through my closet, I decide to do the most normal thing when greeting Weston on a Saturday morning, and that is stay in my pajamas, though I do run a brush through my hair and refresh my face a little.

Do I want to have sex with Weston?

Weirdly, that the question has never crossed my mind. Not once.

Almost every other woman would give their right ovary for a night with Weston Singer. And no, I am not exaggerating.

Shaggy dark hair, piercing blue eyes, strong jaw, full lips, and a panty-dropping smile. And that's only Weston's appearance. His voice is deep and sensual, dripping with bedroom confidence—and his swagger—damn!

During college, he got laid plenty, but he was always more focused on his studies. Now, every couple of weeks, there's a new girl, but she never lasts longer than a week before he gets bored with her and moves on.

I'm the one woman constant in his life, and that's probably because I've never turned him on, and after last night's conversation, I think I have a good idea why.

My parents drilled a competitive drive in me that triggers during one-on-one conversation. When we first met, I must have seemed aggressive, and therefore, never a desirable option.

But if that's the case, what exactly is he offering?

A knock sounds on the door, and I go to greet Weston.

He's brought with him two smoked-salmon bagels from The Bagelry, which are heavenly.

Sitting across the table from him, I can't help but feel self-conscious. We talk a lot less than normal, and if I'm not mistaken, he's avoiding eye contact. I guess he regrets the direction our conversation took. Or maybe he thinks making me a savage in the sheets is aiming too high, far exceeding my potential.

Attempting to act normal, I say, "Hey, I just wanted to thank you for telling me the truth last night. I know it must have made you uncomfortable. We don't have to discuss it again."

Weston comes back with, "You think that's going to get you off the hook?"

I blink, gazing into his intense blue eyes. "Get me off the hook?"

"Don't act like you don't remember our conversation."

"Obviously, I do remember—"

"Then, you should know that I'm going to do everything in my power to help you. I'm gonna turn you into a new kind of savage."

"How thoughtful," I reply, forcing myself to look away from his firm biceps that I always knew were there, but never really looked at before.

He takes my hand into his and forces me to look him in the eyes. Lord help me.

"Now, we're going to take a look at Rosie's programming."

Inwardly, I cringe. Of all the things he could have brought up.

Part of me wants to be angry, but somehow, with a few careless words, he's successfully put a smile on my face.

I arc a brow. "Look at Rosie's programming…how?"

"We're either going to have to reprogram you or figure out how to use it to your advantage. Some guys have a robot fetish, ya know. We just might have to look on Fetish-Forum-dot-com."

I burst out into laughter, though I want to slap him. No one has ever made me laugh as hard as Weston, though it's often at my expense.

"Let's talk a little bit about your first dates," he says. "How are your conversations?"

"I tell them about my work, where I went to school, my ambitions. Of course, I pepper in questions I have for them."

"Let me guess, they're all business-related."

"I mean, it makes sense. I ask them where they went to school, their—"

"You don't have to say anymore. I already know where this is going. The thing is, you impress them enough, so they go in for a second date, and even a third, because they'd be crazy not to. But you fail to ever *'hook'* them."

"Hook them?"

"You're so well-measured. So safe. So secure. And those are all good attributes, but they're not memorable qualities. Jim Franks not going to go home and fantasize all night about your client portfolio."

"Then what do you suggest I talk about?"

"Your passions! Sure, tell them what you do for a living, then follow up with how much you like to travel. Don't go into the boring history of Peru. Instead, discuss backpacking, nature, skinny dipping in Scandinavia."

"I got leeches—"

"Don't mention that—or rather, if you do, make it something to laugh about."

My shoulders slump. "Okay, talk about traveling."

"Not just traveling. Talk about your bucket list, what you would do if you won the lottery, what you're afraid of—can't be work-related, a weird skill you have that has nothing to do with lawyering or data analysis. Your favorite book—fiction. Heck, you can even talk about your guilty pleasure: reality television."

"So, doing that will help me to *'hook'* a man."

"It's a start, but not the finish. You also need to work on your body language."

"I have great posture, so I'm taken seriously—"

"I know-I know about your posture, but when you're on a date, you might want to lean in a little, spike your brow when he says something intriguing, smile more, look away bashfully. The truth is, you're a shark in the courthouse, but that doesn't translate well on a date. Oh, and don't always sound so serious. Use a little slang. Inject some sensuality in your voice. Touch his arm. Sweep loose strands of hair from your face. Like this."

Weston tucks a strand of hair behind my ear, and my body is immediately set ablaze with want.

"See, like that."

Calm down. This is Weston. He's here to help. Don't get your hopes up.

Forcing all thoughts of Weston from my head, I confront the epic truth that has been there for years, ever evading my logical brain: I'm just not cut out for dating.

"Savage, I know you got it in ya. You just need to act with them the way you act with me."

"With you?"

"Yeah. We've been out at least a hundred times together, and you're always so stiff out in public, but when we are kickin' it at your place or mine, you relax. So I know you can do this."

"It's because I know that I never have to be on guard with you."

Although we weren't filthy rich growing up, my family did have considerable wealth. I was always taught not to trust people—that they wanted what we had.

For the most part, that was true. But not with Weston.

Weston's hand covers mine. "I'll never give you a reason to mistrust me."

"Thanks. I'm glad we had this conversation. I'm definitely going to go into my dates differently, with better talking points."

"Oh, you thought we were finished?"

"There's more?"

"We need to go over second dates and places you should go: escape rooms, paintball, those art studios where you get drunk and recreate classics."

"Those are all good suggestions that I will consider."

"And then we need to talk about your sex life."

My cheeks flush with heat, and I have to turn away, so Weston doesn't see the fear in my eyes.

"It's okay, Jenna. You don't have to get nervous or embarrassed around me."

"That must be soooo easy for you to say. Women throw themselves at you. And...there were plenty of rumors going around the college campuses about your... considerable skill level."

"Do you think I was born with it? No, it took practice and a dedication to learning female anatomy."

Somehow I feel my cheeks burn two shades brighter.

"And if you walked into any bar across America, there isn't a red-blooded man that wouldn't take you home, and that's the God's-honest truth. You have magazine-worthy good looks, and I'm not saying that because I'm your friend."

He's not wrong. I was blessed with good looks, but they don't seem to overcome my terrible social skills.

Weston tugs at my hand playfully. "I have a gift for you."

"Oh?"

He grabs a bag he placed on the counter and hands it over to me. I look inside and see a series of movies: There's Something About Mary, 50 First Dates, Charlie's Angels.

"What are these?"

"Each of these movies have kick-ass women in them that are guaranteed to hook a man."

I hold up 50 First Dates. "Really, because this woman suffers from constant amnesia?"

"But...she's still cool."

"Wes, I appreciate you, I really do...but this is a lot to take in, and I don't even know where to start."

Wes holds up a movie. "We start here."

Made in the USA
Middletown, DE
21 February 2021